Jim Henson's™

FLAMES OF THE DARK CRYSTAL

PENGUIN WORKSHOP
An Imprint of Penguin Random House LLC, New York

TM and © 2019 The Jim Henson Company. JIM HENSON's mark and logo, THE DARK CRYSTAL mark and logo, characters, and elements are trademarks of The Jim Henson Company. All rights reserved. First published in hardcover in 2019 by Penguin Workshop. This paperback edition published in 2019 by Penguin Workshop, an imprint of Penguin Random House LLC, New York. PENGUIN and PENGUIN WORKSHOP are trademarks of Penguin Books Ltd, and the W colophon is a registered trademark of Penguin Random House LLC. Printed in the USA.

Visit us online at www.penguinrandomhouse.com.

Library of Congress Control Number: 2019942634

ISBN 9780593095386   10 9 8 7 6 5 4 3 2 1

Jim Henson's

FLAMES
OF THE
DARK CRYSTAL

BY J. M. LEE

ILLUSTRATED BY
CORY GODBEY

Penguin Workshop

We may meet in another life, but not again in this one.

Master urSu, from *The Dark Crystal*

CHAPTER 1

Shadows filled every corner of the world.

Naia could hear water. Could smell thick, damp air all around her. But no matter which way she turned, all she could see was darkness. Reaching out, she felt something wet brush against her fingertips. Then it was gone.

Light flickered. Silver and flashing like a shooting star, or sunlight shining through the dense swamp foliage. Before she could react, it sped away.

Naia burst through a cluster of branches and leaves, wings spreading enough to catch a current of warm jungle air. She was airborne only a moment before her feet struck the hard surface of an apeknot tree branch, and then she was off again. Leaping from branch to branch through the light-dappled canopy, chasing after the silver star that flitted like a bird in front of her.

"Tavra!" she shouted. "Wait up, Silverling!"

Tavra did not slow down. If anything, she took it as a challenge, spreading her gossamer wings and taking flight, zipping through the trees like only a Vapra could. Naia heard the swamp rumble below and grinned. Tavra might have the advantage of flight-worthy wings, but this was the Swamp of Sog. Naia's home.

She jumped from a branch just as a bubble of hot swamp

gas jetted up, filling her wings and launching her high into the treetops. She tilted, riding the current, speeding closer to Tavra. She might catch up yet.

Time slowed as she drifted. Though the swamp was beautiful in its greens and purples and golds, vibrant in the daylight and full of life, something was off. She felt as if she had done this before. But the last time she'd traveled this route, she hadn't had wings. She had only watched Tavra from afar with envy. Wishing she might one day be able to do the same.

And then . . .

Pain lanced through Naia's brow and she stumbled, nearly slipping from a branch. She fell to her knees and clung to the whorled bark to keep from falling as the world went dark for an instant, as if a bird had flown overhead and blocked all three suns at once. Then it was over, the light returned, but . . .

"Wait," she tried to say. "Tavra, wait—"

The swamp and every tree in it shook at a deafening groan from below. The bog churned, bulging, as something enormous rose. Naia covered her ears and squeezed her eyes shut. She didn't want this to happen. Not again. She had no other choice. She couldn't look away forever.

Naia looked down.

A monster breached the surface. Black and purple, scaly and shelled, with tusks like a Nebrie and bone-hard spikes along its skull like a horner. Endless rows of legs of every size and shape emerged from the swamp, pincers and claws, hooves and bony hands. Its face shifted, one moment with bulbous, sad eyes, the next with a flat, reptilian head and a maw big enough to swallow the entire swamp. It let loose a roar, spraying spittle and gore, and Naia could see the blackness inside its gullet was endless, a cavernous tunnel into the abyss at the center of the world.

Silver flashed again. Tavra had drawn her sword.

"Tavra, no!"

Naia's voice was lost in another of the monster's gruesome cries. A moment later, the monster smashed its jaws down around the tree where Tavra had perched. The towering apeknot splintered like a sapling, and Tavra was gone.

Naia stared at the tree where it broke. Its white heartwood stained with violet. A sickness from within. When she turned her eyes once more on the monster, she saw the same illness pulsing through its skin. Violet, glowing veins streaking through every joint of its anatomy. An inky darkness pooling in its maddened eyes as it saw her.

"No," she whispered. "No—"

The monster's jaw unhinged and it lunged. The world shattered to pieces, and Naia was falling. Down, farther and faster, her wings refusing to open as water and debris rained down around her.

Her body struck water, and everything went dark.

Help, Naia wanted to say. Instead, she thought it, projecting it into the murky, liquid nothingness that surrounded her. Dreamfasted it, even, to whoever might be able to hear her. But she was alone. She drifted, sluggish, tired. Wanting to move, heart racing when her limbs refused to obey her. The gills on the sides of her neck and shoulders opened. The water was dank and brackish, but it was better than suffocating. She breathed it in, feeling its cold current revive her. Awaken her. Her fingers tingled, coming back to life.

Her shoulders were sore. Someone was holding her, floating in front of her in the water.

Thank Aughra, a familiar voice said, filling her mind. *I thought you were gone!*

She opened her eyes, and she was no longer in the dark. Instead, she felt as if she were staring into a mirror. No, not a mirror.

Gurjin?

The last time she'd seen her brother, they had parted ways between Aughra's orrery and the Grottan caves. He had been weary then. Exhausted from being a prisoner of the Skeksis and locked away at the Castle of the Crystal. Now he swam before her, his strength restored. The green hue in his skin was vibrant, the spots on his cheeks rich and dark.

What are you doing here? she asked. *Where—*

Her questions were like the key to a locked door that was suddenly flung open. Memories tumbled out: confronting skekSa the Skeksis Mariner on the cliff high above the snowy city of Ha'rar. Her friends, fighting for their lives. Amri and Tavra, sending a message to the Vapra Gelfling. And their escape.

We jumped off the cliff, she mumbled, treading water. *We were trying to get to Onica's boat. But then skekSa's ship . . .*

The waves had split around the ship's bony, horned carapace.

A living sea creature, a monstrous behemoth, enslaved and under the control of Lord skekSa. It had come out of the ocean and swallowed their ship. Naia shook her head and tried to dislodge the horrifying memory from her mind.

But how are you—where are the others? Amri and Kylan, Onica and Tavra and Tae—

skekSa captured them, Gurjin said. *The behemoth swallowed the ship and everyone on it. We're in the beast's mouth right now. Look up.*

There was barely any light in the watery chamber, but Naia's eyes were finally adjusting. Overhead, she saw the belly of Onica's ship, floating aimlessly amid debris. From previous wreckages, no doubt.

After the behemoth's jaw locked shut, gas filled the chamber, Gurjin continued. *It knocked everyone out except me. I was in the water. I was only able to save you before skekSa took the others away . . . Naia, we've got to find them. When skekSa noticed you weren't with them, she said something about using them as bait.*

Naia shook out her hands. Her weary mind struggled to take it in, but she couldn't while her friends were in danger.

Right. Let's go. For now I'm just glad you're here.

Naia and Gurjin climbed out of the water onto a fleshy ridge. The noxious gas had faded, but the air in the behemoth's mouth was dank and musty. Naia shuddered as she noticed a proper walkway made out of wood planks had been built into the behemoth's body. She could only imagine the agony this giant creature must feel. How long had it endured skekSa living inside its body? Treating it as a ship without a heart or soul?

"She took them this way," Gurjin whispered, gesturing to one of the many passageways that led deeper into the creature. Though Naia crept as quietly as she could, and the echoing grumbling and burbling of the behemoth's body were loud enough to cover the sounds of their footsteps, she couldn't help but feel she was being watched. The walls of every passageway twitched and undulated. The ship knew where they were, even if skekSa didn't. It could feel them, just as she could feel an insect if it skittered across the top of her hand.

Naia tried to remember their path so they could get back to the ship once they rescued her friends. Though once on the ship, she wasn't sure how they would escape the locked jaws of the behemoth. One step at a time.

"When Mother was called to Ha'rar with the rest of the *maudra*, I came with," Gurjin offered as they scampered up and down the mazelike passageways. "Mother wanted me to find you. When the Vapra fire lit and the dream-etchings were burned across the citadel, I knew it had to be you. I went looking and found your Sifa ship out in the bay below the cliff. Got out to it just as it was swallowed by skekSa's ship. Glad I did, too. If I hadn't, you'd be with skekSa right now."

The comment rankled Naia, as if it were her fault they were in this predicament. She took a breath and let it roll off her shoulders. There was no point in arguing over who was the more responsible of them right now.

"Mother wanted you to find me?" she asked. "What for?"

Gurjin flattened his ears and hurried ahead of her so she couldn't see the rest of the expression that came across his face.

"I'll tell you later," he said. "I hear something."

It was a deflection, but an honest one. Voices drifted to her ears, muddled through the breathing and twitching of the porous passageway. Familiar voices. Her friends.

After two more turns they stopped. A large circular membrane sat in the center of the wall. It was squeezed shut, like an upright eyelid. Naia had seen a similar doorway in the ship once before, back when she'd been skekSa's guest. Now she leaned in closer. On the other side, she could see hazy lights and hear skekSa's muffled voice.

"We gotta get in there," Gurjin said. He reached out to touch the membrane, but Naia pulled him back.

"If it opens right here, she'll notice," she said. "There has to be another way in. The good news is, if skekSa's in there, it means she's not out here. At least, for now."

They searched up and down the adjoining passageways. The texture of every wall was different, some ridged and hard, some smooth and shivering and slick. With so many pieces of interlocking anatomy, it was hard to believe there wasn't a single alternate way into the room.

Naia felt a puff of air from above. An oval vessel, about the diameter of a barrel, protruded from the ceiling, snapping open and shut in time with the ponderous breath of the behemoth. When it opened, air puffed out, though when it was closed, it was almost invisible.

"There," she said. "That's how we're getting in. Give me a hand?"

Gurjin nodded, bracing his hands on his knee as they'd done countless times climbing trees as children. Naia hopped up until she could grab the lip of the closed valve. When it opened, blowing more dank-smelling air in her face, she swung herself in and quickly turned around to grab Gurjin's hand. She yanked him up, and his feet cleared the opening just in time for it to pop shut again.

They crawled through the sticky air tube toward the voices. It sloped and curved, up and steeply down, until they reached a far end. Naia waited, crouched on all fours, ready to scramble out. She had no idea what was on the other side—would they be hidden from skekSa's view, or would they tumble out right on top of her?

The valve opened, and Naia made her move, Gurjin quick at her ankles. To their fortune, the duct opened near the floor in a crowded corner half obscured by a heavy red curtain. Naia ducked behind the curtain and paused there, trying to calm her breath as silently as possible as she took in the room.

It was a domed atrium, with a vaulted ceiling in scaled panels over their heads where the inside of the behemoth's shell must have been. Like the laboratory, it was lit by a chandelier, brightly glowing with fireless, gold light. Exquisite paintings covered the hexagonal scales of the ceiling, depicting sea Nebrie, hooyim, and other ocean creatures, and sprawled across the flooring was a thick covering of woven kelp or seagrass. Ornate furniture decorated the room in sets: a few Skeksis-size chairs with plush footrests, sculpted stands, and a broad table covered in maps and scrolls and books—all in the black, intricate, almost skeletal style that the Skeksis favored. Stone and metalwork statues accented several shelves and consoles, littered with Sifa trinkets and treasure in gold, silver, and abalone. Piles of jewels and glittering ornaments overflowed from barrels and chests, some of it simply mounded in heaps on the ground.

"Now. You all wait there. Move and I'll kill you . . . I need something for this blasted wound."

The floor shook with heavy steps as a shadow swept in front of the light of the chandelier, and then she came into view.

skekSa. The Skeksis Lord Mariner, tall and plumed with green and blue feathers, cape drenched with seawater and melted snow and ice. She approached a cabinet on the far end of the chamber, her usually graceful stride broken with pain. The stump of her bleeding wrist was wrapped in a knot of black linen torn from her once luxurious gown. She tore through the contents of the cabinet with her three good hands, a deep groan rumbling from her throat.

While she was distracted, Naia pulled back the curtain. By the light from the flames in a crackling fireplace, she saw Onica, their Far-Dreaming ship captain, and Kylan the Spriton Song Teller. Further in the room, beyond skekSa, were two others, braced and alert: Amri and Tae, the Grottan and the Sifa, like a silver moon and a rosy sun beside each other. Naia could tell from the stern, joyless glare on Tae's freckled face, however, that it wasn't Tae. Not really. A tiny shape sparkled like blue glass at her neck, and Naia let out a cautious breath of relief. Tavra would keep them safe.

Naia dreamfasted at Gurjin, speaking between their minds so skekSa couldn't hear them.

The chandelier. Even skekSa can't see in pitch-dark, but Amri can. Maybe it will buy us some time to get that door open. If we can get everyone back to the ship, maybe we can figure out a way to escape.

She drew the dagger that she'd kept at her side for so long. Gurjin's dagger. She pushed it into his hand so he had a weapon. It belonged to him, after all.

Got it, he said, and disappeared between the folds of the curtain.

Naia turned her attention back to the Skeksis and tapped gently on the floor, hoping that Amri's sensitive toes could pick it up. To her relief, his ear twisted back almost immediately. When skekSa turned her back, rummaging through the cabinet and pulling out bottle after bottle of dark-hued spirits, Amri stole a glance. He saw Naia then caught Kylan's eye just as skekSa whirled around with a bottle in claw. She uncorked it and dumped half the bottle down her throat before giving a beak-smacking grunt and drawing a twisted dagger from her belt.

"Now," skekSa said, jabbing at them with her dagger. "Which one of you will scream Naia's name the loudest?"

CHAPTER 2

"How about you, Spriton? You're quite the song teller, aren't you? How about you do us all a favor and call Naia here so we can be done with this time-wasting farce."

The Mariner strode toward the group of captive Gelfling, dark eyes set on Kylan, but the blond Sifa in the group flared her wings.

"Were I you, I would consider letting us go," she said.

skekSa arched a scaly brow, looking the Sifa up and down. "You sound different, little Tae," she said. "Is that a Vapra accent on your tongue? And I thought I blasted you well and good up on the bluff with my thunder egg."

Naia swore under her breath. She had forgotten that skekSa knew Tae, as she knew many of the Sifa Gelfling. But even if skekSa could tell something was off about how the Sifa spoke, what had happened between Tae and Tavra was so complicated. Naia hoped it would be impossible for skekSa to guess that Tae had been badly wounded. That Tavra—one of the All-Maudra's daughters—had lost her Vapra body and was now confined to the form of a crystal-singer spider. And that she was using the spider's magic to move and speak as Tae, whose mind had gone into a deep slumber after her injury.

There was no way that skekSa could guess all that. The

situation even boggled Naia's mind if she thought about it too hard.

Tavra turned so her real, spider body was hidden from skekSa's prying eyes.

"You're not so deadly as you think. Maybe you shouldn't make enemies you can't afford . . . You were a patron lord of the Sifa clan once. Why not throw your lot in with us, and reap the benefits when we overthrow the Emperor?"

"Don't belittle me," skekSa spat, quickly and hotly.

"Isn't it worth considering?" Onica suggested. "You've seen what we can accomplish. You must have seen the Sifa light the fire aboard the *Omerya*, and the Vapra down below in Ha'rar, even as the Skeksis watched from the All-Maudra's citadel. You know, deep in your heart, that we will succeed."

This time, skekSa did not retort right away—and it was her mistake. Gurjin reached the neck of the chandelier. He drew the dagger from his belt and smashed it against the lamps of the chandelier, showering them with glass and sparks. The atrium went dark, and skekSa erupted with rage.

"*NAIA! I will have your head!*"

"This way!"

Naia threw the curtains back, though in the dark, Amri was the only one who could see her. He grabbed the others by the wrists, tugging them toward Naia and the door. Through the shadows and smoke, Naia barely made out Gurjin leaping from the chandelier toward the curtains. If he'd had wings, the descent would have been childling's play, but as it was, he caught the red fabric with a heavy *thump*. He shinnied down the curtain quick as an apeknot-mouse and a moment later reached them where they stood with their backs to the great valve door.

"It won't open," Onica said, pressing her hands against the membrane. "Kylan, try your *firca*. The chamber doors opened to skekSa's whistle before!"

skekSa let loose another angry bellow, still thrashing about in the dark. Tavra grabbed a slender iron candlestick that jutted from one of the piles of treasure—it was no sword, but it was better than nothing. Naia braced herself.

A chattering song flew from Kylan's *firca*, Skeksis-like and eerie coming from the Gelfling instrument. For a moment Naia worried it wouldn't work—that the ship wouldn't respond to Kylan—but then the valve door shuddered and snapped open.

"*Naia!*" skekSa shouted. A crash followed as she tipped a table, and Naia raised her hand to protect her face from a shower of pearls and jewels. "*You stupid girl!*"

With a roar, the Mariner rushed at them. Tavra readied herself, but Naia grabbed a poker from Amri and launched it like a spear. It struck the Skeksis in the chest, but Naia didn't stay to watch. Didn't stay to fight. They ran through the door and down the winding passageways. Gurjin took the lead, followed by Onica and Kylan, while Naia, Amri, and Tavra kept the rear, hoping they would be able to find their way back to their ship before skekSa caught up to them.

"You all right?" Amri asked as they ran. With a start, Naia realized she was looking *up* at him. She'd been so used to his

Grottan crouching, she hadn't realized how tall he was.

"Yeah, but I'll be better once we get to the ship!"

Gurjin's memory served them well. Before long he led them back to the behemoth's mouth. Seeing the little Sifa boat again should have raised Naia's spirits, but it didn't. She'd been trying to take their escape one step at a time, but the part where they got out of the behemoth's mouth had come more quickly than she'd expected.

"Now what?" Kylan panted.

"Maybe we should ask politely?" Amri suggested wryly.

Onica shrugged out of the ragged cloak she'd been wearing. "Let's start by getting to the ship," she said. "Even if we end up having to leave it behind to get out of here, there are weapons there. Fishing spears and nets."

Naia imagined how good it would feel to have a spear in her hand.

"Onica's right," she said. "The strongest swimmers will guide the others. Onica, take Tae and Tavra. Gurjin, take Kylan. Amri, come with me."

In pairs, they leaped into the water. Though Onica wasn't a Drenchen, she was as adept a swimmer as Naia and Gurjin, darting through the water like a crimson hooyim fish. Naia let Amri hold her ankle as she opened her wings, propelling them through the water and quickly taking the lead on their way to the boat. They were almost halfway there before Naia brought them to the surface for Amri to take a breath of air.

"Surfacing so soon?" Amri teased. "I could've made it."

"You just want me to kiss you again," Naia remarked. The last time they'd been underwater together, she had done the breathing for both of them, though at the time, she hadn't thought of it as kissing. Now that she said it out loud, though, her ears tingled.

Amri grinned with a lopsided smile, water lapping against his shoulders.

"Maybe."

It was an odd time to joke around, but Naia felt her shoulders relax. skekSa hadn't caught up with them, though she surely could have guessed where they'd gone. Maybe she'd been injured when the chandelier had come down, or maybe she was more in pain from her wounded wrist than she'd let on. Either way, for the moment they were safe. Maybe things would be all right. Naia smiled when Amri took her hand, and together they swam the rest of the way to Onica's ship. Rope and net dangled over the side, tied to the hull, and they grabbed on.

"Do you feel that?" Amri asked.

He let go of the rigging with one hand, resting his sensitive palm and fingertips on the surface of the water. Though the water was mostly still, Naia felt a trembling prickling along her skin.

"It feels like a current," she said. "Like a draft."

"Like an exit?" Amri asked, ears perking.

Gurjin and Kylan arrived next, with Onica and Tavra shortly thereafter. Onica vaulted up the netting and onto the deck, then leaned over to help Tavra and Kylan. While the others got on board, Naia waited below with Amri and Gurjin.

"What's going on?" Gurjin asked.

Amri waved his palm flat across the surface of the trembling water.

"Back in Grot, most of the tunnels that have water flow can be followed out of the caves eventually. I wonder if there are underwater tunnels here, too. Like gills, or something similar."

Gurjin exchanged glances with Naia. "Even if there are, if they're underwater, we can't take the ship. And if we can't take the ship, I'm not sure we'll all be able to escape in the water. Naia and I have gills, but the rest of you . . ."

"I'm going to check it out."

Before Naia could grab him, Amri let go of the rigging and dived. The last thing she saw were his white toes flipping a spray of cloudy water. Kylan leaned over the aft rail above.

"Where's he going?" he called.

"Kylan, help Tavra and Onica," Naia replied. "We'll be back soon with news!"

They could see Amri below, cheeks puffed with his held breath as he ran his fingers along the wall. As she and Gurjin swam down to meet him, Naia idly tongued inside her own mouth, noticing how the wall looked like a larger—much larger—version of what she could feel with her tongue just below her gum line.

Amri was inspecting a valve in the wall, identical to the one they'd used to get into skekSa's atrium, though this one was completely submerged. If such a thing opened and closed, like a gill or a blood vessel, it could lead almost anywhere. Outside into the depths of the ocean. Somewhere else in the monster's body, just as dangerous.

Amri must have sensed Naia and Gurjin close by, for he turned with a smile on his ballooned cheeks, pointing energetically at the valve. Naia made her way toward him, reaching out to touch him so they could dreamfast, but she paused when the water shivered—

POPPP

The valve sprang open. Water rushed toward it, sucked in at an alarming speed and volume. A bubble of shock burst from Amri's open mouth, and then he was gone.

AMRI!

Naia pumped with her wings, shooting toward the valve in time for it to snap shut. She threw herself against it, pounding on it with her fists and kicking with her feet, but it didn't open.

Open up! Open up, you stupid thing! Give him back!

Gurjin grabbed her shoulder. *Naia, stop!*

Stop? We've got to get this thing open! We have to go after him!

Real fear seeped into her brother's paling face. Terror that went beyond a simple, rational fear of the unknown. *But you don't know where that . . . tube . . . goes!*

She stared at him through the murky water, surprised she had to say it at all.

It doesn't matter where it goes!

Her brother's grip trembled on her arm, but she pulled free. He drifted away from her, glancing back to Kylan and the others on the boat as if he were thinking about leaving her. Her *and* Amri, who had no gills. She imagined her Shadowling friend caught in the current of endless water, lungs filling with sea. Drowning. Alone.

She didn't care what Gurjin did. She had to help Amri.

Open up! She kicked at the valve, struck it with her fists. Whatever it took to get it to open again. *Give him back!*

She struck it once more and was rewarded with a trembling shiver in the water. Naia folded her wings tightly along her back and braced herself. When the valve snapped open, she leaped in, feetfirst.

The water rushed at an incredible speed in the smooth, curved channel. Naia held her arms around her head to protect herself as the water whipped her through turns and twists.

She gasped when she reached the end, dumped out into a new chamber. From the sticky, pulsating walls around her, Naia could tell she was still inside the behemoth ship's body. It was dim and pungent with the smell of fish and decaying seaweed, but at least there was air. She scrambled to her feet, up to her knees in the brackish water. Lying in a coughing puddle nearby was Amri, thumping his own chest in an attempt to get the last drops of water out.

"I think I'm gonna throw up," he wheezed between coughs.

"Really? No smooth lines like 'I'm better now that you're here'?" Naia asked, helping him to his feet. She tried not to show how relieved she was, though her instinct was to hold him tightly and never let him go ever again.

"I'm saving all my smooth lines for next time. You know, the second time I get sucked down a water tube inside a giant marine creature's living body."

The walls of the chamber were slick, like everything else in the behemoth, glistening with faint bioluminescence. Now that Naia knew what to look for, she could make out half a dozen more valves in the wall.

"Look. I think that's a door."

The chamber narrowed on one side, ending in a flattish membrane that looked like the others they'd passed through. She pressed her hand against it, feeling it tighten under her fingertips. She wondered if the ship could truly hear her. Had the valve opened because she'd told it to, or because she'd struck it? Maybe it had only been a coincidence. But if it hadn't, and the ship was really listening, Naia realized maybe she should be kinder. It was a living creature, after all.

"I'm sorry I was rude earlier," she said softly, and the membrane shivered. "I was worried about my friend. We're just trying to get out of here."

Naia stepped back, gasping as the door twitched, about to open.

"Naia, wait!" Amri cried, but he was too late.

A monster loomed on the other side of the doorway. Not skekSa, but a second Skeksis, tall and cloaked in red and gold, a single horn jutting from the top of his head. He held a scepter in one claw, studded with a ruby, a string of pearls and diamonds draped over his shoulders.

skekZok the Ritual Master looked down on them with a scowl so deep, it could have been their graves.

"Going somewhere?" he asked.

CHAPTER 3

"We were just leaving," Amri said. "You wouldn't happen to know the way out, would you?"

"Silence," skekZok growled. He entered the chamber, and Naia slowly backed away, watching the valve door shut behind his curtain of thick red robes and the Skeksis's chilling, humorless gaze.

"These games are over," he said. "This rebellion nonsense is over. It's *all* over."

Through their touch, Naia could feel Amri trying not to flinch away from the Skeksis Ritual Master. She stepped forward, so swiftly that skekZok reared a fraction in surprise.

"Back off," she warned him.

"Naia, don't," Amri said, but she wasn't going to let skekZok bully them any longer. He was the only thing standing between them and the door.

"My *rebel* friends and I got in and out of the castle and away from skekMal the Hunter. Our *nonsense* defeated skekLi the Satirist and a horde of Arathim silk-spitters in the Grottan Sanctuary. You are outnumbered. And you'll be defeated. So back off. I'm not afraid of you."

"You should be," skekZok said. He spat. "The Skeksis will

ruin the Gelfling so utterly, your descendants won't know the names of the seven clans!"

Naia sprang at the Ritual Master, landing full on his chest. Grabbing handfuls of the ornate chains and necklaces that strung his neck, she leaped over his shoulder, pulling the baubles tight. The Skeksis choked, dropping his scepter to grasp at the tangle of chain. Naia turned, bracing herself with her feet on the back of his shoulders, and jerked on the necklaces like reins on a Landstrider.

skekZok let out a strangled grunt, his claws caught in the chains as he tried to prevent her from strangling him.

"How—how dare you—" he gasped, spittle beading around his beak, eyes bulging in his head. *"Gelfling!"*

The word hissed out of his beak like a curse.

Amri took two fistfuls of the Skeksis's skirts and yanked. Knocked off balance with Naia perched on his back, the Ritual Master toppled as easily as a rotten log in the swamp. Naia kicked off his shoulder, swinging around his neck a last time and binding his claws into the lengths of chain. He crashed into a howling, thrashing knot of robes and jewelry.

"The door?" Amri cried as they retreated. Naia stared at the closed valve door, then the smaller membranes that dimpled the wall. She didn't know where any of them went. She couldn't even remember which one had brought them there.

They both jumped as skekZok let out a roar that shook every wall of the chamber. Pearl beads and chain links sprayed like sparks as he ripped free, snarling and climbing to his feet.

All three of them caught sight of his scepter at the same

time. It lay where skekZok had dropped it, barely out of his long Skeksis reach.

"GELFLING!" he roared.

Amri was the first to make it, faster than either Naia or the Ritual Master. He grabbed the scepter in both hands, trying to drag it away—but it was too heavy. Within moments, skekZok towered over him and tore it from his grasp.

"skekTek may need the Drenchen, but he certainly doesn't need *you* alive!"

skekZok swung the scepter just as Naia reached Amri. The clubbed end came down, sure to smash into Amri with the force of all the Ritual Master's wrath. Naia held her breath and leaped.

"NAIA!"

Amri shouted her name. It wasn't just Amri; there was someone else. The sound fell away from Naia's ears as she tried to focus on the voices. For a heartbeat, she had been upright, in motion, throwing herself against Amri and knocking him out of the way. The next, the wet membrane of the chamber floor collided with her cheek.

Pain came next. Blunt at first, drumming through her ears and body. Then sharp as her nerves awoke, catching fire.

She was lying in Amri's arms. Although her sight was blurry, she could see his cheek splattered with red stains. Naia lifted her hand to touch her head. More blood smeared on her hands. He'd torn cloth from his cloak and pressed it against her forehead, but she wasn't sure it would be enough to staunch the river of unending crimson.

At least he was there. At least she wasn't alone.

But what about the second voice? Was that real? It took everything she had to focus. The world swam and her head pounded, but eventually a silhouette formed above her, between them and a defiant skekZok.

"Hold on, Naia," Gurjin said. "Just hold on."

She wanted to ask how he'd gotten there, but she couldn't. Her vision blurred, her senses rolling. She felt tired. Though in the back of her fading mind, she knew it wasn't sleep that nibbled at her fingers and toes.

The door at the far end of the chamber opened. skekSa took in the scene with a sharp inhale, then struck skekZok across the face.

"What have you done, you idiot?" she cried. "skekTek wanted the twins alive!"

skekZok barely reacted to the blow. He exhaled a deep plume of steam, scowling at his bloodied scepter, which shone in the dim lamplight.

"We'll have to kill them all," skekZok grumbled lowly. "We'll tell skekTek they died in transportation, and he'll have to find other twin Gelfling to experiment on."

Amri tightened his arm around Naia, doing everything he could to hold in the life force that was streaming from her wound. skekZok stepped forth, raising his terrible bludgeoning scepter. Gurjin held his ground, protecting Naia from the advancing Skeksis. He knew it wouldn't take much for the Ritual Master to do the same to him as he'd already done to his sister.

"Wait!" skekSa snapped, holding skekZok back. "Wait, you fool. skekTek wanted to see if Gelfling can absorb one another's powers. Isn't that why he wanted *twins?* Naia is very gifted at healing. I've seen it myself."

Though skekZok seemed impatient to get on with covering up his mistake, he hesitated.

"So?"

skekSa pushed past skekZok and spread her three remaining claws out.

"So," she crooned at Gurjin. "Go on, little Drenchen. Take your sister's magic and heal her."

Everything hurt, and Naia felt thick wetness gushing over her face. She tried to lift herself from Amri's arms, but her body wouldn't move, as if she were strapped down by heavy bands of pain.

Take my powers?

Gurjin jerked away when skekSa nudged him with a claw.

"What—" he began. He shook his head. "*Take* her magic?"

"Yes. Don't you want to save her? Don't you love her?"

"Of course I . . ."

skekSa shoved Gurjin down to his knees beside Amri and Naia.

"Then you don't have a choice. Take her Drenchen-healing *vliyaya*. Take it and use it. Do whatever it takes to survive. That's what you Gelfling do, isn't it?"

Was it even possible? Naia thought she felt wet on her cheek, but she didn't know if it was blood or Gurjin's tears of desperation.

"If it's possible," she tried to tell him. *If you can, then you might as well. I'll die otherwise, and then what good will my powers do?*

"Naia . . ."

Naia closed her eyes as darkness crept in, and a numb cold lapped at her fingertips. She wanted to take his hands and press them against the wound, will him to heal her, even though there was no reason to believe that he could. She was the healer. He was the soldier. That was how it had always been. Ever since they'd been young.

Naia had hated it, rejected it, and eventually grown to accept it. Had begun to find her own place when she'd left home for the first time. Realized her powers of dreamfasting, wild and uncontrolled, could be focused. That her healing powers were special.

If Gurjin took all that from her, where did that leave her? Who would she be if she could no longer shine in the world that was full of darkness?

Suddenly there was light.

Saturating her body, bright and warm, like the sun breaking through the clouds of a storm. Naia opened her eyes. Through the brightness she could see her brother's brow crinkled in effort, focusing on her wounds as radiant blue flowed out from the flats of his palms.

Blue light. *Vliyaya*—flames of the blue fire. Gelfling magic.

It was coming from Gurjin.

CHAPTER 4

SkekSa's crisp voice disrupted the stillness.

"Well, what do you know. skekTek's theory was right."

Gurjin's hands blazed with blue flame, the tongues of the magic light curling along Naia's wound as it healed. The magic tingled and itched, stitching her broken veins and skin together until the gash in her forehead had stopped bleeding.

"Right, that's enough," skekSa rumbled. "Can't have you healed up so much you're fighting back, can we? No, no. Just enough to be alive so we can deliver you to the Emperor."

Naia felt more alert with every moment that passed. Her heart raced. They had to escape. skekSa swept a claw out to knock Gurjin aside, but Amri was suddenly in the way, latching on to her arm. She crowed in pain when his sharp Grottan teeth bit.

"Dratted cave lizard!"

Naia, I don't know what to do, Gurjin whispered in dreamfast, still holding the light against her wound for as long as he could. Amri could distract the Mariner for only so long, and even now the Ritual Master lumbered forth, twisting his claws around the handle of his wicked scepter.

Naia's hand drifted to rest against the pulsing membrane of the floor. The only thing she could think to do was pray.

Someone, please. Help us.

skekSa cursed and bashed her claw against the wall. Amri let go, barely avoiding being crushed. He dropped to all fours, but skekZok raised his scepter. Before he brought it down and smashed Amri to pieces, both Skeksis froze as an ugly rumble trembled through the chamber.

"What—Vassa, no—"

The water that pooled in the lower floor of the chamber shivered, cutting short skekSa's startled curse. Naia gasped. She grabbed hold of Gurjin and reached for Amri.

Their fingers tangled just before the valves opened and water gushed into the chamber. skekSa and skekZok cried out in surprise and then panic as they were all plunged underwater. Naia clung to her brother and Amri, hoping she knew what was coming next. A valve on the far end of the chamber opened, sucking Naia, Amri, and Gurjin into it and leaving the thrashing, submerged Skeksis behind.

This time when she spilled out of the tube and tasted air, it was as crisp and clean as clouds in a blue sky. She wiped the water and slime from her face. Her eyes stung from the light, but it was a welcome burn.

They were outside.

From what Naia could tell, they'd landed near where the creature's shoulder met its jaw, deposited in the great folds of the behemoth's scaly neck. Water dripped off the black shell of the behemoth, shining under the midday suns. Where they stood, the Gelfling could see much of the huge creature's body, from its flat, half-submerged head to its domed shell, peaked with enormous horns and spikes.

Breathing holes flared and closed in rippling sequence along the behemoth's neck, some belching water and others sucking in air. They must have come out of one when the great beast had flushed the chamber with water.

"What happened?" Amri sputtered. "Why did we— How—"

Gurjin clambered over the mounds of sea-skin to Naia. Her blood still stained his clothes where she'd been dying in his arms. She touched her wound. It was bumpy but closed. She felt woozy, but she could stand. Maybe even run if she had to. He'd done a good job.

"Naia! Are you—are you all right? Why did skekSa's ship . . ."

Naia touched the beast's neck, cold and clammy and so ancient, her fingers could fit between the creases of scaly, barnacle-encrusted skin. She had prayed for help. Had someone answered?

"The behemoth. I must have dreamfasted with it. It must have heard me . . ."

"What are we going to do now?" Amri asked. "The others are still inside. And look around us . . ."

They did. Though the sun and fresh air tasted more delicious than Naia could have ever imagined, there was no land to be seen. No mountains of Cera-Na or bluffs of Ha'rar broke the horizon. It was flat in every direction, an unending sphere of ocean silver reflecting the brilliant blue sky. She felt dizzy, but she didn't know if it was from the view or her injury.

"There's no way we're getting away from here without the

ship," Gurjin said. Even with gills, they would be unable to swim the unknown distance to the nearest shore.

"And the ship is locked in the behemoth's mouth," Amri added.

The mouth. Naia stared into the dark shadow at the creature's front, where most of its head was lurking below the surface of the deep water. That was where its jaws were locked together, trapping Onica's ship and their friends inside among all the debris.

Vassa—if that was the behemoth's name—groaned. Naia wondered how long it would be before skekSa escaped from the underwater chamber and ordered the ship to submerge again. She pressed her hands against the behemoth's cool neck, leaning. She could feel its life force under her hand, heavy and cold like a deathly mist, swirling against her fingers.

"Then it's time to ask politely," she said.

Naia closed her eyes.

Please, ancient one, she pleaded. *Dreamfast with me.*

She felt it breathe as she breathed; felt its blood flow as hers flowed. A creature so large had to be ancient, and Naia wondered how long it had served skekSa. Had it been captured when it was young and small, or had skekSa conquered it as an adult, after it had known freedom? Either song was equally terrible, and Naia's heart hurt to think of it. All she knew was that the emptiness that faced her now was all that remained of the creature's spirit.

Every creature on Thra had life essence, from the fliers to the crawlers to the swimmers. Even trees and rocks sang the song of Thra, for they were all born of Thra and carried a piece of that melody within them. When Naia had touched the spirit of the Cradle Tree in the Dark Wood, she had heard its song in pieces. Its song, and the song of everything, thrown out of tune by the corrupted Crystal that was the heart of their world.

With a Gelfling partner who was willing to meet minds, dreamfast was like opening a door and falling into the mind-space of another. But when Naia opened her heart to speak with the behemoth, it was like opening a door into nothingness. She stood at the threshold of her consciousness, seeing only void. An unending darkness, though deep in the impenetrable space she heard a distant, pained moan. A cry of wrath, of anger. Of loneliness.

Vassa moaned, long and loud, the tormented sound vibrating through the entirety of its hard black shell. It was fear, and pain. Naia could feel that much, as she stood again on the threshold of the doorway between their minds. Between their hearts, in the dream-space of their dreamfast.

Peering into the abyss, Naia saw a twinkle. The smallest ember, barely kept glowing. Naia wanted to tend that smoldering light. Protect it and nurture it until it blazed again. This creature was in its own pain. Like every being of Thra, it had a will and a song, and both had been taken prisoner by the Skeksis. If she truly wanted to meet minds, Naia had to set aside her own desperation.

I know you must fear skekSa, she said. *I know she must have hurt you for a long time. But you are larger than she is. Stronger. You are a creature of Thra, with a voice of your own. A voice that can sing again, free.*

Naia felt dizzy again, her strength waning. She didn't know how long she had before she lost consciousness. Had Gurjin really taken some of her power in order to heal her?

If you let go of your fear, skekSa will have no power over you. Not now, and not ever again.

The waters shifted. The light grew brighter. Then a cold current hit Naia, chilling her, and she awoke from the dreamfast in a torrent of swirling waves.

Everything shook, water crashing in streams and rivers as the behemoth moved. The ocean churned, bubbles and waves breaking across its surface, and Naia fell to a crouch beside Gurjin and Amri as the body beneath their feet shifted and flexed. Despite her exhaustion, Naia's face ached with a grin as brackish water spewed forth into the sea.

Vassa was opening its mouth.

"Yes!" cried Amri. "You did it!"

He moved to embrace her but stopped short, glancing at the wound on her forehead. Instead, he gave her a smile so bright, she looked away. Gurjin coughed.

"It wasn't me," she murmured. "It was Vassa. Vassa decided this on its own . . ."

"There's Onica's boat," Gurjin called, pointing into the behemoth's opening maw as it filled with daylight. Far below, floating on the water within, was a little Sifa vessel with purple, blue, and crimson sails. She grabbed hold of Gurjin and Amri with either arm, spread her wings, and leaped.

Burdened with the weight of the two boys, her wings barely

broke their descent. The strain sent pain lancing through her shoulder, neck, and then her temple again, and she felt blood on her cheek. As she bled from her reopened wound, the exhaustion and weariness took hold again, and she faltered.

They crashed into the ocean near the ship, but Onica and Kylan had seen them leap from up above. Onica bounded from the ship with rope in hand, and Naia clung to her as she, Kylan, and Tavra pulled them aboard.

The ship rocked violently on the frothing waves. The instant the wind touched the little boat's sails, they filled with a SNAP, and the boat sped across the waves clear of the behemoth's hooked jaw. They surfed on a growing wave as Vassa moved, belching water and debris out into the open sea. As they crossed out of the shadows and into the sunlight, Naia barely noticed Amri catching her as she nearly passed out. Barely noticed Gurjin trying to heal her wound again. She didn't have the strength to tell them she would be fine.

They had escaped.

Vassa let out another deafening roar, but it was like a song to Naia's ears. Powerful and determined, ancient and revived. Its jaws arched open, large enough to devour an island, and then CRASSSSHED closed in a brilliant spray of blue-green ocean. The ship swung up on the huge waves, spindrift touching the deck and Naia's cheeks like dew.

"There's someone out here," Kylan shouted, pointing off the side of the ship. "Someone swimming in the water—they're so fast!"

He sounded far away. They all did. Even Amri, who looked down with black eyes full of worry as she slumped in his lap. Distant and quiet, like a dream.

Naia gazed out to sea. Vassa's bright green eyes as it submerged into the ocean, taking skekSa and skekZok with it. The last thing she saw before she faded was a big, silver-maned creature drenched in seawater, hoisting itself onto the deck with four powerful arms.

CHAPTER 5

Memories flowed like a river from the furthest reaches of her mind. Originating deep in the Swamp of Sog, where she'd been born in the heartwood of Great Smerth. One of two, her mother and father had told her. Destined to follow in Maudra Laesid's footsteps as *maudra* of the proud Drenchen clan, while her twin brother would leave the swamp to serve the Skeksis at the Castle of the Crystal. She would learn to heal while he learned to protect with a sword. And she would stay in Sog, while he would leave, to join the other Gelfling on the outside in the great world beyond the swamp.

That had been her dream for so long. To go on an adventure. To see the world and find her place within it. She'd finally been able to pursue that dream. Set a course for it and chase it down, like a star twinkling on the far horizon.

Warmth touched her fingers in the flow of the water, and she saw a stream of red. She remembered her injury from the blunt end of the Ritual Master's scepter, though the memories were distant. Just out of reach. Gurjin healing her as best he could. The behemoth, Vassa. Then pain and numbness. Darkness.

You can't.

That was Gurjin's voice. But was it a memory? It seemed like something he might have said. *You can't. She can't. It's not the right time.*

Who was he talking to?

It didn't matter. Not now when she was so calm and peaceful here, on the river. She let the shadows flow through her fingertips, swirling into the gentle waves.

After a long time, she could sense a bank on the shoulder of the river. A place where the waves washed against the shore. A place to wake up. She saw her friends. Kylan and Tavra. Onica and Amri. Gurjin. Waiting for her. How long had she been drifting?

She opened her wings, ready to join them.

Naia woke up in a small cave with four walls of gold and taupe rock, its ceiling reinforced by sun-whitened driftwood. Daylight poured in through the doorway, which was much bigger and rounder than one made for a Gelfling. The ceiling, too, was higher than a Gelfling would need, and decorated with paintings of the stars and their pathways, the three suns and the three moons, and the infinite wisdom shared between them. It reminded her of a hut she had visited once before in the Dark Wood.

"Naia?"

Amri sat beside her, a mortar bowl held between his bare feet and a pestle in his hand, grinding herbs into red and indigo dust. He nearly knocked the bowl over as he leaped up, leaning over her with those big black eyes. She reached out, frowning.

"How long was I out?" she asked. "Your hair . . ."

His pale cheeks flushed as he realized why she was staring. The half of his head that was usually cut short had grown out, a bit shaggy and strange-looking, since it was usually shaved close to the skin.

"A while," he said, glancing away. "Twelve days."

"Twelve days!" she exclaimed. She sat up slowly. Nothing hurt, but she could tell her body was heavy from disuse. "Where are we? Is everyone all right?"

"We're all fine. Gurjin's been healing you slowly since we arrived."

Gurjin had never used healing *vliyaya* before. What had happened? What was it skekSa had said? She touched her forehead. The wound was closed, replaced by new skin.

"Then it's true. Gurjin really did absorb my powers."

Naia wasn't sure what that meant for her. Or for him. For the both of them. Was it something she would reabsorb over time? Or was it permanent? Either way, she couldn't worry about it now. She had her life because of it. She was in no position to be upset. Whatever had happened was done.

"Yeah. He learned fast, especially with urTih's help. I guess he had to, without you."

He hadn't looked back at her yet, soft pink ears at an angle. An emotion was hovering around him like the scent of a flower, but he wouldn't bring it to life with words.

"Are you all right?" she asked.

"You—" he began, then stopped. Then started again. "You shouldn't have followed me down that tube. Back in the behemoth. It was really dangerous. You could have died."

"So could you. That's why I did it."

His cheeks turned pink, then red. "You got hurt because of me."

"I got hurt because of the Skeksis."

"You jumped in without thinking!"

"I jumped in because I care about you!" she replied hotly. Then it was her turn to blush, and she added in a mutter, "And anyway, I thought about it plenty. I can breathe underwater and you can't."

Their voices must have caught the attention of the others, for the sunlight flickered as Kylan and Gurjin came rushing in through the oval doorway. When he saw her sitting up, Gurjin's expression faltered with emotion.

"I was worried you weren't going to wake up," he said, trying to sound aloof, though his voice cracked. When he hugged her gently but firmly, she felt an invisible breath of relief.

"I hear I have you to thank," Naia said.

"He's been fretting every day," Kylan added. He put his hand on Naia's ankle and squeezed. "We're all glad you're better."

"I'll go find Tavra and Onica and let them know the good news," Amri said suddenly, and hurried out of the cave without another word. Naia watched him go, feeling a chill, though the air was warm and dry.

"What's wrong?" Kylan asked, seemingly unaware of the draft.

"I'm fine. Where are we? How did we get here?"

"The Swimmer. urSan," Gurjin said. "She was waiting for us outside skekSa's ship. She helped us dock Onica's ship in Ha'rar and took us all the way down the Black River."

Naia closed her eyes, remembering her dream of the river.

Perhaps her mind had known, at least in part, what had been going on in the waking world.

"But the Black River flows north to Ha'rar," she said. "urSan took us against the current? How, and how far?"

A bigger shadow filled the doorway, nearly blocking out the light until the long-necked creature moved all the way inside. She had an indigo mane streaked with silver, tied in braids along her prominent brow that reminded Naia of skekSa's beak. Her robes were silver and blue and green—hues of the Silver Sea—strung here and there with obsidian cord that shimmered like the Black River.

Amri was at the Mystic's back with Onica and their golden-haired Sifa friend. From how the latter walked, back straight and shoulders proud, Naia could tell it was still Tavra in control. Even after the journey that had given Naia time to recover, it seemed Tae's mind had not yet healed enough to wake.

"The Sifa Far-Dreamer's ship could not navigate the shallow river, so I pulled a raft," urSan said. "The Black River is broad, but it is not the swiftest in all the world. We should be safe here until you are well enough to continue your quest."

She flourished her four powerful arms and twitched her long tail. It might have been to demonstrate her prowess in the water, but all Naia could see was the stump on her right hand. The mirrored injury of the one Tae had given skekSa.

Naia tried not to let it bother her. If they hadn't taken skekSa's hand, she could very well have been strong enough to keep them from escaping. And then where would they be?

"Safe," Naia echoed. "And where is . . . *here?*"

urSan moved closer to Naia, lifting her locs and smoothing her forehead where her wound had been with a gentle, strong hand. Then she stepped back, out of the way so there was nothing between Naia and the doorway.

"See for yourself," she said.

The cave was one of dozens clustered throughout a walkway that curved along a spiral-shaped canyon. The morning was cool in the bottom of the valley, with dew glistening, and the air was sweet with incense and wildflowers. The way the morning sun caught the dust reminded Naia of being below water, surrounded by rippling golden shafts and curtains of light. Punctuating the gentle valley were towers of stacked stones, conjoined into pillars by time and the elements. The boulders and monuments were of every size, some coming up only to Naia's knee, while others towered high overhead. Some were covered with cloth, intricately embroidered and sewn, others painted and engraved with more symbols of time and space.

A glitter caught Naia's eye amid all the shades of gold and ivory and bronze. Something shining and white within the bodies of the beautiful rocks, catching the light of the Three Brothers as they passed through gauzy clouds overhead.

"Crystal veins," she said. "Healthy ones. Ones that haven't been darkened by the sickness of the Crystal. So there *are* places still unaffected. Still healthy."

"Seems that way," Gurjin muttered, almost as if he was bothered by it. Before Naia could ask what the problem was, he

cleared his throat and added, "Amri's been calling this place the Mystic Valley."

She glanced at the Shadowling. "Why?"

"Well, it's a valley, and—"

Naia jumped when the stones that surrounded them moved. It was only then that she realized some of the stones were not stones at all. As if coming to life from the earth itself, three broad-backed, long-tailed creatures rose from where they had been sitting. One with a bandaged eye, in front of a hearth, lighting incense. One with a stringed instrument in hand. Another familiar face with eye-prisms perched on his rounded nose.

". . . it's pretty mystical," Amri finished.

Naia glanced back across the faces of the Mystics—the urRu, the counterparts to the Skeksis. She had never seen so many of the magnificent, strange creatures in one place before. But she frowned when she took in urLii's bespectacled face.

"Aren't you supposed to be in the Sanctuary, guarding skekLi?"

"I was, yes," he agreed. "But as things change with the Gelfling—as you light the fires of resistance, as Aughra and Thra asked you to—things, too, have changed with the Skeksis."

"The Emperor sent reinforcements to the Caves of Grot. They overpowered the Grottan there and were able to free skekLi," Amri said quietly.

Naia didn't know how to react. In her imagination she saw it all, thousands of Arathim crawling between the caverns and tunnels, leaving trails of sticky white web. The poor Grottan, already weary from losing Domrak, fighting with the last of their strength to save all that remained for them to call home.

And the worst of it, that the Skeksis they had imprisoned there had been freed. A Skeksis they could have killed, if they'd gathered their strength. If skekLi had been destroyed when they'd confronted him in the Sanctuary, would this have happened? Had Naia and her friends made a mistake in leaving him alive? She tried not to think about what could have been or should have been, but it was hard not to imagine that the destruction in Domrak could have been prevented. How many Grottan they might have saved.

In the end, it was just more proof that the Skeksis had to be defeated. Once and for all.

"Did Maudra Argot manage to save some of the Grottan, at least?" she asked.

"When I left, they had managed to flee," urLii said. "I'm sorry I wasn't able to do more. Maudra Argot and the Grottan are resourceful, though, and they can navigate those caves better without me. I could barely find my way back and forth to the Tomb, after all."

Naia tried to hold on to hope. Because of their travels to Grot, they'd found the Sanctuary Tree. They'd been able to send Kylan's message dream-stitched among its pink petals. And of course, if they hadn't gone to Grot, she wouldn't have met Amri.

She reached out and caught his hand, squeezing.

"I'm sorry," she said.

He pulled away and pushed his hands into his cloak. "Me too. We just have to believe in Maudra Argot. She didn't get to be the oldest living *maudra* for nothing . . . she'll figure something out."

"She will," Naia tried to assure him.

"There isn't anything we can do right now, anyway," he said. An awkward silence followed, filling with all the things Naia wanted to say but didn't.

Kylan cleared his throat. "I suppose you should be introduced. This is urZah the Ritual Guardian and urTih the Alchemist . . . urZah is connected to skekZok. The same way the Hunter skekMal is connected to urVa."

Naia took in urZah the Ritual Guardian, long and wide with his simple, sticklike instrument that was nothing like skekZok's gilt scepter. The peaceful Mystic's eyes were far away, as if he were looking past her into a space that existed just out of sight.

"Master urSu wanted to speak with you and your brother, when you woke," he said. He hunched closer to the ground than the other Mystics, wide and low, and held a long instrument in his hand, parallel to the ground. The end of it was a cup, like that on a soup ladle, but it was far too shallow and small to actually eat from.

The Mystic Master. Naia hadn't known such a creature had even existed until that moment, but when urZah spoke his title, she knew there was no one else she wanted to meet more.

urSan's big head swept through the dusty air, her serpentine back curving to the very tip of her tail as she walked away. She pointed with three hands and a single stump.

"Follow the ravine until you see a spiral stair overgrown with medicine moss. But you should be forewarned," urSan began. "Here in the valley, a friend of yours has been recovering from a grave injury. We did not reveal his presence until now because we feared it might upset you. He is not well, and there is nothing you can do. But the Master is tending him, so when you go to see the Master, you will also see your friend."

Naia was already on her feet.

"A friend? Who?"

"It is urVa," urSan said. "urVa the Archer."

CHAPTER 6

The ravine stretched out of the center of the valley like two arms, one pointing east and the other west. Naia led the way, leaving the others behind as her stride quickened. urVa was here, and urSan hadn't told them? Not even her friends, while she'd been unconscious?

At least Gurjin and the others didn't know, either, Naia told herself. It would have been far worse if they had been holding out on her, too.

Naia's head throbbed dully at the thought, and she slowed her pace. She'd been unconscious and Gurjin had been healing her faithfully, if what Amri had said was true. Yet she still didn't feel completely herself. Not yet, anyway. Her heart pounded, as if it hadn't beat in ages, and her fingers tingled and twitched with exhaustion.

Weak. That was the word for it. Weak and tired. She trudged on, slowly but no less diligently. She couldn't be weak now. *Wake up, body. Wake up, heart. We can't let the others down now.*

A bulge in the canyon wall stuck out like a knot in a tree, overgrown with dusty golden moss and a few prickly flowering vines. A rope-and-stick ladder dangled below, wide and sturdy enough for a Mystic to climb. Naia had to stretch to reach each rung, her hands barely wrapping around the thick, sanded boughs. At the top of the ladder was a shallow landing and a simple carved doorway, shaded by the protruding rock form and its slinking vines. Without waiting for the others to join her, Naia brushed the foliage aside and went in.

"urVa?"

The winding chamber had pockets of sunlight, warm and golden, shining through round holes in the ceiling. The air smelled of water and herbs. Naia recognized some of the flowers and plants tied on strings to dry from the low ceiling: sogflower and mustleroot and bundles of gently glowing lichens. The tunnel barely widened before it ended, and there Naia caught her breath in her teeth.

The stump of an old tree, just big enough to fit in the cave tunnel, sat before them. Its exterior had been sanded and whittled until smooth and was draped with quilts and fabrics. The stump rested on its side, roots that had once been in the earth now fanning out and upward, braided together by strong hands and tied with twine to form a kind of basket. Resting along the body of the stump, heavy head cradled by the basket of roots, was a Mystic with deep etchings in his face and brow over his closed eyes. Bandages packed with moss were tied to his four arms, along his shoulders, neck, and tail, and his white mane was stained auburn in places from the blood of wounds that refused to heal. His breath sounded like dry leaves in autumn.

"urVa," Naia whispered. She couldn't move, as if she'd sunk into the hard rock floor up to her ankles, as she heard the footsteps and voices of her friends coming down the tunnel.

Another urRu tended urVa. He was large, like all the Mystics, but still graceful and elegant, four long arms slightly spread so his hands floated over urVa's body. *This must be urSu,* Naia realized. The Mystic Master. With great effort, she stepped closer, gingerly touching the matted hair along the Mystic Archer's back.

"What happened to him?" she asked.

"We do not know," the Master replied. His voice was not low, as Naia might have expected from the Master of the Mystic urRu; rather it sat higher in her ears, like wind blowing across the tops of mountains or through a canopy of tall trees. He didn't seem to mind that Naia hadn't introduced herself, nor did he seem surprised as her friends joined them. He waved a hand over the unconscious Archer, letting droplets of water fall from his square fingertips into the other Mystic's white mane.

"Was he attacked?" Kylan gasped when he saw. Gurjin and Amri came next, and by the time Onica and Tavra arrived, there was hardly any room left in the little chamber. A gentle breeze flitted through the openings in the ceiling, but other than that and the sound of urVa's fragile breathing, it was silent.

"All we know is that whatever befell urVa did not fall lightly," Master urSu said.

Naia held her hands over urVa's wounds, afraid to touch him, as if he might break. She could see the shape of some of the injuries from the patterns of blood in the bandages.

"These wounds are from blades and arrows and maybe teeth," she said.

"Who could have done this?" Amri asked. "And why?"

"Maybe a darkened creature," Onica suggested. That was a fair guess, based on the brutality of the wounds, but something about it didn't seem right. Darkened creatures, as vicious as they could be, didn't wield metal blades. Especially not the kind that would have cut so deeply and cleanly.

"Or a Skeksis," Gurjin said.

Naia tore her attention from urVa, though her palms ached to try to heal him. She wasn't even sure if Gelfling *vliyaya* would work on the urRu . . . or if she had any power left to heal, after what had happened on skekSa's ship.

"Master urSu," she said, finally introducing herself. "My name is Naia. I'm the daughter of Maudra Laesid, of the Drenchen. This is my brother, Gurjin." She introduced the others one at a time, and with each name spoken, urSu nodded gently, his careful, discerning eyes meeting each of theirs, as if locking the memory of their faces and identities into his mind forever.

"Welcome, Gelfling of the seven clans," urSu said. He gestured with one of his big hands for them to sit. There was meager room in the small cavern, but enough for the two Mystics and the six Gelfling.

"We're not seven yet," Kylan murmured. "Our Dousan allies are fortifying in the Crystal Sea."

"And Rian of the Stonewood clan is off on a different journey," Gurjin added.

Rian. Naia hadn't thought about the arrogant ex-soldier in a while. She wondered how he was doing, on his special errand from Aughra. While she and her friends had been sent to light the fires of resistance, he had been sent to find *something*, though what it was he was seeking had been kept a secret. Naia and her friends had heard nothing from him since then.

"Hm. And rightly so," urSu replied. "We know you have many questions, and we have much to share with you, young Gelfling. Ask."

"The Skeksis." Naia asked the question that she had been asking for what seemed like forever: "How have they corrupted the Crystal of Truth, and why? And how can we stop them from hurting the Gelfling? How do we defeat them?"

He was unsurprised by her barrage of questions, like a shore buffeted by waves. He reached up to lift a large, shallow bowl from a shelf and set it on the floor before them. The vessel was filled nearly to the brim with cloudy blue-green water, smelling of the salt and minerals that kept its waters misty.

"Yes. Very good. Before we address the Skeksis, and how the world is now, we must understand how this world was once, and what it became. We must understand the urSkeks."

"urSkek?" Tavra said. "What is that?"

urSu waved a hand in a wide arc, dispersing the steam that rose from the bowl of clouded green water. Then he waved another hand, in the other direction. The steam spread, growing from the trembling water, spilling across the floor like a living thing. It reminded Naia of the dream-space they'd shared with Aughra, blurring the line between reality and thought.

"Nearly two thousand trine past," urSu began, "the Three

Brother Suns aligned in the sky. One on top of the other, unleashing a pillar of light. Aughra was there that day. The voice of Thra."

Visions of shadow and light flickered in the wide pool of water that shivered in the bowl, and Naia saw images reflected in the water and across the rolling mist. Conjured by urSu's magic, clear as a painting or a memory in a dreamfast: Mother Aughra, standing atop a high cliff. Watching the suns collide in the sky. A flash, a spear of pure light. Aughra's screams as she tried to look away—and what remained when it was over. Eighteen glowing figures with long ivory faces. They wore shining robes the color of daylight, with slender arms like tree boughs and blazing shapes atop their heads that branched and tangled like fire.

"The urSkeks," urSu said, his voice like the sound of the vision itself. It was by his power they were seeing this unimaginable sight. "Beings from another world. Sent here on the light of the solar eclipse—the great conjoining of the suns in the sky. The gateway opened by the power of the Crystal of Truth, which connects this world to others . . ."

urSu waved his hands once more, and the vision of the ghostly, glowing urSkeks dissipated. Eighteen, Naia had counted. Twice-Nine. The same number of Skeksis. Her hands clenched in her lap as she waited for the rest, though part of her already knew instinctively where urSu's story would take them.

"The urSkeks came from a world where one is all," he said. "Where one is none. But these urSkeks were different. They were rife with discord, filled with desire. Desire for *more*. Because of this, they came to this place. They befriended Aughra. They showed her the wisdom of their race, which she, in turn, showed the Gelfling."

When the steam coalesced once more, it was with the image of time passing. The suns and moons raced across the sky in rapid succession, and Naia saw Aughra. Then Gelfling, rising from the land among the other flowers and creatures. They learned to channel fire and water, to turn the earth and to respect all life.

"One thousand trine passed before the suns began another conjunction. The urSkeks, feeling they had done well, converged on the Crystal. Thinking that when the light of the triple sun struck it, the gateway would open once more for them to return home. But . . ."

Naia saw the urSkeks, gathered around the Crystal in the castle where it floated, high above the floor in the chamber where she had seen it herself. In this vision, it was clear and brilliant. Pure as ice, singing with the voice of eternity. The song of Thra. As the three suns converged overhead, the light came once more—

But then, chaos. Screams. Light and dark were torn apart, like twin shadows cast from a single sun. Where there had been eighteen, now there were thirty-six: the urSkeks, by the light of the Crystal, had split in two.

"Skeksis and urRu," Naia whispered. "You were once . . . one."

"We still are one. But split. The Crystal's power did not deliver us to our home. Instead, it saw the imperfection that remained in our hearts. It saw we still were restless. It rejected us. And so our second lesson began."

Naia held her breath, heart pounding, as she watched the melee unfurl below the Crystal. The Skeksis and urRu—not yet lords or Mystics—newly born, shrieking and moaning. Clutching themselves and staring into the bewildered eyes of their other halves. Naia couldn't imagine the pain and fear they must have felt—if they felt those things at all—couldn't imagine what it might be like to be seared apart by the Crystal, awakening to find herself looking into the eyes of her worst self.

Or the other way around. To see her best self staring back at her, knowing it meant *she* was the other half.

A Skeksis fell, bleeding from a wound he'd taken in the confusion. At the same time, his Mystic half stumbled, and together the two died, having seen only moments of life in this new configuration. Naia watched in horror as the others hardly noticed, too embroiled in their panic and mourning.

A flash of light broke the din. All stopped and gazed upward, where a dread shining splashed like a fountain.

One of the Skeksis had struck the Crystal with a scepter. The immortal, invincible-seeming Crystal flashed and hummed, vibrating with light and power. Naia could feel the pain of the Crystal in that moment, even separated by so many trine. She could feel it in her heart, knew the song of agony.

A single shard flew from the wound where the scepter had pierced it. All eyes tracked its spiral through the air. Then it dropped into the chute below the Crystal, glittering like an escaping tear.

As it vanished, so did the vision. Naia let out the breath she had been holding and realized her hand was clenched around Amri's. She let go and wiped the wetness on her cheek.

"They cracked the Crystal," she said.

"Yes, we did," urSu replied.

"You didn't, the Skeksis did," Gurjin said, but the Mystic Master shook his head.

"We are the Skeksis. As they are us. It was we who cracked the Crystal. We who lost the shard. We who left the Crystal incomplete, as we are incomplete. It is our final lesson. A gift from Thra, so we may be tested. For without the shard, we cannot heal the Crystal. And without the Crystal intact, we cannot return from whence we came. When final judgment comes, only then will we know whether we might leave this world as urSkeks once again."

"Do the Skeksis know this?" Tavra asked. "Do they remember being urSkeks, as you do?"

"It is hard to say," urSu said. "They did, once. But they have become consumed by desire for this material world. Distracted by riches and the adoration of the Gelfling. Drunk on the delight of power. It has been nearly one thousand trine again since we split in twain. In that time, many have forgotten . . . but not skekSo."

Emperor skekSo. The one who ruled even the Skeksis, who sat in the castle with the Crystal held in chains. Whose reign had enslaved the Heart of Thra, and upon whose orders the Gelfling were being drained of their essence.

"You are his counterpart." Naia's statement could have come out a question, but she knew in her heart it was simply the truth.

"You and the Emperor. You used to be one."

Gently urSu nodded, so low and long it was nearly a bow. "That is why I was the one charged with sharing this information with you, Naia of the Drenchen," he said. "This you must know, so you may know what you must do."

Naia had met the Emperor only once, when she'd stood in the Skeksis throne room beside Tavra. She had been meek, then— hiding behind Tavra, unsure what to think of the burning eyes that looked upon her. But now, knowing what the Emperor and his lords had done to the Crystal, she wanted nothing more than to stand before him once more, dagger in hand. She would not be meek the next time they met.

More than ever before, Naia wanted to obliterate them from Thra and every other world. Permanently, so they could no longer wreak their corruption upon worlds that did not belong to them. So they could no longer poison the world that was trying with all its might to endure.

But could they be stopped? Were the Gelfling strong enough? And even if the Skeksis could be killed, a darkness waited on the other side. Naia had seen what happened to the Mystics when the Skeksis were harmed. What happened to one reflected upon the other. Cuts and scars. urSan's missing hand. urTih's bandaged eye. Naia had never paused to think how far their connection went. But now that she had seen what had happened in the shadow and light of the Crystal, she knew.

"The Skeksis have to be stopped," she said. "But . . ."

She couldn't finish. Couldn't say the words out loud and bring them to life, not in the faces of the creatures who would ultimately pay the price for what she and the Gelfling were planning. She could barely look at the resting Archer, heart heavy with the knowing.

"If skekMal dies, so will urVa," Amri said, the first to say it out loud. "Same with all the Skeksis and Mystics."

The terrible truth hovered like the scent of death. Naia had known for a long time that the Skeksis and the Mystics were connected, but none of them could have guessed how or why. When urVa was hurt, so was skekMal. So was the opposite just as true. But no one had ever confirmed whether or not a Skeksis might die if their Mystic counterpart did—though she could have guessed it might be the case, Naia had never considered the thought too closely. Especially not when considering the larger goal she had kept in the forefront of her mind: unite the Gelfling and defeat the Skeksis.

But what did that defeat look like? Surely, if all the Gelfling united and the Skeksis called them into war, *defeat* would actually mean *death*. Naia was not so modest to say she had never imagined killing a Skeksis before, especially not after what they had done to her friends and family. Had she been given the chance before to drive a dagger into Emperor skekSo's heart, she would have done it without a second thought. What other way was there to make their defeat permanent? They were powerful and strong, and they held the Crystal captive. How could the Gelfling possibly defeat them, if not through force?

Naia stared at poor urVa and the bloodstained bandages

that dressed him at almost every joint. Fractured bones and torn muscles, cut and bruised skin. If skekMal had been killed by whomever he had fought, urVa would have died alongside him. urVa, who had helped them, taught them, and saved them. She couldn't let that happen.

Her chest hurt from holding her breath. The truth of their predicament came closer and closer to the surface until she couldn't push it away any longer. She felt a tear roll out of the corner of her eye, laden with the sting of pain and despair.

"We can't win," she said. "Anything we do to the Skeksis happens to the Mystics."

"That doesn't mean we can't win," Gurjin said, almost silently. He was trying to be reassuring, but there was no strength in his voice. He was just as distressed as she was.

"How are we supposed to defeat them if we can't hurt them?" she asked. "If we can't kill them? When they have no hesitation killing us? But we *can't* kill them. It's not right. If we do, we'll be just as bad as them!"

There it was. Out in the open, straightforward and simple. The tiny room fell into a deep silence, though Naia's words seemed to echo forever. *We can't kill them. We can't kill them.*

"But Aughra told us to unite the Gelfling," Gurjin said. "She told Rian to find something. She and Thra must have a plan. We have to be patient and trust them."

"Do you really believe that?" Naia snapped, unspent emotions bubbling to the surface. "You really think that everything we've done so far—everything Rian is doing—can somehow stop the

Skeksis without hurting them? Without hurting the Mystics? And if Aughra knows so much, then where is she, eh? Why hasn't she said anything?"

She bit her tongue. Her friends stared back at her with varying expressions of discomfort. Kylan licked his lips as if he were going to reply, but he kept quiet. Naia sucked in a breath, but it didn't help. She felt as if every anxiety she'd pushed down was rushing out and she couldn't stop it.

"All this time, we've been rallying the Gelfling to rise. To stand up to the Skeksis. All this time, we've been preparing them to fight. But to what end? When we finally call on them to confront the Skeksis, how will we fight them? If not swords and spears, then what—songs and prayers?"

Gurjin was the first and only to respond to her, and only in a tone of voice like one would use to scold a child.

"Naia," he said sternly. "Calm down. The last thing we need is you going off and doing something without thinking again."

The air in the chamber felt thicker by the moment. Before she suffocated, smothered by the dim light and the dispassionate look on her brother's face, Naia shouldered past her friends, mumbling, "I've got to get some air."

With carefully calculated steps, she put poor urVa and the others behind her, escaping the dark chamber for the sunlit valley outside.

CHAPTER 7

Once she'd swung down the rope ladder to the dusty earth, Naia struck out into the ravine away from the center encampment, arms folded tightly across her chest, listening to her footsteps echo against the walls of the empty-seeming canyon.

It wasn't empty. Not really. She caught sight of skittering, furry lizards chasing bugs for their breakfast. Birds flying overhead. Shrubs and mosses growing from between the rocks, and the occasional smooth-barked tree winding its way upward with lacy golden leaves. She even saw urLii emerging from one of the caves with a wide yawn, his quill and book in hand. The valley of stones was full of life, but even so, Naia felt alone.

Naia watched the slow movement of the suns cast shadows on the dusty valley walls. Her mother had told her that when her grandmother had been Naia's age, it was extremely rare that all three suns were seen in the sky at once. When it happened, it was only briefly, with the third sun skirting just above the horizon. But now, many trine later, Naia could see all three clearly, even at the bottom of the canyon with the steep walls on either side. She had noticed it on her first days out of the swamp, but she hadn't thought anything of it. Hadn't paused to consider what the writing in urVa's hut had meant, when Kylan had read it aloud.

When single shine the triple suns, the writing had said. It had been meaningless then, written by a strange, distracted philosopher who lived in a hovel in the middle of the Dark Wood.

"Or when single shines the triple sun," Naia murmured to herself, remembering what urSu had called it. The triple sun. When the three suns became one. It was the light of that triple sun that had brought the urSkeks.

Light glinted. Running through the smoothed walls of the valley on the endless streams of crystal filaments. They were nearly invisible, blending in with the rest of the dusty stone until struck full of light from the suns. Naia reached out to touch the thin crystal veins, but the threadlike mineral was so delicate she could scarcely feel it, much less hear its song.

The crystal veins were what connected Thra to its heart, just as the veins in Naia's body flowed with her lifeblood, in and out of her heart in an endless cycle. She touched the rock, wishing the veins might speak to her now. Pure white, yet untouched by the darkening seeping from the Crystal like a sickness.

"Hear anything?"

Amri picked his way over the rocks. Naia didn't protest when he stood beside her, putting his hand where hers had been, pink finger pads soft against the rock.

"No," she said. "I'm . . . No."

"I tried that when we first came here. While Gurjin was healing you and we weren't sure if you were going to make it . . . but I didn't hear anything then. Haven't tried since."

"I'm sorry I worried you."

He shrugged. He wouldn't meet her eyes, though before when they'd been on skekSa's ship, he'd been all grins and winks, even when they'd been trapped in the behemoth ship and chased by a Skeksis. It hadn't been dreamfasting, but it was close—like they had begun to know each other. As if she could look into him and see inside and was offering the same to him when he looked at her.

But now when she looked, she couldn't see as deeply. What had changed? News of Domrak, maybe, or now the revelation that their plans to defeat the Skeksis were dashed to pieces? Either way, Naia didn't blame him for the aloofness. Not now, anyway.

"It's all right," he said. "It's . . ."

He narrowed his eyes at the wall, focusing in thought. He crouched, legs and back bending gracefully as he slid his hands down the stone surface. It reminded Naia of how her mother healed: tracing the lines of a living body, sensing its shape and energy. He pulled his hair back and pressed his bared ear against the stone, closing his eyes. Then unfolded and stood straight once more, tall and slender, and pointed.

"I think I *do* hear something. This way."

Their path took them farther from the center of the valley, where the way narrowed into a thin passage barely wide enough for Naia and Amri to walk in single file.

Amri stopped in front of a wedge-shaped hole, where the crystal veins they had been following interlaced, streaming together to form bigger ribbons of the glittering, rough mineral. The braided, tangled veins vanished into the tunnel.

"I can hear the network of crystal growing stronger inside.

There must be places throughout the valley where it happens," Amri said as they stood before the cave entrance and considered its inky darkness. Naia nodded.

"Let's go," she said.

Almost immediately, the way fell into blackness. As they went deeper, Amri's eyes widened, absorbing the shadows. He became almost another Gelfling in the dark; the timidness and squintiness melted away, revealing a confidence that bordered on audacity. Naia knew it was who he really was, coming to life like a night-blooming flower.

As he guided her over jagged stalagmites and under hanging stalactites, Naia felt as if she were crawling between the fangs of another enormous beast.

"I'm sorry about what happened in Grot," she said. If that *was* what was bothering him, maybe now that they were alone, he would open up about it. She wanted him to. She wanted to comfort him.

But all he said was, "Me too."

Just when it became so dark that she might as well have had her eyes closed, light came again. Softer, this time, the kind of light that came from within. Naia blinked away the shadows and focused as they neared, then let out a long breath of awe.

Buried at the back of the tunnel, hundreds of tiny crystal veins converged, tangling in a dizzying swirl of white and blue and gold. Where they converged, a huge cluster of crystal jutted from the wall, piercing the shadows with its light. It was the biggest crystal cluster Naia had ever seen, aside from the Crystal itself—almost as large as her two hands folded together, pointed and glistening like the icicles that shone from the eaves in Ha'rar.

"It's beautiful," she breathed. She wanted to touch it, feel the pure, gentle light that ebbed and flowed from it like the breath from a living being. The two of them huddled closer, letting the light of the crystal shine on their faces. Even Amri sat close, unflinching. This light was not the kind that strained or hurt his Grottan eyes.

The elation of finding the crystal faded when Naia noticed a discoloration on one of the cluster spires. She curled her lips in, letting out a sorry breath when she saw the tinge of purple that crept across one of the tiniest facets. It was so small it looked like a tiny bruise. Something that might heal in time, fade away into nothing, only a blemish on the face of the stone. But Naia knew better.

"Even here," she said. "Somewhere so beautiful and hidden. Even here, the darkness of the Crystal spreads."

"I don't think anywhere is safe," Amri said quietly as they regarded the violet mark. "Not until we heal the Crystal itself."

"And we barely know how to do that," Naia added. She sighed and tugged on her locs, wishing for all the world she could heal the Crystal like she could heal cuts and bruises, and even broken bones. Or at least, like she used to be able to.

Naia looked down, holding her hands palm up and spreading her fingers, and focused, the way her mother had taught her even when she was very young. The light was dim and weak, though still there. Like a tiny ember in a dying bed of coals or the last bit of moss glowing at daybreak. Nowhere near the radiant beams of light that had come forth in the past.

It really was true. Gurjin had absorbed her powers. Not everything, but enough that Naia wasn't sure what she was capable of anymore. In the realm of healing, or anything else.

"Naia, what . . ." When Amri saw the dim blue light rising from her hands, he changed his question: "You're going to try to heal it? I don't know if that's a good idea . . ."

The blue light in her hands pulsed with her heartbeat, in time with the shining of the Crystal. She and the Crystal—the Gelfling and Thra. They were connected, mother and child. Not like the monsters who had come from another world and ruined everything.

"They came here and told us lies. Told us they would protect the Crystal and did the opposite. They broke it and lost the shard. This isn't even their land—who are they to break the heart of our world, and then call *us* the traitors and rebels?"

Amri put a cool hand on her shoulder. Gently, but firmly.

"I know, but—"

"Even though they were powerful and frightening," she went on, "I always thought they could be stopped. I always thought that if we were strong enough—if we lit enough fires, if we united the Gelfling. If we did everything Aughra and Thra told us to do, we could *stop* them. But now I know we can't. We can't kill the Skeksis, because we can't kill the Mystics. We can't stop them. I can't stop them."

"But the Crystal is so big, Naia—so much bigger than you.

Healing is giving. If you try to heal it, you might give up too much—"

"I still have to try. Even if Gurjin took most of my power to heal me, I've got to have a little left. Enough to do something."

"Naia, wait—" He grabbed her wrist, but she pushed past him, thrusting her hand full of healing light against the purple-tinted spire of crystal. "No!"

He threw himself against her, but he was too late. Energy bolted through their bodies like lightning, sucking her breath from her lungs.

When she came to, she was slumped against the cave wall, Amri beside her. They'd been knocked across the tiny cavern by the arc of light that had come from the vein.

"Amri," she said. She shook his shoulder.

"What happened?" he mumbled, reaching up to touch the scratch on his cheek.

"Hold still. You're hurt."

Hurt. Because of what she'd tried to do. The light faded from her hand as guilt seeped out of her stomach. She willed it to return. Willed it and, at the same time, hoped Amri wouldn't notice the dull panic throwing itself against the inside of her chest. The blue light flickered, and she swore under her breath. If she couldn't even heal Amri, then how could she possibly have thought she could heal the Crystal?

"It's not working," she whispered.

"Naia, it's fine," he reassured her. "I've had my share of bruises and scratches from cave rocks."

He touched her wrist, gently pushing her hand away. She helped him to sit up, and together they gazed at the blighted crystal cluster, the only thing that lit the tiny cavern. He pressed his hand against his cheek, though the bleeding was already slowing. Naia's stomach hurt. She couldn't even heal a tiny scratch—they were lucky it hadn't been worse.

"I'm sorry," she said again.

He reached out to her, eager to leave but unwilling to go without her.

"Let's just get out of here," he said.

She agreed by taking his hand. The two of them left the cluster of slowly darkening crystal behind, buried deep in the wall of the cave like a bad dream.

CHAPTER 8

The two of them climbed up the edge of the valley to walk along the upper ridge on the way back. The Skarith Land sprawled in every direction, radiant in every color. To the north were the lush greens and blues and purples of the endless Dark Wood, punctured on the west side by the deep black Castle of the Crystal, rising like a claw from the ground. To the northwest, beyond the castle, was a shining gold sheen that marked the Crystal Sea desert; to the northeast, the gray, craggy Grottan mountains and the high hills where Aughra's orrery was perched like a bell-bird's nest. And at their backs to the south were flat, rolling plains of yellow-green grass blotted with patches of violet and pink wildflowers. Far beyond the Spriton Plains was dense fog that pulled at Naia's heart. The Swamp of Sog, the southernmost border of the Skarith Basin.

It was an easy journey, compared to the steep cliffs in Ha'rar or the dangerous, sharp crags in the Caves of Grot. Naia tried to enjoy it. Tried to let the beautiful wonder of their world take away the tired defeat that gnawed at the bottom of her stomach.

"If we're here, south of the Dark Wood," she murmured, trying to ease the silence, "you must have been on the river with urSan for a long time."

Amri nodded, folding his arms. Naia watched him stare out over the magnificent vista, his cheeks and ears slowly turning pink. Although she never thought he could be mistaken for a Vapra, pale cheeks that blushed quickly were an endearing something he shared with the Silverlings.

"Please forgive me?" she asked again. He had barely responded when they'd been in the cave.

He met her eyes, though there was still something shielded about him. Even after what they'd gone through in the cave.

"Of course I forgive you," he said. "We're friends."

"Friends?" she repeated. An embarrassed laugh wormed its way out of her throat. "Oh."

Friends. Of course.

"There you are!" Kylan grunted, slightly out of breath as he climbed on top of a boulder, up ahead between them and the central heart of the valley. "Come quickly. urVa is awake!"

Naia and Amri exchanged glances, then ran after their Spriton friend.

urVa was indeed awake, though his eyes remained half closed and his breath barely moved the dust that drifted in the sunbeams. The others made room for Naia when she arrived, moving swiftly to where urVa's head rested. His hand trembled when he reached for her, and she held his big hand in both of hers.

"Little Gelfling . . ."

"You're awake," she whispered. "urVa, what happened? Who did this to you?"

"Indeed . . ." For the first time, he seemed to recognize her, his dark eyes catching a glimmer of light. "Oh, Naia. There you are. How goes the lighting of the Gelfling fires?"

"We've lit three. The Gelfling hearths burst into blue flames and etched the story . . ." Naia sighed and stroked a lock of urVa's pale hair. "I wish you could have seen it."

"The blue flames will make whole what was once undone," the Mystic said. "Will seal what has been sundered."

Naia clamped her hands together. "Will . . . seal? Aughra called them the fires of resistance. Why not the fires of rebellion? The fires of revolution?"

"Because this is not about war. We cannot forcefully remove the darkness in others. We can only find balance with the darkness within ourselves . . ."

"But the Skeksis—" Naia interrupted herself when she heard her voice rising. She closed her mouth and took a breath. "How are we supposed to win if all we do is *resist*?"

"*Resistance* . . . is a word with many meanings," he replied after a long, ponderous thought. "This world is ill. Its heart has been infected. When an organism senses an infection, it reacts in response. Healing elements that might not have been present before."

"Menders," Amri whispered. urVa nodded.

"Yes. Menders. That is a fine term. You see, over time, the organism develops a resistance to infection. Because of the menders. The fires . . . are part of Thra's process of resistance . . ."

Everything he was saying reminded Naia of her training in healing. Her mother had not limited her teachings to *vliyaya*, of course; there were many ways to heal, not all of which involved using precious life-essence magic. Medicines and herbs, knowing how bones were arranged in the body. Remembering which brightly colored flowers were poisonous, and of those poisonous ones, which could be converted to salves when boiled or burned or left in the sun.

"Thra is an organism, like a Gelfling or a tree," she said. "The menders are its way of trying to heal itself. The fires are the sign. Like . . . like a fever. An indication that the body is sick and trying to recover, and a way for the body to fix itself. And resistance . . ."

"Yes," was all urVa said. "As when the body builds a resistance to an illness which once plagued it. You menders. Will endure the deterioration caused by the Skeksis. You will find . . . the way."

Naia's eyes stung. "I don't know, urVa. I don't know how we can do it. We can't destroy the Skeksis. Not if it means destroying you, too. It wouldn't be right."

urVa folded his fingers around her hands so they were safe in his palm. To her surprise, he chuckled, an old, slow, familiar sound.

"For every one," he said, "there is another."

The old mantra settled onto Naia like a comforting quilt. Hands enclosed in his, warmed by the light coming from above, she felt the knot of anger in her stomach loosen. Shedding its coils. There was no doubt in the Archer's voice, as fragile as it was.

"Another way," Naia echoed. She wiped her eyes with the back of her hand. "We'll find another way."

"Very good, my little Naia," urVa said. Then his eyes closed, his head growing heavy and still again. Naia stroked his mane and sighed.

"I've been asleep for too long," she said. "But urVa still believes in me. In us. It's time we make a plan and continue on our path."

"Even if we know now that we can't kill the Skeksis?" Tavra asked, raising a brow.

"Yes," Naia said. What was done was done, and it was time to set her sights ahead, again. "We will find another way. And in the meantime, we will light the fires and unite the Gelfling."

They left urSu to tend urVa, walking in silence. Gurjin glanced at the cut on Amri's cheek, sighing and shaking his head, though he didn't ask about it. After that, Amri lagged behind, but Naia let him. She didn't know what to say to either of them right now.

They found a place near the cooking fire, where one of the Mystics stirred a large cauldron. Gurjin stretched his arms out as they all took a seat in the soft sand.

"We've discussed our options a bit while you were recovering. Kylan, would you like to do the honors?"

"Oh!" Kylan chirped, bright and eager to dispel the dreary mood. "Yes. Naia, it's so wonderful. urSan's been sharing her maps and charts with me since we've been here. She has maps of every region she's traveled in the Skarith Land. Up and down the Black River, into the desert—all along the Silver Sea and the Sifan Coast."

He took his book from his traveling pack, along with a few other rolled map scrolls. Naia could understand the figures of the land that were drawn on the map, though she couldn't read any of the writing. Where the maps in Kylan's book had always seemed digestible, small regions illustrated in heavy detail, urSan's sprawling scroll seemed to encompass the entire world.

"This is the valley where we are," Kylan said, pointing. "Near the headwaters of the Black River. We're very near Sami Thicket and not far from Stone-in-the-Wood. And I've marked here, and here, too. Domrak and Sog."

Naia nodded. "The four clans we haven't visited yet. The Spriton, the Stonewood, the Grottan, and the Drenchen."

Gurjin sat on Kylan's other side and traced a line with his finger. "Exactly. Domrak and the Swamp of Sog are equally distant, but in opposite directions. It makes sense for us to split up."

"No," Naia protested. "We're stronger in numbers."

"But we're more than we were," Gurjin said. "You and I need to get back to Sog. Kylan can come with us, since Sami Thicket is on the way. Onica, Tavra, and Amri will go to Grot and Stone-in-the-Wood. It makes the most sense."

Naia looked at the map. From where they were now, there was a path that went north toward Stone-in-the-Wood and Domrak, and a different one that went south through Sami Thicket to Sog. Staying together would more than double their traveling time. She hated it, but Gurjin was right.

"Well . . . what do you think, Tavra?" she asked, hoping the seasoned soldier might have a compelling reason for them to stay together. Tavra reviewed the map, cupping an elbow in one hand and tapping her cheek with the other. But when Onica touched her shoulder, leaned in, and whispered something in her ear, Tavra looked away from the scrolls and parchments. Instead, she looked at Amri, then Naia.

"I think Amri should go with the three of you. Onica and I will go north without him."

"But he's Grottan," Gurjin insisted, even though Amri still hadn't said anything, not even about his own fate. "Don't you think he should go north with you? To meet with his clan?"

"No," Tavra said with an air of finality. "I can navigate Domrak without him. The mountains will be infested with Arathim, and the Skeksis will be scouring the Dark Wood and the pathways to Ha'rar. It will be easier for us to travel alone. And after that, Onica and I must return Tae's body to Maudra Ethri and the Sifa in Cera-Na, where she can rest until her mind recovers. It will be a long and harrowing journey."

Gurjin bunched up his face. "But—"

"Therefore, we will go alone. The rest of you will go south to Sog."

"Maybe we should let Amri decide," Onica spoke up. Kylan nodded and all eyes turned to the Shadowling.

"Onica's right," Kylan said. "Amri, what do *you* want to do?"

Amri's ears flattened at the attention, thin lips quirking nervously. Naia thought for a moment he would say what she didn't want him to: that he preferred to part ways with them and go north. That maybe whatever had changed between the two of them would propel him even farther away from her.

It's just as well, anyway, she thought. She wasn't his *maudra.*

He should do what he felt was best. She was ready for him to say just that when he cleared his throat and sat up straight.

"If it's all the same, I'd like to go south to Sog," he said. "Tavra's right. It'll be easier for them to travel in a smaller number. And I'm really only familiar with Domrak. The Dark Wood, even Ha'rar and Cera-Na—I won't be any help there." In the end he shrugged and added, "Anyway. I've always wanted to see the Spriton Plains and the Swamp of Sog."

Tavra nodded with approval. "After we meet with Maudra Fara and Maudra Argot, light the fires of the Stonewood and the Grottan, Onica and I will make our way back to Cera-Na."

Naia realized Tavra was dressed in traveling gear, with new sandals made of dusty tan suede and hemp rope. She and Onica were preparing to depart soon.

It was a sad and sudden realization. Naia wanted to hold on to Tavra and Onica, so tight they could never leave her side. She had come to rely on them both, regarded them as older sisters. But she also knew that it was the right thing to return Tae's body to Maudra Ethri, where her mind could heal in safety with her clan.

"It will not be goodbye forever," Onica said, reaching out and squeezing Naia's hand. "We'll surely meet again when all the fires are lit and the Gelfling gather to confront the Skeksis."

Naia nodded, glum but understanding. This was the way that made the most sense, even if it meant saying goodbye. At least she didn't have to say goodbye to Amri.

Naia realized everyone was watching her, even the two Mystics who had sat on the other side of the fire, quiet as the stones that lined the valley. They were all waiting for her. Though Tavra was the warrior daughter of the All-Maudra, and Onica a Far-Dreamer who could speak to Thra. Though Gurjin had been a soldier at the Castle of the Crystal. Though Kylan had learned every song ever told in all of Gelfling tradition, and though Amri could hear the voices of the earth and knew all the wisdom stored in the Tomb of Relics. Though the gift of healing had been taken from her, leaving her angry and confused. Though all these things, it was Naia's response they waited upon.

"Then that is what we'll do," she said.

"Very good," Tavra said, rising. "Now that we've charted our course, Naia, would you come with me? I'd like to have a word with you alone."

CHAPTER 9

When they were out of earshot from the others at the cook fire, Tavra knelt below a tree. A moment later, her eyes closed and her chin drooped. She fell fast asleep, and the sapphire spider stirred, detaching from Tae's neck and creeping down her shoulder. Naia knelt beside them, shaded by the tree's wide leaves, and held out her hand so Tavra could stand in her palm, close enough that she could hear the crystal spider's quiet voice.

"Would you try . . . dreamfasting with me?"

In answer, Naia closed her eyes. She pictured Tavra in her Gelfling form, tall and elegant, with pale skin and long silver hair streaked with lavender. She opened her mind to dreamfast, using the memory of Tavra's true nature to guide her.

Though she had a different form, Tavra had not forgotten this most essential Gelfling tradition. The dreamfast began almost immediately. In her mind's eye, Naia saw them in the valley of stones, Tavra seated across from her, dressed in her Silverling armor. Sword at her hip, gossamer wings at her back like a cloak of prismatic ice. Naia smiled.

"How are you feeling?" Tavra asked in the dreamfast.

In the place where their minds were linked, where the dream-space existed only between the two of them, Naia's emotions were

a jumble. She held back as much as she could, but as soon as she opened her mouth, everything rushed out.

"I don't know," she confessed. "I'm going to keep trying. I don't know how to give up, and urVa seems to think I can find another way . . . but what if I can't? Everyone is following me, but I'm not even sure I know the way myself. Not even Gurjin seems to trust me right now. I feel like he's holding back."

"Gurjin is trying to look out for you," Tavra said mildly, as if she didn't care either way whether Naia believed her.

"And then there's Amri! I felt like we were, I don't know. *Connecting.* I thought maybe he . . . But then he said we were just friends. I feel like everyone is pulling away from me."

"We all handle emotions differently, especially during difficult times," Tavra replied kindly. "You and Gurjin may be twins, but you've had very different experiences. You cannot walk the same path forever, but that doesn't mean you are alone. And as for Amri, well. Perhaps you should look a little closer."

Naia coughed, cheeks warming. She wasn't sure what *that* meant.

"Anyway. You wanted to speak to me?"

"Ah, yes."

Tavra's ears twisted backward, her cheeks coloring. She shook her head, sighed. All the usual fidgets that she used to make when she struggled to speak the truth. She had been trained from a young age to be a soldier, and the daughter of the All-Maudra. She put her duties first and her own feelings second. It wasn't the truth that was difficult for her, but speaking from the heart.

"When we first met, I thought you were a naive and brash little thing," Tavra said finally. "You never did as you were told. You were stubborn and self-centered."

"Thanks, I think," Naia said with a snort.

"But I came to believe in your strong will. I came to understand that your brashness and naivete were a garden in which bravery could grow, unbridled by the restraints of the outside world or the worries about what other people might think of you. In that garden has grown the truest, purest courage I have ever seen."

Naia's cheeks burned. She said nothing, and Tavra continued.

"What I mean to say is, I am so very proud of you, Naia. I am so proud of all you have overcome, and how you continue to grow. It is something I have meant to tell you for a long time, but now that our paths lead apart for a time, I wanted to be sure I told you. It is something I wish I could have told others before my chance was gone."

"You mean Seladon and Brea?" Naia asked. Tavra's sisters.

Tavra hung her head and closed her eyes, ears angling back. For an instant, her image wavered, and Naia saw a tiny, crystal-bodied spider. But the vision returned, and Tavra sighed, spreading her hands so her palms filled with the sunlight of the dream-space.

"I may never be able to speak with either of my sisters again," she said. "Just as my mother will never be able to speak to any of her daughters again. Because of the Skeksis, and because of the era in which we now must survive, time has become so precious. More precious than I anticipated. We must hold close those we love, more now than ever before."

A tug came from deep within Naia's heart, like a ribbon had been tied there and someone was pulling on it. Without thinking, she threw her arms around Tavra's shoulders and squeezed her as tightly as she could. In the dreamfast, it was if she were really there. Warm and solid, breath caught in surprise—then strong and protective when she put her arms around Naia and returned her embrace.

"You've changed, too," Naia said when she leaned back. "I used to think you looked down on all us lowly non-Vapra. I thought you couldn't possibly have anything to teach me. But we were both wrong, and I'm not ashamed to say it. All I know is I'll miss you, Silverling."

Tavra put her hand on Naia's cheek. Naia could hear another sound, coming from the waking world. It was Kylan's *firca*, joining the Mystic musician near the fire. The dreamfast faded, and with it, so did the memory of Tavra's touch. Naia opened her eyes to the spider standing in her hands.

"But we'll meet again," she finished. "When we lead the Gelfling of all seven clans to victory, torches burning bright."

"We will certainly try," Tavra said.

The others rose when Naia and Tavra returned. They all knew it was time to say farewell. Tavra held out her hand, and one at a time they linked fingers around wrists.

"We go to light the fires within the hearts of the Stonewood and the Grottan," Tavra said. "Amri, please give us your trust as we make our way to Domrak. We will find your people and do whatever we can to ensure the safety of those who remain."

Amri nodded solemnly. "I believe in you."

"We will meet again, when the torches emerge from the darkness," Onica said, fixing Naia with her ocean-green gaze. Though the others could sound as confident and sure as they wanted, there was something invincible about the Sifa Far-Dreamer. Something undeniable about her reassurance. "We will resist, though we may not know what that means. If we continue to seek the light, I believe we will endure. Good luck, Naia. Kylan. Amri. Gurjin."

"And to you, Far-Dreamer," Naia said.

With that, their goodbyes were over. Tavra put the map in her belt where a sword had once been. Naia watched the two Gelfling wave a last time, then head off to the northeast, hand in hand.

She looked over her shoulder at the three boys who waited for her. Though she would miss Tavra's knowledge and skill with a sword, and Onica's warmth and sage wisdom, she realized it was the female companionship that she would miss the most.

"We might as well get going, too," Gurjin said. "Sog's still a long way off."

It felt odd, to leave just like that, but then again they had never intended to arrive in this peaceful, quiet valley at all. Naia took a last look, capturing the vision in her memory. As she did, her eyes landed on the gentle hands of urSol the Chanter, who had stood sipping his *ta* the whole time they'd been discussing.

"I will tell the others that you've gone," he said.

Naia bowed. "Thank you. And please give my thanks to urSan, when you see her next. For rescuing us, and her hospitality. And to Master urSu for his wisdom. And please take care of urVa—know we won't hurt the Skeksis. Not anymore."

Naia felt like a child with so many little things to say, so quickly, one after the other. And at the end of it all, she didn't even have a solution. Not even as they prepared to leave the Mystic Valley. Continuing along the path they'd made for themselves, though the goal Naia had once been so sure of was now a cloud changing shape in high wind, nearly dissipated altogether.

"We'll find another way," she said. "We'll have to."

urSol's nod was as long and graceful as a tree bough bobbing in the wind.

"You will," he said, and turned away.

CHAPTER 10

Naia stretched her arms and legs as they walked. Her strength was returning, and her limberness, even after all the time asleep, and the world didn't feel as if it might suddenly fall out from under her. The journey to Sami Thicket, and then to Sog, would not be as difficult as traveling through the highlands or the mountains, and especially not so harrowing as the freezing bluffs that surrounded Ha'rar. But now that the Skeksis knew the Gelfling were rebelling, nothing would be easy. Not anymore, not even a long walk through the open Spriton Plains.

A few times, she tried to summon the blue light to her hands. To mend broken blades of grass, or soothe the wing of a hopping bug that landed on her sleeve. But whenever she tried, the light flickered and went out—or never came at all. After a while, she stopped trying.

It was strange to travel south, back into territory Naia knew better and better the farther they went. For so long she had been forging ahead into places she'd heard of only in songs. Always relying on others for directions, hoping they could find their way from landmark to landmark. Never knowing exactly how far things might be or what dangers might lie in between. Each Gelfling clan knew their own little world, but few traveled far beyond it.

Once, Naia had been no different. But now that she had seen the blue Grottan caves and the wintry Ha'rar bluffs, she could understand why. Thra was vast and full of life. But while precious, *life* was not always safe. It took only one misstep or misunderstanding for a moment of wonder to become one of terror, whether it was getting lost in the depths of the Dark Wood or blundering into the strangling grasp of mountain finger-vines.

The trees thinned until they receded altogether. Naia and the others crested a hill and stood at the top, looking down into the vast plains that rolled before them like the waves of the sea at low tide. A herd of furry creatures grazed in a flock a ways off while great gusts of wind swept across the gentle hills. Naia listened to the grasses sliding against one another, took in a deep breath, smelling the sweet scent of wildflowers.

"How does it feel to be back?" Amri asked Kylan.

The song teller's black braid moved with the wind, his collar ruffled as he gazed out on the land that was his home. "I don't know," he said. He lowered his hand so the tufts of the tall grass touched his palm. "It's bittersweet."

Amri swiveled his ears, looking back and forth between Kylan and Naia.

"What do you mean?"

Kylan shrugged. "This land is where I was born and grew up. But it's also the land where the Hunter took my parents, and where I could never fit in with the other Spriton in Sami Thicket . . . I ran away. I suppose I never told you that."

The confession came out with an odd confidence. When

Kylan had run away from Sami Thicket and joined her, he'd been a different person. Awkward and clumsy, a musician who was more interested in song-telling than throwing a spear like the rest of the Spriton his age. He'd left because he had felt he had no other choice, resisted thinking of it as running away.

The way he said it now, claiming what he'd done, made Naia smile. He was no longer the nervous, timid boy who came to life only when his hands played his lute and the songs of lore came singing from his lips. That courage had grown in him. Now he wielded it against darkened creatures. Against Gelfling-eating plants and Arathim. Even the Skeksis Lords.

"Maudra Mera will be surprised to see you," she said. "How far do you think it is to Sami Thicket?"

Kylan held up a hand, shielding his eyes and scanning the land. He pointed to a distant spot, almost obscured by the hills and the wisps of low-lying clouds.

"That'll be it. There will be plenty of streams and places to rest along the way."

"Fine," Gurjin said. "But we won't be resting long. We'll stop to fill our waterskins, but we need to keep our pace."

It seemed like a thing Naia should have said, as the leader. But he was right, and it wasn't like she disagreed.

They walked the better part of the day across the plains, passing through meadow rife with nectar-sweet flowers and thick fields of tall, whistling stalks that swayed over their heads. When the suns reached their highest, Amri pulled on his hood and walked with his hand on Kylan's back for guidance. Naia tried not to wonder why he hadn't asked for her shoulder, when he always had in the past. Tried not to worry about why it mattered or why she cared when it was all the same in the end. Friends helping friends.

While they walked, Kylan told Gurjin the song of all they had done. As she listened to him recall their adventures leading up to meeting Gurjin again aboard skekSa's ship, Naia felt almost as though he were telling the song to a stranger. Gurjin, her brother, with whom she'd been raised side by side. Her other half. Until the truth about the Skeksis had come out, anyway. Now she felt as though she hardly knew him. Was it because of everything that had happened to them since then? Dangerous, life-threatening things—beautiful, life-changing things, too. Kylan sang of those things even now: While Gurjin had been held captive at the castle, Naia had found her wings. While he had returned south to Sog to warn the Drenchen, Naia and her new friends had traveled as far north as Ha'rar. Those great moments had happened to them separately.

It was all a part of growing up. And in doing so, perhaps it was inevitable that they would grow apart.

When evening came, they found a little creek and set up camp for the night. The breeze calmed as the air cooled. Between the smoke from the fire and the quiet bubbling of the creek, it seemed like it might be a perfect night.

"What's Maudra Mera like?" Gurjin asked as he poked at the fire. Amri shed his hood and picked up one of the spits, spearing a fruit from their traveling pouch and propping it over the flames.

"I mean, I've heard a bit about her from friends at the castle, but what should we expect? How easy will it be to convince her to join us?"

Kylan put his own fruit in the fire and watched the rind crackle and smolder, popping open so the sweet juice inside bubbled out.

"Not very," he said. "After my parents died, Maudra Mera looked after me herself, so I got to know her very well. How she is both in private and when she stands before the Skeksis. I know that she fears them, more than anything. Fears their power and their strength, and believes the best way to protect her clan is to do whatever it takes to maintain the Skeksis' favor."

"Tae told us what happened when the six *maudra* gathered in Ha'rar to bless Seladon as the new All-Maudra," Amri added. "It was the Skeksis that killed All-Maudra Mayrin, and the Skeksis who put Seladon in charge. Maudra Mera blessed Seladon's ascent, so in a way, she's already sided with the Skeksis."

Kylan nodded slowly, then changed his mind and shook his head. "That's not really fair. Seladon is the oldest of Mayrin's daughters. She would have become All-Maudra whether or not the Skeksis were the ones behind Mayrin's death. Just as Naia will become *maudra* of the Drenchen, no matter the circumstances of her mother's retirement."

Naia shifted her weight. "Let's try to avoid thinking of those two things in the same thought," she said. She had always known that would be her future, but she didn't want to think about it happening so soon, and she certainly didn't want to be lumped in the same sentence as Seladon. Naia had never met Tavra's older sister, but her reputation as a keeper to the old ways preceded her. If what Tavra said was true, Seladon—like Maudra Mera—would do whatever it took to be sure the Skeksis treated the Vapra well.

Kylan sighed and said, "Maudra Mera will be difficult to convince, if only because she has been so loyal to the Skeksis for so long . . . and because for so long, it has worked."

"Save the Spriton at the sacrifice of Gelfling from other clans," Naia said. "The last time I was here, she was only nice to me because she wanted favor with my mother."

"Don't forget that Maudra Fara was the same in Stone-in-the-Wood," Kylan replied. He was right; Maudra Fara had been more cordial about it, but the fact was she'd cared more about the Stonewood Gelfling than she'd cared about Naia and Kylan—or even Rian, who was one of her own.

"All of the *maudra* seem to care only about their own clans," Amri murmured. "Even Maudra Argot. Everywhere we go, the *maudra* are preoccupied only with how to save their clan. They don't care about what happens to everyone else . . . It can't stay this way if the Gelfling are going to survive."

"I think that's part of lighting these fires," Gurjin replied, staring into the crackling flames of their own little campfire. He leaned back. "Back at the castle, the guards came from all over. But even so, the Skeksis always had these ways of drawing lines between us. After Mira went missing, the Skeksis started telling everyone it was a Stonewood that did it. Sure enough, even though we all acted like friends the day before, everyone turned on Rian and the other Stonewood. Like they were all waiting for a reason . . . like we'd been taught to think of each other as different, even though we're all Gelfling."

"What about you?" Naia asked. "You're Rian's best friend, aren't you?"

"After Mira, maybe," Gurjin chuckled, though it was sad. "When the Skeksis told everyone it was a Stonewood, yeah. For a moment I wondered if maybe Rian had done something. Stonewood are supposed to be stubborn and aggressive, and Rian's not exactly the opposite of that. It took his dreamfast to make me believe."

"It wasn't until the Skeksis came that we were divided and learned to think of ourselves as different," Kylan sighed.

"And it was the Skeksis who ordained the All-Maudra," Naia added. "And who chose the Vapra."

The picture was growing clearer, like a reflection in urSu's bowl of water as the ripples slowly stilled. The image of a fertile land, Gelfling growing like sprouts. One breed of flower with seven varieties, growing in a million beautiful colors. Then the light of the Great Conjunction split the urSkeks. The Skeksis, whose wise, cruel minds knew how to make the most of the Gelfling, their new loyal subjects. By plucking one of the flowers and declaring it the most beautiful of all.

This was the history of the Gelfling and the Skeksis. The Skeksis had charted the course and laid out the trail, and the Gelfling had followed it without even knowing. For almost a thousand trine, it had been this way. Now it was finally time for their ways to converge.

"Even if Maudra Mera fears the Skeksis, and even if she's sworn loyalty to Seladon as the All-Maudra, we'll find a way to persuade her," Amri said. "She fears the Skeksis because she wants their protection. She wants their protection because she loves her clan."

"It was the same with Maudra Ethri, who wanted to sail away from the Skeksis to save the Sifa," Kylan added.

"Yeah! She wanted to run because she loved her clan, and it was that love that gave her the courage to stay and fight. Remember?" Amri caught Naia's eyes eagerly with his, then blushed as if it were an accident before he pulled his hood down again.

"Remember . . ."

Ethri and the Sifa. Periss and the Dousan. Even Tavra and the Vapra. She set aside her doubts. About the Skeksis and how to endure them. How to heal the Crystal and Thra. If she fixated on the mystery of the stars and never looked down, it was only a matter of time before she tripped. It was her friends that were right in front of her. Not the Skeksis or the Mystics or the broken Crystal. They were relying on her to find the path and lead them down it, and she would not fail them.

"It is that love that we will nurture in Maudra Mera until it blooms into a fire," she finished.

"Well, we will certainly try," Kylan said, plucking his supper from the fire. The rest of them did the same, and they ate beneath the stars as the Sister Moons crept into the sky.

CHAPTER 11

On the second morning of their journey to Sami Thicket, Naia woke to the sound of furtive footsteps approaching on tiptoe.

She opened her eyes without moving. Gurjin was facing her, just as alert and still. They waited until the footsteps were on the other side of the small line of trees that circled their campsite, Naia slowly twisting her ear to catch the whispers:

"Drenchen? How did they get past the rangers?"

"Who cares. Get ready."

The dim shadow of two long spears rippled over Naia's shoulder. She moved her hand on top of a big rock that was resting in the grass beside her head. A twig snapped. As the owners of the two voices charged out from the trees, Naia and Gurjin leaped up, Naia catching the closer attacker's spear in the crook of her elbow and smashing her rock against its shaft so it broke in half. To her right, the other spear snapped as Gurjin cut it to pieces with his dagger. Somewhere at her back, Kylan yelped.

Two Spriton in light leather armor stood, mouths agape, holding their broken spears in numb hands. They were dark-skinned, like Kylan, one a familiar boy with black hair and the other a girl with dark blue locs, her bright green wings half-splayed in surprise. Naia dropped her rock and picked up the end of the spear with the point, holding it out and daring them to move while Kylan and Amri rose from their bedding.

"Hi," Naia said. "Good morning."

"G-good morning," the girl stammered. She spread her fingers, dropping the remains of her spear. "No need to do anything brash—"

"Like jumping on sleeping travelers with spears drawn?" Gurjin asked, waving with his dagger for the other Spriton to drop what was left of his spear, too. He did, and Gurjin kicked the pieces of wood away.

"Listen, maybe this is all a misunderstanding," the girl said. She nodded with her chin over their shoulders. Naia assumed she was gesturing to Kylan and Amri, but she didn't take her eyes off the two Spriton to look. "We never see Drenchen north of Sami Thicket, but I see you're with one of our . . ."

The sentence fell awkwardly out of the girl's mouth when Kylan stepped between Naia and Gurjin. The boy gasped.

"*Kylan?*"

"Hello, Lun," Kylan said to the boy. Then to the girl, "And Gereni."

When she heard the boy's name, Naia knew how she had recognized him. When she had first come to Sami Thicket, he had been sitting with Maudra Mera, preparing food for the Skeksis. She moved aside for Kylan and lowered the point of her half spear, though she didn't toss it aside just yet.

"Kylan—we thought you— Where did you *go?*" Gereni asked.

Over him, she looked back and forth between Naia, Gurjin, and Amri, who had come to stand on Naia's other side. "And who are these people?"

"Friends. What are you two doing scouting so far from Sami Thicket?"

Lun pursed his lips and gave Naia and Gurjin a suspicious look from the corner of his eye. "Why don't you come back to Sami Thicket, and Maudra Mera can explain."

"Great!" Gurjin said, slinging his dagger at his hip. "The more the merrier. Wait a moment while we pack up our things, would you?"

"Not *you*," Lun snorted. "We've had enough of your kind of late. It's your fault we're scouting way out here, anyway! And I don't even know *what* you are."

The last he said to Amri, who raised a brow and said, "Wow. All right."

Gurjin exchanged a look with Naia. "Charming, aren't they? My favorite at the castle, too. They always knew how to make people feel welcome."

"Weren't we just talking about this last night?" Naia asked under her breath. Then aloud, "Listen. We're friends of Kylan's and we're not interested in fighting with you. We have important information for Maudra Mera. I'd appreciate your help in making sure we reach her."

"I'm not going back to Sami Thicket without them," Kylan said. Lun didn't move, not in his expression or any other part of his body, but Gereni seemed friendlier. At the very least, she'd been relieved to see him. Kylan saw it, too, and appealed to her. "We've been traveling south for days. Whatever's happened between the Spriton and the Drenchen, we're not a part of it. You can trust them. Like you'd trust me."

Gereni turned an ear toward him, assessing the other three Gelfling that stood before her. Naia crossed her arms and waited until the Spriton girl folded up her wings and nodded.

"Fine."

While they packed up their camp as quickly as they could, Naia listened to Lun and Gereni argue.

"Gereni, we can't trust the Drenchen, even if Kylan says so. They could be spies from Maudra Laesid's encampment!"

"Even if they are, at least they're in our sights," Gereni replied sternly. "And don't you recognize them? They're Naia and Gurjin. The two that have been traveling the world spreading the rumors about the Skeksis."

"Wait, go back. Maudra Laesid's what now?" Gurjin asked.

The two Spriton looked over their shoulders as the group of them started walking, leaving the cold, damp embers of their campfire behind. Kylan shouldered their pack, and Naia slipped the spear head in her belt just in case.

"I suppose if you've been north all this time, you wouldn't know," Lun said with a little curl of the lip. "Maudra Laesid's brought the Drenchen north of the swamp. They're marching on the Castle of the Crystal."

"What?" Naia hissed. "She wouldn't—" She stopped herself before she could finish, though, because it wasn't true. Her mother was a great warrior, stubborn and righteous. There was no doubting she would raise her spear against the Skeksis if she felt the time was right.

"So you're saying she would," Amri said.

"Unfortunately," she replied grimly.

"She would, and did," Gereni continued. "But she cannot cross the Spriton Plains without our leave, and Lord skekUng has ordered us to stop them. Though after what happened in Stone-in-the-Wood, I wonder if we should let them through."

"What happened in Stone-in-the-Wood?" Naia asked. But Gereni and Lun's patience had expired, and neither of them answered. All Naia could think of was what they had already guessed, since hearing what had happened when Seladon had taken the crown of the All-Maudra. It was Maudra Fara and Maudra Laesid who had declined to bless her ascent, and now it was Stone-in-the-Wood where something had happened, and the border of Sog where something else soon might.

They walked behind Lun and Gereni for most of the morning and into the afternoon. Naia kept looking beyond each hill, waiting to see the cluster of dense trees that hid the Spriton village of Sami Thicket, but whenever she looked, she saw only more grass-covered hills under a sky full of soft white clouds. By sunset, they came around a hill pierced with a light gray boulder, and suddenly they had arrived.

A small forest grew in a pocket of hills, and in the emerald and cinnamon trees Naia could see watchtowers, ladders, and other signs of Gelfling life. Torches were lit against the evening, shedding red light on the path into the village. Two Spriton sentries came out to greet Lun and Gereni, eyes widening when they recognized Kylan. They gathered around him, hardly noticing the other three Gelfling who had arrived with him.

"Is that Kylan? Mera's little story stitcher!"

"We thought you got eaten by a ruffnaw!"

Kylan cleared his throat and stepped aside, making room for Naia, Gurjin, and Amri. It was strange to see him surrounded by the athletic Spriton scouts with their armor and spears. She had forgotten that, among the Spriton, Kylan's skill as a song teller bore little weight. It was the reason he had left, after all.

"We're here to speak with Maudra Mera," Kylan said evenly. "This is Naia, Maudra Laesid's eldest daughter and the one who will become *maudra* after her. We need to know what's going on with the Drenchen, and quickly."

The scouts took note, and Lun waved them on. "Don't worry. We'll take them to Maudra Mera. Come on."

A footpath had been cleared between the entrance to the thicket and the village itself: a ring of wood and clay homes arranged around a center pavilion where the hearth fire burned. As they stepped foot into the center space, Kylan's thin lips were pressed tight, his hand holding on to the *firca* hanging around his neck. His gaze was steadfast, directed across the pavilion to the big round house that belonged to Maudra Mera. Whatever his feelings were about returning to the place from which he'd run, he was determined.

"You don't have to escort us all the way there, Lun," he said.

"I know the way. If Naia and Gurjin try to run, or do whatever it is you think they'll do, I'm sure you'll see it from over here."

Lun opened his mouth to protest, but Gereni held out a hand. "Fine. But be warned. Everyone has been called to duty since the Drenchen approached the border. If you try to run through the thicket, we'll see you. And we'll catch you."

Naia tried not to roll her eyes, and Gurjin tossed an overly dramatic salute. "Understood, captain!" he said. Then, "Ouch!" when Naia thumped him hard in the arm.

"Your friends are rude," Amri commented wryly as they left the two scouts behind and approached Maudra Mera's house. Kylan walked ahead, shoulders squared, his stride growing bolder with each step. He raised his chin and lowered his hands to his sides.

"They're not my friends," he said. "I was an embarrassment when I left, and they never came to find me. Neither they nor Maudra Mera care about me or what we've been through. No one is going to be nice to us, but it doesn't matter. They never were before, and it doesn't change what we need to do."

Maudra Mera opened her door as they drew close enough to knock. She was not tall like many of the younger Spriton, dwarfed by her red and brown robes embroidered with fine needlework and beads. Her shining black hair was braided and tied in loops at her back between her wings. She looked upon Kylan with a face that seemed wearier than the last time Naia had seen her.

"Maudra Mera—" Kylan began, calm and braced for her reprehension. But all his anticipation was for naught. His squared shoulders softened, his knees trembling as Maudra Mera grabbed him by the shirt and yanked him down, wrapping both arms around him and squeezing him as tightly as she could.

"Oh, my little Kylan," she whispered into his shoulder, and Naia could swear she saw a tear glistening in the corner of the *maudra's* eye. "You came home."

"I did," Kylan said when he found his voice. He stood back so Maudra Mera could see his accompaniment. She looked upon them with varying levels of wariness, saving a particularly hard-eyed grimace for Naia. "We've come from . . . well, a great many places. But we have important news for you, about what you must do if we're going to . . . withstand the Skeksis."

Maudra Mera huffed through her nose, and Naia wondered if she was going to kick them out.

"I promise I've got nothing to do with what my mother is doing," Naia assured her. "I'm here as Kylan's friend, and as a messenger for Aughra, Thra, and the rest of the Gelfling clans. If you tell me what's going on with my mother, I may be able to help both of you."

This wasn't about making sure the Spriton or the Drenchen were victorious. It was about finding the right way through. Naia hoped Maudra Mera could sense her earnestness. Maudra Mera's eyes had already dried from the emotion of seeing Kylan again, hardening her into the shrewd, focused *maudra* that Naia remembered.

"I see. Yes, come in, my soggy dear. And all of you. We have much to discuss."

She brought them inside, waving them to the large slab of timber that served as her table. The smell of the wood and clay mingled with the sweet and bitter scents of fabric dye and thread. Tapestries hung on the walls, adorned with ribbons, bells, and the occasional pair of dangling, half-finished shoes.

"So you've finally come home after running off and making me sick with worry," Maudra Mera said, circling the table as they sat around it. "I sent a message by swoothu to Maudra Fara when the Skeksis came looking for you. They took Lun's sisters instead. Maudra Fara never replied to my message, and after that, I could only assume they'd captured you. You could have at least sent word to me that you were safe."

She wasn't lying. Maudra Fara had brought that very message to them in Stone-in-the-Wood, but Kylan had thrown it in the fire. The song teller grimaced.

"I'm sorry."

"If all the rumors are true, you've joined the resistance against the Skeksis, isn't it? I heard from someone that it was you that sent the message on the pink petals. Though I managed to avoid touching any of the cursed things myself."

Naia spoke up when Kylan looked down at his hands, curling his fingers into his palms.

"Maudra Mera, please. Kylan's sorry about what's happened and that he didn't send word to you. That's why we're here. We've been given the task by Aughra to meet with the seven clans and light the fires of resistance against the Skeksis. They've defiled the Crystal, and they're feeding on the Gelfling. They're disrupting the way of Thra. We have to unite, all seven of us, if we're going to be strong enough to survive."

"I've heard about these so-called fires of resistance," Maudra Mera said sharply. "You know what I think about it? Nonsense. Of course the Skeksis have defiled the Crystal. Of course they feed on us. I'm sure that's the fate that has befallen Lun's sisters. None of this should shock anyone. Why do you think I've been so loyal to them all this time? Why do you think I grovel at their feet and kiss their gold and silver rings?"

"So now you obey their command without thinking?" Naia asked. "Stopping the Drenchen from crossing the Spriton Plains? That's not staying out of the Skeksis' affairs—that's taking their side."

"You Drenchen—you and your mother are going to get your entire clan killed, going up against the Lords of the Castle this way. We all know what happens to *maudra* who stand up to the Skeksis."

"All-Maudra Mayrin died because she stood up for what was right," Kylan said. "Maudra Mera, please. I know you fear the Skeksis and what they can do—"

Maudra Mera let out a gasp of anger, wings flaring at her shoulders as she drew up to her full, if still diminutive, height. "Yes, I do! I fear them more than death itself—and Mayrin and Fara should have, too. It would have been safer for them to stay out of the Skeksis' affairs!"

And Fara? An ugly chill crawled down Naia's neck.

"Mera. What happened in Stone-in-the-Wood?" she asked.

Maudra Mera's cheeks dimpled as she clenched her teeth, her brow etched with worry and dread and the weight of terrible news.

"You didn't hear?" she asked coldly. "After she returned from All-Maudra Seladon's blessing, Maudra Fara rallied her Stonewood soldiers and took them to attack the Skeksis at the Castle of the Crystal. Though she brought every Gelfling of fighting age to the battle, the Skeksis knew they were coming. While you and your lot traipsed across the land lighting fires of resistance, Maudra Fara and the Stonewood were soundly defeated. Killed or captured and brought to the castle to be drained."

Naia felt as if she might sink into the ground, eaten up by the infinite darkness that lay buried beneath the crust of the earth. She wanted to say it couldn't be true, but the graveness in the Spriton *maudra*'s thin, wiry body told her it was.

"As of four nights past," Maudra Mera finished, "mighty Stone-in-the-Wood is no more."

CHAPTER 12

Naia remembered the moment they'd been told All-Maudra Mayrin had been murdered. This was similar, like being struck in the back of the head. Without warning, without the chance to brace themselves. And now they could only stumble in the hopes they wouldn't fall.

"This can't be," Kylan said. "Stone-in-the-Wood? If Maudra Fara planned to take the fight to the castle . . . then why . . ."

"The Skeksis knew long before she and her warriors had left," Maudra Mera replied. "Whether it was the Arathim or some other spies that told them, it doesn't matter. They ambushed Maudra Fara as she attacked the castle. When the Stonewood retreated, they pursued her. All the way back to Stone-in-the-Wood, which they destroyed as a threat to us all. Since then, the Skeksis have been ranging with their terrible monsters hunting down any survivors . . . even as far as Sami Thicket!"

A pang drove itself deep into Naia's gut. "The Skeksis have been here?"

"Indeed," Maudra Mera snapped with a glare so hard, Naia flinched. "Lord skekSa the Mariner was here herself, looking for you Drenchen *rebels*."

"skekSa . . ."

"Yes. She told me that if I were to see you, I should hold you prisoner for her until she returned! Can you imagine? And with what happened in Stone-in-the-Wood . . ."

So she'd survived her ship when it had plunged down into the ocean . . . *Of course she'd survived*, Naia scolded herself. urSan had been alive when they'd met her in the Mystic Valley. If urSan was alive, then so was skekSa. Alive and so ruthless in her pursuit, she'd reached Sami Thicket before Naia and her friends, probably while they'd been recovering with the Mystics.

"Are you going to do as she said?" Gurjin asked.

"If she finds out you've been here and I don't, then what will become of the Spriton?" The Spriton *maudra*'s gaze softened. She turned and cupped Kylan's face in her hands. "I've been losing my mind with worry, Kylan. I don't know what to do! But at least if you're here in Sami Thicket, I can keep you safe—"

Kylan clenched his fists on the table.

"I don't need to be kept safe! Especially not if skekSa is out looking for us . . . All *four* of us. Naia, Gurjin, Amri, *and* me. And Tavra, the All-Maudra's daughter. And a Sifa Far-Dreamer, and Rian. If you're going to take them captive, you'll have to take me, too. Our resistance against the Skeksis was a task given to us by Aughra herself."

"Aughra!" Maudra Mera laughed, though it was strained. "Aughra, who turned her only eye away from the Gelfling once the Skeksis appeared? It was the Skeksis who helped us. The Skeksis now who threaten us. The Skeksis who we must fear and obey. Unless you have another proven way for us to defeat them."

There it was again. Defeating the Skeksis. Stopping them forever. One time, not too long ago, Naia would have had an answer to that. But now she didn't. No one did.

"Maudra Mera, please," Naia tried once more. "Maudra Fara lost to the Skeksis because she was alone. If the Spriton join us—"

"I have seen sixty-four trine of Skeksis rule, Naia," Mera interrupted. "I have seen more of it than you and more than even your mother. I know what the Emperor is like. I know the path he will take. Now that their eyes have turned on us, the Gelfling, I can see no other way to survive. This is the path that is laid before us. Subservience and survival is our destiny. We cannot deny what is plain before our eyes. We must instead do with it what we can. It is our duty as *maudra*—mine *and* yours—to ensure the survival of our clans."

Maudra Mera swept up and waved them sharply to the door. Kylan followed without protest, pulling Naia up to do the same. The four of them followed her back out to the pavilion. No guards waited, and Maudra Mera didn't call for any. Naia glanced at Kylan.

"So you're . . . *not* taking us captive for skekSa?" he asked.

"I will permit you to remain in Sami Thicket until tomorrow," Mera said. "But you must not wander into the wood, and you must be prepared to depart first thing in the morning. Am I making myself clear?"

"Very," Naia said.

And with that, Maudra Mera left them, like a pair of sandals half-finished. Naia folded and refolded her arms. The news of

Stone-in-the-Wood was a sign that the Skeksis were now wide-awake to the Gelfling resistance. What had been a secret was out in the open, and there was no way to call it back. And what had been Naia's solution was no longer an option. And on top of all that, skekSa was after them with a personal grudge.

"Do you think Maudra Mera's right?" Amri asked. "Will your mother attack the Spriton?"

Naia tilted her head back, wishing all her worries would tumble out so she could think clearly. A thin veil of clouds were stretched across the sky, shedding light rain that quickly dried under the heat of the hearth fire and the torches that were being lit around the pavilion. The Spriton were preparing for their communal supper, probably of roasted squash as usual, and the flames in the hearth were big enough to make enough of the stuff for all of the villagers.

"Not unless they attack first," Gurjin said. "So long as things remain this way, no one will get hurt. We have to stay calm and not cause trouble. That'd only make it worse."

"But how long can things stay like this?" Kylan asked. "The scales are in balance, but barely. The moment one of the two clans makes any move, the other will react. It's only a matter of time. And the Skeksis . . ."

Naia gazed across the pavilion, watching the Spriton make ready for supper. The distant clanging of a hammer on an anvil reminded her of someone tapping their foot, waiting. Just a reminder that time was always passing, whether they wanted it to or not.

"Then we'll just have to light the Spriton fire before it comes to that," she said.

"So what do we do now?" Gurjin asked. "How do we change her mind?"

"I could try to talk to Maudra Mera alone, but I don't know that it'll make a difference," Kylan said. "She can only see one path. One future."

Amri sighed. "Too bad she can't see the dream-etchings that happened when the other fires were lit. It might inspire her."

When they'd joined hands with Maudra Ethri, Onica, and the other Sifa aboard the *Omerya*, lit the Sifa fire, the mystic flames had etched their song across the coral ship's deck. The same etchings had appeared in the cloisters of the Dousan Wellspring, and even now the song of the Vapra was emblazoned on the crystalline citadel in Ha'rar.

"We could dreamfast with her and show her," Naia suggested.

"It won't make a difference to her," Kylan said. "Whether we tell her or show her in dreamfast. Those are the songs of the other clans. Maudra Mera is concerned only with the Spriton."

"Eel-feathers," Naia swore. Dreamfasts were only of things that had already happened. A sharing of memories, not hopes. None of them were Far-Dreamers like Onica. Telling the songs of the future in dreamfast was out of their grasp.

Naia straightened as an idea bolted up her spine and down her arms.

"What if we show her without dreamfasting? What if we show all the Spriton a vision of the future?"

"How, Far-Dreaming?" Amri asked. "Onica is probably already in Domrak by now."

Naia pointed at Kylan's *firca* where it hung at his breast.

"We don't need a Far-Dreamer. We have a song teller. What's the difference between a memory of the past, or an idea of what could happen in the future? Maybe we can't show Maudra Mera what *will* happen, but when you tell songs, Kylan . . . it's magic. You could tell a song of how things *could* be."

Kylan looked down at the *firca*, then back at Naia. "I can't make up that kind of song on the fly."

"You've done it before. The song you told Rian—Jarra-Jen and the Dew Tree?"

Kylan's ears flattened. "That was different. I was just trying to make him feel better. This is more important—the whole fate of the Spriton could be riding on whether I tell the song properly. I don't think I can do it."

The fleeting sparkle of hope fizzled out, and Naia drooped again. She couldn't make Kylan do it, and even if she could, if he didn't believe in himself, there was no way anyone else was going to.

"What's going on over there?" Amri asked, nodding with his chin toward a group of Spriton maneuvering a wood handcart close to the hearth where the food was being prepared. The cart handlers weren't dressed in the heavier leather of a spear thrower, instead outfitted in lightweight armor. They stood by while the food preparers collected squash rinds, stems, and branches and tossed them into the cart.

"Looks like feed," Gurjin said. "That's the kind of stuff we fed the Landstriders and the armaligs back at the castle."

"But out here in the plains, the Landstriders forage," Kylan murmured. "There's plenty for the small herds we keep, in the thicket and the meadows nearby."

"Then what—or who—are they feeding?"

They watched as the cart was filled, nearly overflowing with produce. Then the Spriton at the front lit a torch from the cooking fire and led the way while the three in the rear pushed the cart along the dirt path that led out of the far edge of the pavilion into the forest.

"Remember how Maudra Mera was very adamant that we don't wander into the wood?" Amri said, arching a brow. Naia nodded.

"Yes, I do. You remember that, Gurjin?"

"Yeah," he said. She waited for the twinkle of curiosity to light in his eye. Instead, he said, "And I think maybe we should do as she said. We're already treading lightly here. If she finds out we've gone sneaking around, she'll probably kick us out sooner, and how will we light the fire with the Spriton then?"

Naia frowned. There was a time when her brother would have been the first to suggest following the wagon drivers. She remembered his hesitation to go after Amri on skekSa's ship, too. Another sign of how they were growing apart.

"Then you don't have to come," she said. "But I'm going to find out what's going on."

She didn't wait for him to agree. Amri followed her, and

then Kylan. Gurjin sighed, and the four of them headed into the thicket together.

They followed the Spriton as they wheeled their cart all the way out of the thicket, to the far side where the hills dipped into a gentle valley. Naia and the others scampered after, staying just far enough away. The moment they crested the hill, they froze.

The valley glittered with torchlight. Naia hadn't seen it from the other side as they'd approached Sami Thicket, hidden by the wood and meadow grass. Tall, dark shapes moved in the valley, and the misty night air murmured with the snorting, nasal grunting of the long-legged, wide-eared creatures that flocked below. Naia didn't need Amri's night vision to know what she was seeing.

"Landstriders," she gasped.

Dozens of them, the buckles of their riding gear shining in the dim torchlight. Spriton warriors groomed and dressed them for battle, some of the Gelfling wearing pointed black and shining armor and billowing capes.

"There are so many of them," Amri said. "Are there usually?"

"No," Kylan said, the single word like a stone.

Gurjin grimaced. "Those Gelfling in the black armor—they're not Spriton. They're guards from the Castle of the Crystal."

"So the Skeksis sent reinforcements when they asked the Spriton to stop the Drenchen from advancing?" Amri asked. "Naia, what are we going to do?"

The rotten feeling in her gut grew bigger by the moment. The anger wouldn't do anything to solve the problem, but she didn't know what else to feel in that moment. Amri's question echoed through her head, louder every time she couldn't calm it with an answer: *What are we going to do?*

She took a deep breath. This wasn't a time to get lost with worry.

"Depends on what they're doing," Naia said. "Amri, can you see?"

He gave her a sideways glance. "Just because I can see in the dark doesn't mean I know anything about Landstrider gear," he quipped wryly. "What am I looking for?"

"Look at their legs," Gurjin suggested. "Are they armored?"

Naia scanned the creatures below, even though she knew Amri would be able to make a much better assessment. One of the Landstriders let out a piercing whistle through its bony proboscis as a Spriton came too close with a torch. Its rider pulled it away by the reins, though the grumpy creature still kicked up clods of dirt with its hooves. It was finally sated by the cherry-squash rinds being distributed by the Spriton wagon drivers, but not before Naia saw black panels of leather strapped to its long, thin legs.

"There's something strapped on near the knees," Amri said, just as Naia noticed the same thing. "It's hard to tell if it's armor from here, though. And not all the Landstriders are wearing it. Why, what does it mean?"

"If they're armored, it means they're more likely preparing for a blockade," Gurjin said. "Armor weighs them down and restricts their movements, but it would help protect them against enemies on foot. You would never take a fully armored Landstrider into a headlong attack. It wouldn't be able to run or maneuver. Maudra

Mera is just preparing the Landstriders to make a stand and defend in case the Drenchen come."

Naia frowned.

"But Amri said they're not all armored. If Maudra Mera wanted to ambush the Drenchen first at night, with full force, wouldn't it be more strategic if some of the Landstriders were armored and some weren't?"

Naia couldn't stop imagining what damage they and their riders could do to the Drenchen sleeping out under the open sky. Out of their element, whose wings couldn't carry them like the Spriton, and whose unshod feet were used to the soft swamp. Not the prickly, rocky earth and the biting brambles. If the Spriton brought the Landstriders against the Drenchen, especially in the dead of the night, the Drenchen would surely lose. Maybe permanently, if Maudra Mera's fear of the Skeksis made her ruthless. If that happened, no amount of time would be able to restore what might be lost.

"It's always more strategic to have both," Gurjin said, but he wasn't swayed. He crossed his arms. "I still think she's preparing for defense in case the Drenchen come."

"Then why are they armored *now*? At the end of the evening like this? Look at that soldier—he's in full gear, spear in hand."

"He could be preparing to go on patrol," Gurjin replied. "If she's expecting the Drenchen, naturally they have to be prepared. It takes time to dress a Landstrider, and they can be fussy about change. If the Drenchen approached suddenly and the guards had to jump quickly into the saddle and rush into battle, the Landstriders might spook."

Naia took in the scene below, trying not to bristle. Gurjin might have the experience of working with Landstrider riders and guards from the Castle of the Crystal, but it still didn't feel right.

"What do you think, Kylan?" Gurjin asked. The song teller had been quiet as they'd assessed the scene. "Do you think Maudra Mera is preparing to strike tonight, or do you think they're keeping at the ready to form a blockade?"

Kylan pressed his lips into a flat line.

"I don't know anything about Landstriders and war, but I know Maudra Mera. She is afraid of the Skeksis, most certainly, and if the Drenchen come to Sami Thicket with spears bared, she won't hesitate to bring the Landstriders against them. But as it is, I have to agree with Gurjin on this one. I don't think she's the type to ambush anyone in the middle of the night. Especially if she hasn't been attacked first."

"So that's that, then," Gurjin said, before Naia could protest. "They're forming a blockade. No one's going into battle tonight. We found out what's going on, and it doesn't change anything that we've already learned. Let's get out of here before they see us snooping around. If Maudra Mera finds out, she might take us captive after all."

Without waiting, Gurjin spun toward Sami Thicket, and Kylan was quick to follow. Amri waited with Naia, following only after she let out a huff and took off after them.

"That's that, huh?" Naia said as they hurried through the wood. "You didn't even ask Amri."

"No offense, but Amri wasn't a castle guard around Landstriders or a Spriton who knows his *maudra*," Gurjin said.

A dozen replies bubbled up, but Naia bit them all back. At least, at first.

"I know you think I'm overreacting," she said. "But if I am, then you're underreacting. You saw yourself that those riders weren't just scouts going on patrol. They were in full combat armor. All that, and you won't even consider the idea that she might be planning to attack."

"She's not planning an attack! It doesn't make any sense. The Drenchen are far away, and Maudra Mera isn't going to risk a confrontation. She's shrewd, but she doesn't want to hurt other Gelfling. Why would she strike first when she doesn't have to? You can't assume Maudra Mera is going to attack the Drenchen tonight just because it's what *you* would do!"

Naia almost missed a step. His words seemed unnecessarily harsh, and they stung.

"That's *not* what I would do."

"We'll figure out what to do tomorrow. You'll see. The suns are going to come up tomorrow, and those Landstriders are going to be right where we left them. You have to trust that the Spriton don't want to go to war any more than the Drenchen."

Naia bit her tongue. She didn't want to believe that the Spriton were preparing an ambush, but she had seen Maudra Mera grovel before the Skeksis. She had seen the fear.

"Gurjin . . ."

He let out a big sigh and put his hands on her shoulders.

It was something a big brother would do, as if he had forgotten they were the same age.

"You're always jumping without looking. It's going to get you hurt. *Please*, promise me you won't do anything brash."

She stepped back, out from under his hands.

"You've changed," she said.

He let his hands drop. She waited for them to ball into fists, but they didn't. He pressed his lips together and shouldered past her, heading through the last trees before the wood gave way to the Sami Thicket pavilion.

Kylan cleared his throat after an uncomfortable moment, then said, "I guess I'll find a place to sleep for the night."

Then he followed Gurjin, and Naia was alone with Amri. He hadn't said a word during the whole exchange with Gurjin, and now she wondered if she was going to get a scolding from him, too. Or maybe he would say nothing. She didn't know which would be worse.

"Naia, I . . ."

He trailed off almost before he started. She watched his gaze, as if he were thinking about something else. He glanced down at her and she thought he might say something. But he didn't, and they returned the rest of the way to the pavilion in silence.

CHAPTER 13

Gereni found them later and offered her family's garden for their sleeping place for the night. The hut was on the edge of the pavilion, between the central area of the small village and the thicket itself. Behind the hut was a patch of earth, turned up and soft from a recent harvest. They put down hay and quilts and lay down below the viny trellises, watching the light of the hearth fire flicker off the trees that bordered the thicket.

Gurjin said nothing as he pulled his cloak over his head and went to sleep. Naia almost asked Kylan to tell a song, if even just for the silence to end. But she didn't, worried that it would be asking too much of him. Instead, she watched the sky as Amri settled next to Kylan.

"Doing all right?" the Shadowling asked quietly.

"No," Kylan replied. "There's so much to take in. Maudra Mera, skekSa, the Drenchen, the Landstriders." *Naia and Gurjin fighting,* he almost seemed to add. Naia wished she were part of the conversation. Wished she could encourage her friends while they encouraged her. But she kept her nose out of it.

"I don't know what to make of any of it," Kylan went on. "I don't know how we're going to rally the Spriton while everything else is going on."

"We will. Get some sleep."

Naia lay awake staring at the sky through the trees. Back in the pavilion, the hearth fire dimmed as the night went on, simmering to smoldering embers in the circle of big stones. The Spriton voices quieted, and before long everyone in Sami Thicket was asleep.

Everyone except Naia. She couldn't stop thinking about the Landstriders, despite Kylan's reassurance. She tried to remind herself of what Gurjin had said. She had to trust that the Spriton didn't want to fight the Drenchen. She had to believe that if neither of the clans attacked first, no one would be hurt. But the two clans had been rivals for as long as anyone could remember—just as the Spriton and the Stonewood, the Grottan and the Vapra. It had never been all-out war, but that was only because there had never been a reason.

And now there was. Fear and survival instinct. Choosing sides. Was this, too, a part of the Skeksis' long plan for the Gelfling? Drawing lines, separating the Gelfling into clans. Carefully calculated in a precarious balance that was kept in check only by the power of the Skeksis and the Crystal they held hostage. And now, pushing the Gelfling into a choice between attacking first or being ambushed themselves. Eat or be eaten. Strike first or lose everything. It was a cycle that begot itself, so long as fear played a part. The Skeksis didn't even have to leave the castle to see the Drenchen and the Spriton destroy one another.

She got up when she couldn't lie awake any longer. Taking care not to disturb the others, she stretched her legs, walking the dirt path that wound on the thicket side of the village huts. Now and then she looked between the huts into the empty pavilion. Only the perimeter torches were lit, and she was the only one about. In the village, at least. No doubt the guards back in the valley were awake, sharpening their spears and making ready for battle.

Whispering caught her ear and she stopped, waiting in the shadow of a hut, as a pair of Spriton entered the pavilion from the far end, the trail that led through the wood to the camp. When she realized they were heading toward Maudra Mera's home, Naia skirted the huts to get closer. By the time Maudra Mera opened her door, Naia was close enough to see the intricacies in the *maudra's* sleeping braids.

The two Spriton were dressed in lightweight scouting gear. In the seemingly empty pavilion, they didn't bother taking the conversation inside.

"The Drenchen have advanced much further than we anticipated," one of the Spriton reported, hushed but urgently. "They seem to be camped for the night, but at this rate they will pass through by morning."

Maudra Mera cursed under her breath. There was a long pause.

"I didn't want it to come to this. This is the worst thing that could have happened! How ready is Captain Arla?"

"Ready as she can be. But we weren't expecting to engage the Drenchen so close to Sami Thicket. Arla is worried about what might happen here if we wait until the morning. She recommends we strike first. Tonight."

Being right didn't feel as good as Naia would have liked. It didn't feel good at all.

"What are we going to do?"

Naia gasped loudly, nearly jumping out of her skin at the silky voice that whispered in her ear. Maudra Mera and the two scouts went silent, ears straining, and Naia clamped a hand on her own mouth to keep from making any noise.

"Let's take this conversation inside," Maudra Mera said.

Naia let out the breath she'd shut in her mouth with her hand once they'd gone. Then she punched Amri in the shoulder.

"Don't creep up on me like that!"

"Sorry. Creeping is kind of my thing." He rubbed his arm, and the humor faded quickly from his voice. "Naia, I heard what they just said. Should we go in and try to talk her out of it?"

Naia's heart beat quicker. She didn't know if Maudra Mera would listen to her. She thought about leaving Sami Thicket and trying to find her mother and the Drenchen, but even with Amri's help, finding her clan would be difficult. Maybe impossible.

She and Amri froze when the door opened again and the two Spriton left at a fast pace. They were headed back to their camp, equipped with orders from the *maudra* that could determine the fate of Drenchen and Spriton alike. Naia watched them disappear into the wood, slipping out of her fingers. Everything was moving so quickly and wrongly, and she was helpless to stop it.

Or was she?

Naia tried to be as honest and quick as possible as she faced her Shadowling friend.

"The fires of resistance are about unity. I don't understand everything, but I know there's no way we'll be able to light them if our two clans are at war."

"But if we warn the Drenchen, we'll just be helping them hurt the Spriton. And if we help the Spriton, we'll be hurting the Drenchen. And either way, it's not going to stop them from fighting each other."

War begot war. Eat or be eaten. Naia grimaced, knowing what she had to do.

"That's why we need to stop them *both*. Now. Before either of them can make the first move against the other."

Amri nodded slowly, ears rising as he understood what she was about to do.

"What about Gurjin and Kylan?"

"We don't have time to get them. And I don't trust Gurjin to help. He'd be against this. I'll understand if you decide not to come with me."

Naia braced herself for disappointment, though every nerve was coming to life in her fingers and toes. Ready to run, as fast as she could. Ready to do the only thing she could think of to prevent the Spriton and the Drenchen from going to war.

Amri only shook his head, serious eyes flashing in the moonlight.

"I don't know if it's a good idea. But I know that I believe in you."

Though she had hardly expected to be so elated by such simple words at a time like this, Naia's heart sang.

The two of them ran along the dirt path into the wood, hoping they could beat the scouts back to the camp. Naia strained to be as quiet as Amri, who seemed to fly over the brittle twigs and dry leaves that covered the forest floor. Though they'd often joked about his strange, creeping way, she realized as they darted under the sparse trees that he was really rather graceful. Silent and sure-footed, just another dash of black and silver in the twilight wood.

When they reached the hill overlooking the camp, Naia could see the Spriton scouts calling for their captain. Soon, the orders would be given, and it would be too late. Once the Landstrider riders charged, there would be no stopping them until the Drenchen camp was defeated.

"I'm going down," she said to Amri.

"What do you want me to do?"

"Do whatever you can to spook the Landstriders as far from the camp as possible. You can do that, can't you? With your creepy Grottan ways?"

He flashed a smile. "Oh, yes."

"Great. Then do that."

"Naia." He grabbed her arm just before she was out of reach. "Please be careful."

She didn't know how to respond to that, or the intense look he gave her as he said it, so she just nodded and turned away.

The Spriton didn't notice her until she was nearly in their midst, bursting into the camp where the Landstriders flocked to feed. She grabbed a large torch from where it was thrust into the earth, whipping it back and forth so it showered the grass with embers.

"What's going on— Stop her!"

The Spriton and the castle guards scrambled to react, but they were too late. The embers struck the grass and the skins of the tents, and the Landstriders reared and bucked as Naia waved the torch wildly. Hooves and long legs as dense as trees thrashed in the air, the valley erupted into the whistling and baying of the spooked beasts.

When three of the Landstriders crested the hill that surrounded the valley, they slowed, as if reconsidering their escape. Then the echoing call of a Grottan hollerbat rippled across the clear night. The haunting cry seemed to come from hundreds of voices all at once, and the Landstriders bolted, galloping away over the lip of the valley.

Naia leaped on top of one of the supply tents, kicking up the hay that thatched the roof until it showered across the feed area. *Bola* whizzed by her head and feet, but she was used to sensing the movement of the rock-and-ropes in the air. She danced from tent to tent, lighting them as she went. The flames devoured the dry thatching and the equipment within—crates of Skeksis weapons and Landstrider riding tack. Gelfling ran below her, both escaping the growing fire and trying to chase the Landstriders that were quickly bucking their riders and bolting from the camp.

A *bola* finally caught her, tangling around her ankle and throwing her off balance. She flung the torch into the center of the camp as she fell, clobbered by Spriton and castle guards.

But now it was the Spriton who were too late, their operation ruined. As they hauled her up, dragging her away from the smoking, flame-engulfed camp, she could see the spooked Landstriders galloping up the hill, reins and rigging in shambles, scattering across the night-blanketed plains. Guards shouted for more water from the river to quench the flames, which were already dying in the damp night air and under the buckets from the Landstrider watering troughs.

The guards who held Naia bound her wrists. They had no words for her, and she wasn't surprised. What was there to say? She watched silently and passively as the chaos melted into steady action, the air clouded with smoke and ash instead of the bright tongues of fire.

The guards wrestled her upright when fresh torchlight glowed, coming down the hill from the direction of the thicket.

"Maudra Mera is coming," one of the guards finally said to her. "You'll get what you deserve."

Naia kept her breathing steady, though her heart was racing in anticipation of what was to come. She would tell Maudra Mera the truth. There was no reason to lie. She'd done what she'd done to save the Drenchen and the Spriton. To buy time to reason with both her mother and with Maudra Mera. It was the safest way to protect as many people as she could.

Her heart calmed, at least a little. She'd done what she'd done for a reason. She had been careful to destroy only the supplies from the castle. She had made sure no one had been hurt. She didn't expect Maudra Mera to be happy with her—far from it—

but she didn't need her to. She only needed her to understand.

Naia prepared those words, and others, as she waited for Maudra Mera to arrive. Readied them on her tongue for when the *maudra* inevitably asked her why she'd done it.

But for all her effort, Naia's knees still wavered as the *maudra's* entourage entered the center of the camp. Not because of Maudra Mera, but because of the two Gelfling who stood at her shoulders. Kylan, gaping in disbelief—and Gurjin, gray-blue eyes hard as a river stone and angrier than she had ever seen.

CHAPTER 14

"I had hoped maybe, after traveling the world beyond your putrid Swamp of Sog, you might have learned some common sense!" Maudra Mera exploded. She looked like she wanted to grab Naia in her thin hands and shake her. "I have been so kind to you. Even the first time. I let you rest in Sami Thicket. I gave you shoes. For Thra's sake, I gave you Kylan!"

The Spriton *maudra*'s exclamations felt like pebbles, bouncing off Naia's chest. She felt them, but they were insignificant compared to the growing tension between her and Gurjin. His fists were clenched at his side, ears flat and cheeks pinched. She waited, and it came.

"Naia, *what were you thinking?*"

Even Maudra Mera quieted, stepping aside when Gurjin stormed forth. Naia met him, back straight, eyes level.

"I overheard her guards in the middle of the night," she replied. "They were going to attack the Drenchen."

"So you did *this?*" He flung a hand, gesturing to the smoke and shouting that had become of the Spriton camp. "Naia! You could have hurt someone!"

"But I didn't."

"You betrayed Maudra Mera's trust ... You betrayed *my* trust!"

"I had to," she retorted, trying to keep any emotion from her voice. Trying not to show how much the last bit hurt. All around them, the Spriton watched. Even Kylan, who knew better than to get in between her and Gurjin. "I didn't tell you because I knew you'd react like this!"

"As if I'm the one overreacting! You launch yourself at every shadow, dagger drawn. Like you're looking for a fight to—I don't know, *prove* something. You leap into danger without worrying what might happen—"

"I *can't* worry!" Naia cried. "We can't win if I hesitate like you. At every turn, you balk! Back on skekSa's ship. Earlier tonight. You've changed, Gurjin. Since when are you scared of jumping into a hole before you know where it leads?"

Gurjin stared at her with cold eyes. "Since Mira did that and it ended up getting her killed!"

Naia snapped her mouth shut at the name. Mira, the Vapra soldier friend of Rian and Gurjin's, whom Naia would never meet. Her life had been lost. Even the last vial of her life essence had disappeared down the throat of the Skeksis Chamberlain. Imbuing him with her power. Absorbing her life essence for himself, if only temporarily, before she vanished altogether.

"At least I'm trying to do something," Naia growled. "Even after you stole my—"

"This isn't going to help anyone!" Maudra Mera shouted. "When your mother finds out we're without our Landstriders, she will attack—ruthlessly, and swiftly. How do you plan to make reparations for what you've done?"

Naia put her fight with Gurjin behind her. Where it belonged.

"My mother has no quarrel with the Spriton—even if you *did* side with the Skeksis. If you don't point your spears at her, she won't bring hers to you. She is fair and honorable."

"Honor is a petty thing on the battlefield. You were not born yet when your mother was proving herself as a Drenchen warrior fit to be *maudra* after your grandmother. When Maudra Laesid hears what you've done and brings her Drenchen brutes through Sami Thicket to disband us as a lesson to the Skeksis, she will not call it dishonorable. She will call it *strategy*."

"You're wrong," Naia said. Her mother was coolheaded. Stubborn, yes, but reasonable. Yet Maudra Mera was so convinced, it was hard not to imagine, if just for a moment, that she might be right.

Maudra Mera was not swayed.

"Open your eyes, Naia. There is only one path here, especially after what you've done. If you would open your eyes, you would see it so clearly and accept the direction in which it leads." Maudra Mera turned sharply away to address the Spriton. "Back to Sami Thicket, my Spriton. My honorable guards of the castle. We must prepare. For if I am right, the Drenchen will be here by morning with spears drawn."

"What about her?" asked Lun, pointing a spear at Naia.

"I'll take responsibility for her." Kylan stepped forward, addressing Maudra Mera directly. "Your soldiers don't have the resources to guard her. Not if the Drenchen will be here soon. So at least let me take this responsibility. I give you my word I'll protect the Spriton operation the best that I can."

Maudra Mera hesitated only a moment.

"Very well, Kylan. You may be the only one who can control her, anyway. Now, come along, the rest of you."

Orderly and without question, the Spriton obeyed, marching up the hill, back to the village. Gurjin gave Naia a last glance before turning his back on her and going with them.

Kylan stood beside her as the Spriton parted around them, leaving them in the smoldering remains of the camp Naia had ruined.

"Kylan . . . ," Naia began. She couldn't tell how he was feeling, but the longer they stood there in silence, the more she realized he was angry. He hadn't yelled like Gurjin had, and he had even volunteered to become her warden, but he wasn't happy with her. "Listen. I know you're not pleased with what I did. But we need to figure out how we're going to light the Spriton fire—"

"*We?* Seems to me you had no trouble coming up with a plan on your own."

She huffed. "I'm sorry. But—"

"Apologies don't have *buts.*"

Naia focused on unclenching her fists and taking a deep breath and letting it out. She was going to do this properly.

"I'm sorry," she said, making sure she meant every syllable.

Honesty worked. Kylan let out a big sigh.

"It's not even what you did," he said. "It's that you did it without telling me and Gurjin. After all we've been through together. I thought you trusted me. I thought we were a team. But you really made me feel like a stranger tonight."

His voice cracked a little at the end. Naia felt awful, more awful than she had when Maudra Mera had yelled at her or when she'd fought with Gurjin. This, of all things, was not what she'd meant to do. She'd felt as if everyone was withdrawing from her, ever since the Mystic Valley. But now she wondered if maybe she was the one pushing the others away.

Shadows moved in the smoky air, and Amri slipped out of the darkness between two tents.

"Everyone's gone back to the village," he said. "Naia, are you all right?"

She nodded. "Good job with the Landstriders."

"Thanks. Though I'll admit, I always wanted to ride a Landstrider. Not spook the ghost out of them."

The three of them followed the path away from the camp, back to Sami Thicket. The pavilion was crowded with the soldiers and the other Spriton hurrying to prepare for a battle Naia felt was more and more imminent.

"Do you really believe your mother won't attack?" Kylan asked.

"I don't know what I believe anymore," Naia replied. "Kylan . . . I really am sorry about not telling you before." Kylan bobbed his head.

"I know," he said. "It was because you had to make a decision and you felt like you had to make it alone. I know it's your destiny to become a leader. I just don't ever want it to be at the cost of losing you as a friend."

Naia grabbed his shoulders with both hands.

"You'll never lose me as a friend," she said. "I promise."

He returned her embrace. When they parted, Kylan looked as relieved as Naia felt. They stood at the edge of the pavilion and watched. Some of the Landstriders had been recovered, their tall legs and big ears casting bizarre shadows as they galloped past the fire blazing in the hearth at the center of the pavilion. But there were not nearly the number there had been, and in the dead of the night, the Spriton had been caught by surprise.

"We have to stop them," Amri whispered. "We have to stop them from attacking. But I don't know how. It's just like with the Skeksis. We can't attack them, so how are we supposed to defeat them? How do we end a war without fighting?"

She wondered if the other Gelfling clans they'd already met were doing the same—taking up swords and spears and preparing to fight. The violence would only grow upon itself. Feeding itself. A monster that fed on its own hatred and fear. The Skeksis were the ones that had created the monster and let it loose upon itself.

"We have to do something," she whispered.

But what? Naia held her breath as she watched the torches of war light. Killing the Skeksis was wrong for what it would do to the Mystics. She knew that now. But even more than that, killing the Skeksis would not kill the dark thing they'd awakened in the Gelfling. Like the darkened creatures that had looked into the purple crystal veins, the Gelfling clans had been corrupted in their own way. And turning their hatred and anger against the Skeksis would do nothing but feed the darkness within them, until it consumed itself and them entirely.

Naia and Amri both jumped when Kylan pushed past them, a stern ripple creasing his brow.

"Kylan—where are you going?"

"Meet me at the hearth," he said, voice laden with determination. "This song teller has something to say."

CHAPTER 15

Naia was waiting for Kylan as he marched past Maudra Mera, toward the hearth that blazed at the center of the pavilion. He climbed up onto the stone wall that kept the fire contained and lifted his *firca*. The single, piercing note silenced every voice in the pavilion. Even the Landstriders stopped, turning to find the silhouette of the little Spriton song teller standing in front of the fire.

In the hush that followed, someone whispered, "Is that Kylan?"

"What is he doing?" Maudra Mera asked, staring from beside Naia.

"Listen," Naia said. "Listen, and see."

Once he had everyone's attention, Kylan lowered his *firca*. The outline of his shoulders wavered in the fire and heat of the Spriton hearth, betraying a tiny tremble of nervousness. Then he raised his lute and sang.

> Let me tell you a song of another time
> In a world green and good, in an age of wonder
> Three Suns crossed above for a thousand trine
> Three Moons in the river flowing under

Then a shaft of light fell from the sky
And eighteen stars descended

Some of the Spriton paused to heed to the song teller, while others had stopped for only a moment to take note of him before going back to sharpening their spears and readying for battle. But the longer Kylan sang, the stronger his spell became. Slowly, one at a time, the Spriton stopped to listen.

For a thousand trine, the stars watched the land
With wisdom of fire and death and life
Then the Crystal cracked at their impatient hand
Thus our world split into an age of strife

Two races then appeared: the gentle Mystics
And the cruel Skeksis

At first, as Kylan sang, Naia heard his voice. The rich words in song, but that was all they were: words, that rang through her ears, riding the notes of his lute. But as she listened and watched, she felt something begin, as it always did when Kylan sang. The words and the music held one another. Closer and tighter, dancing through her mind. As they did, they gave life to new sensations. She could see the light of the urSkeks descending to Thra, could feel the heat of their radiance burning through the sky. Even the scent of the Crystal Chamber—dust and the metallic sour of space burned by the energy that erupted outward when the

Crystal cracked—filled her nostrils though she knew she stood far from the castle and the chamber, the air full of trees and grass and the smoke from the Spriton hearth.

> The Mystics forsook the castle and vanished
> While the Skeksis remained with the Crystal of Truth
> They forgot the star-world from which they'd been banished
> Their eyes turned to Thra, craving power and youth
>
> They drank deep of the nectar from the flowers of Thra:
> The Seven Gelfling Clans
>
> The Skeksis supped on our Gelfling essence
> While deep in the castle, o'er a shaft of air and fire
> In pain and in need, its light evanescent
> The Crystal of Truth dangled blighted and dire
>
> But when the Gelfling learned what had happened:
> The Seven Clans resisted
> Oh yes, the Seven Clans resisted

All the Spriton were listening now. Even Maudra Mera. They saw it, heard it, smelled it. Every Gelfling in the pavilion was held, enraptured, by the song teller's spell. It was a kind of magic unlike any other. Perhaps, she thought, a magic to which Gelfling were particularly susceptible, for no matter the clan, songs were as close to the hearts of Gelfling as their *vliya*.

The Sifa were first, in the bay of Cera-Na
Gem-Eyed Ethri and a Far-Dreamer with fiery hair
Gazed into the hearth on the coral *Omerya*
Fanned the fire of resistance with the fresh ocean air

The Dousan were second, in the dark of a storm
Two brothers at odds: one captain, one thief
Joined hands and blew on the summoning horn
Lightning fire resurrected the great Wellspring Tree

Alas, the Skeksis saw the fire of the Gelfling spread
They ruined Stone-in-the-Wood. Killed the All-Maudra dead

The Vapra were third, in the dark of their night
Till a Shadowling climbed the ice cliffs by the sea
Brought the Hidden Moon up to the snowiest height
Let her message of hope light the Waystar tree

Naia saw Onica and Maudra Ethri aboard *Omerya*. She felt the cold electricity of the storm over the Wellspring, the hard sand whipping her face in the pitch-dark. The murky depths of the oasis, where she and Amri had found the last living roots of the Wellspring Tree buried in mud. Amri leading them through the blustering night to the Waystar grove. Tavra's noble voice as she'd spoken to the Vapra and reassured them that not all was lost. That there was hope, despite the things that had befallen them.

Beside her, Amri looked on with the same pride that Naia felt, eyes alight with the same thrill. This was their story. Where they had entered the unending song of Thra. The resistance of the Seven Clans, the lighters of the Seven Fires. Aughra's menders.

Naia tried to find Gurjin among the crowd. He was standing across the pavilion with a group of Spriton in castle guard uniforms. To her surprise, he was looking at her. Not in anger but with the same hope that she felt.

She let out the breath she had been holding.

I'm sorry, she thought. Said, in her mind. She didn't know if their dreamfast link was strong enough while there was such a rift between them. A rift she wanted to mend. She didn't know if he'd heard her until he dipped his head.

I'm sorry, too.

She smiled and turned back to Kylan. The song teller hesitated, strumming his lute as his eyes found Naia's. He'd sung of the past and their successes, but now came the important part. The part they'd talked about, where his song weaved the dreams of the present and showed the Spriton what the future could bring.

She met his eyes and nodded.

I know you can do it, she told him without words. He must have understood her because he nodded back and sang:

Charged by the Skeksis to raise up their spears

The Spriton were fourth in the rolling green plains

They listened, were wise, cleared the smoke of their fears

Saw the path ahead lit with all seven blue flames

And so four of the seven Gelfling flames were won

More than half where there had been none

Whispers rose like smoke as Kylan stood at the hearth fire in Sami Thicket and sang to the Spriton of the deeds they had done, if only in his imagination. Naia felt the fingers of inspiration tickling up her back as Kylan painted a picture of his heroic clan, brave and wise, taking hold of their futures despite the Skeksis Emperor's scepter looming over their heads. Despite what had happened to their neighbor clan in Stone-in-the-Wood.

"Could this be?" Naia overheard a Spriton warrior ask her fellow.

"If the Spriton were to join the others, it would be the turning point," another replied. "But if we don't . . ."

"Shush," hissed yet another. "Let him finish!"

It was no longer a memory that Kylan was describing, but a hope for the future. What came next would be more of the same; one song teller's dream of what could be yet to come, shared with his people through the dreamfast of song.

Please, let them see, Naia prayed. To Thra and to the Crystal. Maybe to Kylan, too. It was his hope that guided their imaginations now. It was his belief of how things could be. His words in his song. And his memories had formed the message that they'd sent on the petals of the Sanctuary Tree. This time, it was up to him to tell the song that was in his heart.

The Grottan were fifth, in deep caves once called home

Below the Sanctuary Tree, holding darkness at bay

Then came flickering fires—they were no longer alone

And the darkness was banished by their shadowy flame

Sixth came the Drenchen under Sog's Great Smerth

As the *maudra*'s fierce daughter finally returned

She had helped light the fires, from the fifth to the first

And when she came home a hero, the blue fire burned

Naia shivered when Kylan sang the words about her. Her triumphant return to Great Smerth. Stepping into the golden-green light that drenched the Glenfoot with warmth. Her mother and father waiting, her sisters diving from the branches of the great Drenchen tree to meet her. Her clan gathering under Great Smerth's watchful shade, ready. Believing in her. Reaching out when she did, knotting fingers unto wrist in an unbreakable braid of hands.

The vision was so overwhelming she didn't notice Amri's hand in hers until he squeezed.

"So it will be," he said quietly. Decisively. "So it will be."

The fire would light. Through all her other doubts, that was a thing she held on to more tightly than ever.

"And then . . . ," she whispered.

Kylan's song had brought them to the sixth fire. The near future—nearer than seemed possible, as if it were racing toward them.

But no one knew what would happen once the seventh fire was lit, and all the clans had committed themselves to resisting the Skeksis. It seemed whenever they asked what would happen when all seven fires were lit, they were never answered. Neither by Aughra, nor a Far-Dreamer, nor Thra itself. For so long Naia had believed the fires would awaken the greatest spirit in the Gelfling of all—the will to fight back and defeat the Skeksis. Now she knew that was not their future, but like Maudra Mera, she had struggled to see a new path. A new goal to lay her sights upon.

Naia fixed her eyes on Kylan as he stood before the Spriton hearth fire. Perhaps after all this time, it would be a song teller who had the answer.

Only one fire remained, till all were lit for good
All eyes turned to the ruins of Stone-in-the-Wood

There the Gelfling clans unite
There the Gelfling fires light
The dream-flames etched on a sacred wall
And there the Skeksis Lords will fall

She saw it as he sang it, clear as day and night. In the ruins of Stone-in-the-Wood, the Gelfling came together. Kylan's song told of strife resolved, the flames of the different clans combined into a single fire. One which blazed so brightly that it might drown out the shadows of the Skeksis. Not with weapons and war, but with light and song, in harmony with their world.

The fire was distant, in their future, but Naia could hear it. Feel it, like the presence of loved ones in another room. And she knew that when the time came, the flames would be so bright and pure, their light would reach the Crystal itself.

Kylan's lute rang in the heavy air, reverberating as if the song might be over. Then, with the resolution of a master, he played the last refrain:

> What all started with the Crystal shattering
> This song teller's ballad of the Gelfling Gathering

All was still, all silent. Until Maudra Mera stepped forward, spear in hand.

"Is this a Far-Dream, or just a song?" she asked, loud voice uncharacteristically awestruck as well. Kylan didn't answer, breathing too heavily to respond. Wide-eyed, Maudra Mera turned to Naia and asked again in a different way: "Is it true?"

Naia held out her hand, palm up.

"It could be," she said.

Maudra Mera looked at Naia's hand, then down to her own, where she held her spear. Naia held her breath, wondering if this could be the moment. The moment, like with Maudra Ethri or with Erimon of the Dousan, that the leader of the Spriton changed her mind.

Kylan hopped down from the hearth and approached the two of them where they stood, surrounded by the Spriton in the center of Sami Thicket's pavilion. Maudra Mera let out a pained sigh.

"Naia. Kylan. I understand what you're trying to do."

"You told us that you couldn't see another future," Naia said. It was bordering on interrupting, but she couldn't bite her tongue forever. She raised her voice, hoping all the Gelfling in the pavilion could hear her plea to their *maudra*. "So Kylan has shown you one! The future in his heart. Can you see, now? Can you imagine what kind of future the Gelfling could have if the Spriton join them?"

"I can see a version of the future if we follow a path, but if the Spriton were to turn on the Skeksis and light this—this *fire of resistance*—that would only be one step. The path diverges again and again," Maudra Mera said.

"So we keep our eyes and ears open," Kylan said. "And when the path diverges, we look and listen. And choose the path that leads us to the future we seek. For a time, we may walk alone, and in those times it is easy to become lost. But I believe that if we listen and sing the same song, those paths will converge. Become *one*. Wide enough for us all to walk side by side. Together."

Maudra Mera was no longer angry, no longer had the edge of annoyance or the shadow of fear lurking in her sharp, dark eyes.

"I fear the two of you do not understand how large the world is that you walk," she said with a short sigh. It was the breath of a mother whose children had grown, a *maudra* who saw danger in their future but didn't know how to stop it. She held Kylan by the shoulders.

"I told your parents, years ago. When your mother left to build her homestead with that Stonewood out in the field. I *told* her, it was dangerous. Falling in love with a Stonewood, leaving the plains that were her home. Leaving her clan. But she didn't listen. She told me that if she didn't leave Sami Thicket, she would spend the rest of her years wishing she had. Then she left, and together, they built a home on the border of the Dark Wood. Where you were born, Kylan. And for many years, I thought that perhaps I had been wrong."

"And then the Hunter came," Kylan said, voice unwavering. "And after I went to live with you in Sami Thicket, I thought for many years you were right. But Maudra Mera, listen and understand. Our lives change every moment. You weren't right to try to stop my mother, and you weren't wrong during the years she and my father lived happily on the edge of the Dark Wood. Right and wrong change, or don't exist at all. I left Sami Thicket feeling as if I would bring shame to my entire clan because I couldn't throw a rock-and-rope. I returned as the song teller who spread the word of the Skeksis betrayal on the petals of the Sanctuary Tree, and who fought off skekMal the Hunter with a stone from a Drenchen *bola*."

A horn rang out across the quiet pavilion.

Naia gulped. The soldiers that had stood in silence, listening to Kylan, turned at the alarum. More horns blew, until the thicket around the village was vibrating with the sound. Already she could hear the clamoring of soldiers calling orders to each other. Raising their spears and shields. The black silhouettes of their weapons cut through the light of their war torches, burning hot and red.

At first Naia wondered if skekSa had returned. But then she realized it was not a Skeksis who had been sighted. Naia heard familiar drums, the knocking of wooden spears and heavy footsteps.

"The Drenchen?" Amri asked, ears twisting to the sides.

"The Drenchen," Naia agreed, heart sinking.

Kylan looked away from Maudra Mera and gazed across the pavilion, as if he might meet the eyes of every Spriton that stood there, dressed for battle, even as the Drenchen forces entered the thicket. As Naia turned her ears, she could hear their footsteps coming through the wood that surrounded the village, made out the clanging of the alarm bells and one of the Spriton blowing on the horn.

"We make our own destinies," Kylan told the Spriton. "For every step we take, we claim our futures. And now, we must all step together. In time, toward a tomorrow we may only be able to dream of."

No one answered. Maudra Mera gazed upon Kylan the Song Teller, everything about her softening with some emotion Naia couldn't fully understand. It was something like pride and something like concern. Worry and invigoration, all wrapped in one. Kylan put his hands on hers where they were still resting on his shoulders.

"Call on the Spriton to put down their spears," he said. "Call on the Spriton now to shun the order of the Skeksis. Rebel by refusing to fight one another—"

The clamoring of armor interrupted him. Three guards, short of breath, burst into the edge of the pavilion from the woods.

"Without the Landstriders, we couldn't hold them off—

Maudra Laesid and an entourage of twenty warriors, armed with *bola* and spear and net!"

Naia bit back a chill. They had not won the Spriton over yet, and now . . . Maudra Mera glared at Naia and Gurjin. They were about to be put to the real test.

"You say we make our futures. I want to be sure of ours. If I call on the Spriton to lay down their weapons against the Drenchen, we will be vulnerable. But you say you can persuade your mother to call off her attack on the Skeksis that will bring their wrath upon us all. Convince her to let go of her call to war and join the other Gelfling in resistance. Do you still think you can?"

"Yes," Naia said without hesitation.

Maudra Mera raised her chin, regal and hardened. She let go of Kylan's shoulders and faced the entrance of the village. Naia saw the shadows of the warriors coming through the wood and the great, serpentine back of an enormous flying eel.

"All right, then," Maudra Mera said through clenched jaw. "Prove it."

CHAPTER 16

Naia and Gurjin stood at Maudra Mera's side as the Drenchen warriors entered the Spriton pavilion.

There were three phalanxes, the foremost two made of spear- and *bola*-throwers in thick leather armor, their hair tied back for battle in green and blue string. Unlike the female Spriton, Vapra, and Sifa warriors Naia had seen in her travels, the Drenchen women were dressed nearly the same as men, carrying heavier armament where a Spriton might have taken a lighter dagger or dart reed. Drenchen wings were not for flying, and there were no deep swamps or lakes in the Spriton Plains.

The third phalanx was smaller, approaching last just ahead of a slithering beast Naia recognized. A giant flying eel, moving steadily across the soil of the wood and onto the stones of the pavilion, her front half raised with furred fins splayed to keep her balance. She was Chapyora, the *maudra's* muski, and seated on her neck just behind her head was Maudra Laesid herself.

The pavilion was still and quiet as Chapyora bore Maudra Laesid into the center, gently lowering her thick-maned head so Naia's mother could dismount. One of the warriors in the *maudra's* phalanx approached with a long spear, which Laesid used as a staff and crutch as she approached Maudra Mera, Naia, and Gurjin.

She was tall for a Gelfling, though her height made her missing leg that much more noticeable. Her skin was a deep green, her bead-and-ribbon-wound locs brushing the back of her knee, glowing with bioluminescent moss in the dim firelight. Across her shoulders hung a cape of midnight, black and shimmering with violet, blue, and green. The *maudra*'s cloak, passed down through generation after generation.

Her brow was stern, but it broke when she laid eyes on her children.

"Naia," she said. "Gurjin—you found her."

Naia wanted to embrace her mother, but now was not the time. Not in front of all the Spriton and their *maudra* who had just put an ultimatum on Naia's shoulders: Convince her mother to call off her attack, and they would light the fire of resistance. Though she hadn't seen her mother for many unum, she held back her impulse and bowed instead.

"Mother. Gurjin found me indeed, off the coast of Ha'rar. I'm glad to see you."

"And what are you doing here?"

"Maudra Mera agreed to speak with me. We were in the middle of coming to an . . . understanding when you arrived."

"Hm."

Maudra Laesid took note of Naia's restraint, dipping her chin and waving her guard away. She cleared her throat and raised her voice.

"Maudra Mera. What you see before you is only a portion of our full force. We have seen your Landstriders scattered across the plains in disarray, and so I see no further need to raise my hand against you. However, I will not hesitate to do whatever is necessary if you do not step aside and allow us passage to the Castle of the Crystal, where we will rain rage upon the traitorous Skeksis until they surrender their prisoners and the Crystal to its true keepers, the Gelfling of Thra."

Naia swallowed, though her mouth was suddenly dry. For as long as she could remember, her mother's voice was one of immobile strength, as tall and sturdy as Great Smerth and with stubborn roots that grew just as deep. That voice was one that had kept her and her siblings safe—both from the dangers of the swamp and from each other's squabbling—and the one that had taught her to use her healing *vliyaya* as well as to throw a spear from Chapyora's back as she raced through the apeknot canopy.

But it had always been her mother's voice, not her *maudra's*. One she knew to be full of love and devotion, loyalty and protection.

Now she heard it as an outsider might. As Maudra Mera surely did, though to her credit the tinier *maudra* did not give any ground. Her back did not even tremble.

"As she mentioned, your daughter and I were discussing this as you arrived," she said. "And I believe, following that discussion, Naia has something to tell you."

Naia braced herself as the weight of every gaze settled on her shoulders, the heaviest of all being the blue-eyed one from her mother. She felt Gurjin and Amri beside her, Kylan nearby. Though she was glad for the three of them there, in that moment, strangely enough, the one she wished for was Tavra. Another daughter of a *maudra*, who had seen many a confrontation between Gelfling clan leaders. She would have known what to do.

But Tavra wasn't there. Naia drew in a breath, held her chin up as her mother did.

"Mother. As you've probably heard, I was asked by Aughra to meet with each Gelfling clan and prepare them to unite against the Skeksis."

"And I bring my torch this night," Laesid said, gesturing. The Drenchen warriors raised their flames in response, a chain of bobbing golden lights. "No harm will come to the Spriton if they let us pass. Our quarrel is not with them."

"If you bring it this night, it will only be to join the ashes of the one brought by Maudra Fara at Stone-in-the-Wood," Naia said, and at least this time when she spoke, her mother sighed.

"A sad day for all Gelfling, when Stone-in-the-Wood fell," she said grimly. "But had the Drenchen been at her side when she brought her attack, perhaps we would be reminiscing a victory instead of defeat. But what's done is done. The Skeksis expended energy to defend against Maudra Fara and the Stonewood; now is the best time for us to attack, before they recuperate."

"The Skeksis expended hardly anything defeating the Stonewood," Maudra Mera replied hotly. "As you know, they still had Landstriders to send us in an effort to hold you."

"Landstriders, which you could easily turn north instead of south," Laesid replied. "Join us, Maudra Mera. Light your fire of resistance, as my daughter has encouraged you. Think of what a force we could become if we added your strength to ours. Your flying spear-throwers and Landstriders, with my stone warriors and eels?"

Naia stepped between the two, facing her mother.

"We can't," she said. "The Skeksis cannot be killed."

Maudra Laesid snorted. "Anything alive can be killed. Or are you saying they are immortal?"

"No," Naia said. "But their deaths come at an immeasurable cost. Killing them will not save the Gelfling. Violence will only bring more violence. Maudra Fara was defeated not because she was weak but because she went against them alone."

"Naia, we cannot wait for all seven clans," Laesid replied, misunderstanding. "You may have traveled the world with words, but words are light and easy to bear. Swords and spears—warriors and soldiers—are not. We need to act now, while we can."

"That's not what—"

"You have never seen war," Maudra Laesid interrupted, raising her voice. "And for that I am grateful! But you childlings know nothing of these things. Even if all seven clans agree to join us, it will be many unum before their armies can reach the Dark Wood."

Naia could hold back no longer.

"It's not about armies!" she cried. It didn't sound grown-up, or *maudra*-ly, but she didn't know what else to do. "Mother! Warriors and soldiers cannot cleanse the darkening or heal the rifts that divide us—killing the Skeksis will not save the Crystal!"

Maudra Laesid paused, and Naia tried to still the pounding of her heart. She waited for another argument, but one didn't come. At least, not immediately. Had something she'd said finally gotten through? Before the moment slipped away, Naia appealed one last time.

"*Please.* You taught me that the Drenchen are healers as well as warriors. In one hand we hold the knife that cuts, in the other the light that heals. In this moment, on this night, be the light that heals."

Gurjin stepped to Naia's side, finally finding his voice. "At least hold off and give us a chance to find another way," he said.

Laesid's cheeks dimpled as she clenched her jaw. A long breath passed between them, as if she held Naia's and Gurjin's pleas in her hand. Weighing them, pondering their meaning.

"Maudra Laesid, if I may," Kylan spoke up. "You were perhaps the first to believe the Skeksis had turned against the Gelfling . . . because of your unwavering love for your children, because you trusted them without question. If not for your faith in them, you wouldn't be here, willing to risk everything to protect them."

"Remember that belief in them," Amri added. "And believe in them now."

Maudra Laesid sighed, and Naia realized even the staunchest of boulders could be moved. Far away, she heard the distant grumbling of thunder as a cold wind raced across the trees that surrounded the pavilion.

"Very well," Laesid said. "We will fall back, and I will listen to what you have to say. But know that if I am not satisfied by your alternatives, I will press on."

"We'll see about that," Maudra Mera said. She drew herself up, sucking in breath so sharp, Naia thought she might spit.

Maudra Laesid had agreed to hold her attack; now would Maudra Mera uphold her part of the bargain?

Maudra Mera turned toward the hearth and waved her hand with a decisive, swift gesture. Then, with far more authority and volume than Naia thought could be contained in her little body, she called out, "Spriton! Come to the hearth we have kept alight for countless generations. Come! Now! Swiftly!"

The Spriton did as she commanded, as quickly and with as much diligence as could be expected from a clan with such a shrewd and discerning *maudra*. They murmured to one another around the hearth, abuzz with hushed conversation.

"Go," Naia said to Kylan. "Join them. Lead them."

The firelight surrounding the pavilion danced against Kylan's shining hair and the bone *firca* hanging at his breast. He was no longer the timid bard she'd crossed paths with so many days and nights ago.

"Come with me," he said to Naia, Gurjin, and Amri. Naia glanced back to her mother once, trying to reassure her that this was the way. Then she joined the Spriton around the hearth, as Maudra Mera climbed to the spot on the hearthstone where Kylan had told his song.

"It has always been my duty to protect you all," Maudra Mera began. "And you know that I will do whatever it takes to find our success. In the field, in the wood. Once, in the courtyards of the castle palace for the favor of the Skeksis Lords. But no longer that. This night we saw a vision of what could be. We saw a vision and proof that it is not a cloud in the sky, but a flower petal on the wind. Difficult to catch, but not uncatchable. So now, my beloved Spriton. Lay down your spears and hold each other tightly. If you believe, then I will believe. We have seen the path, and I will lead you down it as surely as I am able, to where it joins the seven clans in victory, as the seven fires rise and the Skeksis fall."

The Spriton hesitated at their *maudra*'s command, glancing over their shoulders at the Drenchen who stood at their backs, armored and armed.

Kylan was the first to step forward, holding out his hands to show his empty palms. He took Maudra Mera's hand in his and squeezed when Naia stepped beside him to take his other.

One spear lowered, set against the stones of the pavilion. Then another. Amri grabbed Naia's free hand as the Spriton warriors threw down their weapons in a cascade of steel and wood, joining hands at last.

Blue fire exploded from the hearth, ascending into the sky three hundred times as high. Its tongues rippled in every color of the rainbow, across the night like a magnificent pillar, as if a star had erupted from the earth and was shooting into the heavens.

The Spriton fire was lit.

CHAPTER 17

Spriton and Drenchen alike stared at the tower of flame ascending from the Sami Thicket hearth.

As its ever-changing light fell upon the stones of the pavilion and the clay and rock of the Spriton homes, the air smelled of cosmic smoke and stardust. Etchings—*dream*-etchings, like the ones that had been burned into the deck of the *Omerya*, across the walls of the Dousan cloister, and even on the Vapra citadel—spilled across the pavilion.

The pictographs told the tale that Kylan had already sung: the previous three fires lit and how. Added to the end of the unraveling story were Spriton warriors, spears in hand in the saddles of the gallant Landstriders. Gathered in a circle around their hearth fire, listening to a song teller with a forked *firca* hanging at his breast.

Kylan stared at his image when he saw it, touching the real *firca* with his hand. Naia grinned until her cheeks hurt, shaking him gently by the shoulder.

"You did that," she said.

Naia waited to see if the shadows of the other Gelfling would appear, as they had before. Glimpses through the fires, out into the places across the world where the other ones were burning.

It was part of the magic of the flames; she didn't understand why or how, but that was the way of Thra. It had given them this gift, and she hoped they would be able to use it to unite.

"There!"

Silhouettes materialized. Gelfling faces, moving in and out of the rippling tongues of multicolored flame. The burst of smoke and fire settled, like boiling water falling to a simmer, and as it calmed, the faces started to come into focus—

Naia and the others jumped back as a new explosion of fire erupted from the hearth, charging the burning spectacle with a rush of renewed color, as vivid and dazzling as if it had just been lit.

"What's happening?" Amri cried, shielding his eyes.

The light from the fire burned across the pavilion, revealing new pictographs: An enormous stone tree, with petaled branches withering above and stone roots growing deep below. A small group of Gelfling huddled deep in a crypt below the mountains, surrounded by crawling, multi-legged shapes.

"The Sanctuary Tree?" Amri gasped. "Then . . ."

Chills raced up Naia's back.

"I think another fire was just lit," she said. "In Domrak."

"Look!" Kylan called.

In the haze of the flames, the figures reappeared. One familiar figure in particular. More solidly than ever before, as if he were right there on the other side of the screen of fire. He was standing in a dark cave, with a few other Gelfling beside him.

"Rian!" she called, heart pounding.

"Aughra's Eye!" he replied. That was Rian's voice, all right. "Naia? Kylan—Gurjin!"

"Hey!" Gurjin called with a wave. "So you're alive, after all!"

"Rian, where are you?" Naia asked. "And tell us quickly—the last time we saw through the fires, it didn't last long!"

As they stood across the fire from one another, Naia began to feel the presence of others. In the streaks of light blue flames, she saw the sails of a majestic coral ship, a scarlet-haired Sifa captain. In the gold, she saw the shadow of the Dousan Wellspring Tree, heard the voices of monks calling the others to the fire. Something had happened.

"We're in the Tomb of Relics," Rian said. "It's a long story— but I found it. The weapon Aughra sent me to find."

"Weapon?" Amri breathed.

Rian held something up. It looked like a sword, but Naia could barely make it out. The fire was already fading. They didn't have much time left.

"If we're seeing you—then you lit the Grottan fire?"

"Yes!"

Where one moon had been in the sky, shedding its light upon the night, suddenly there were two. Gurjin let out a whoop.

"We're here with the Spriton!" he said. "We lit the one here, too!"

"Only two left," Rian said with a smile. The fire ebbed for a moment and Naia thought it had gone out. It returned, still rippling with shifting jewel tones—but it was fading fast.

"We go next to Sog to light the Drenchen fire," Naia shouted, hoping he could hear her. "Are Tavra and Onica with you?"

But the fire's colors washed away, burning back into red and gold and yellow. Whatever magic connected the fires of the Gelfling resistance, that doorway was closed again. At least until the next fire was lit.

"He did it!" Gurjin cried. "Rian lit the Grottan fire!"

Naia's cheeks ached, and she realized she was smiling.

"Huh," she said, cracking a grin. It felt good. "I guess he's good for something, after all."

Maudra Mera came to stand between Naia and Gurjin, staring into the fire.

"Now only two remain," she said. She looked upon the etchings that now covered the pavilion, nearly end to end. The same that graced the *Omerya*, the cloisters, the citadel—and now the Grottan Tomb of Relics as well. "These fires . . . they are more than symbols of our resistance. I believe they may be the fires of prophecy."

"Fires of prophecy?" Naia asked her mother as she joined them.

"There is an old song that the Gelfling were shaped of earth and wind, lightning and water, shadow and light. But it was the spark of fire that brought us to life. That is why our essence is called *vliya*—blue fire. Fire burns at the heart of our world; the Heart of Thra was forged in it. We, too, burn with it. That is why the center of every Gelfling clan is the hearth . . . or so it used to be."

Maudra Mera looked back at the hearth, and Naia

remembered the first time she had seen it. A hearth burned in the center of Great Smerth, too. Even the Grottan, deep in the caves, had joined one another in song around a hearth—as had the Dousan, in the rare days they returned to the Wellspring from their travels in the Crystal Sea.

"There are scrolls in the Tomb that mention this. They say fires of fate spoke to the Gelfling on the day we were born," Amri said softly.

"Some songs say it was Thra's word," Kylan agreed. "Before Thra had words to speak. Some say it may have been Mother Aughra that whispered the song to us, when the Gelfling were nothing but seedlings."

Aughra. The voice of Thra.

Master urSu's words came to Naia in that moment, echoing Kylan's. That's what he had called Aughra: Thra's voice. She hadn't thought anything of it then, but now she wondered what the old Mystic had meant by it. The fires of prophecy were a sign, but Naia had always thought of them as Thra's sign to the Gelfling. Now she wondered if maybe they were the Gelfling's sign to Thra. To its heart and to its voice—to the Crystal and to Aughra—that the Gelfling were uniting and coming to save it.

Maudra Mera folded her hands. "Whoever spoke to us, that fire burns within us still. And now it blazes beyond us, as a sign of our strength. These fires will light the way indeed. I am sorry for doubting you."

Kylan smiled. Then he opened an arm and stepped toward her, only half expecting to be greeted with the same. He sighed when

Maudra Mera wrapped him in her arms, holding him tightly.

"I know you must leave again, though I wish for everything you would stay here in Sami Thicket where I can keep you safe," she said.

"You'll be all right if skekSa returns?" Naia asked.

"We'll be better than all right if that pirate shows her snout here again," Maudra Mera retorted. "When a Spriton leaps, she leaps with both feet. There will be no standing on the line between Skeksis and Gelfling here. So go on, then. Get out of my sight, before I change my mind."

She pushed him away, wiping her face with her flouncing sleeve. Kylan laughed and kissed her forehead.

"I'll be back, Maudra," he said. "And I won't hesitate to make you proud."

"I am already quite proud," she huffed. Then she turned away and faced the Spriton warriors. "Spriton! You've done well tonight. Bring out the food and feast, for our work is not yet done. The Skeksis will soon hear that we have turned against them, and we must fortify and be ready!"

As quickly as they'd joined hands around the hearth, the Spriton jumped in response to their *maudra*'s commands. Naia and Gurjin, Kylan, and Amri remained with Naia's mother and her flying eel.

"I did not know," Maudra Laesid said. She gravely looked upon her children and their friends. "I did not know that you had been given a task such as this. I did not know the clans were being awakened in this way, lighting these fires. And I certainly did not know that your friend Rian had been sent to retrieve a weapon to wield against the Skeksis."

A weapon. An instrument of war. Naia swallowed, trying not to let uneasiness get the better of her.

"What are you saying?" she asked.

Maudra Laesid gave a hearty snort, gesturing to the Spriton.

"I'm saying you do not need to convince me. I will not let these pesky Grasslings best the Drenchen in our rebellion against the Skeksis. We will return to Sog and light the Drenchen fire immediately . . . but first."

Naia and Gurjin yelped in unison as Maudra Laesid dropped her spear, embracing both of them at once. They held her in return, and Naia buried her face in her mother's locs. She smelled of soil and apeknot leaves, flowers and fresh water. Home.

"I missed you so much," Naia mumbled. "I wanted to come home, but I couldn't. Not until it was time."

"I know. Gurjin told me how strong you'd become." Maudra Laesid leaned back, holding their shoulders to keep her balance. Amri picked up her spear and held it out. She looked at him as she took it, then Kylan. She smiled and said, "You must introduce me to your handsome friends."

Naia chuckled at first, though once her mother had said it, she realized it might be true.

"They're Amri and Kylan. Amri joined us when we went to the Tomb of Relics ourselves . . . and I met Kylan on one of my first days after I left the swamp. They've been with me ever since. Tavra, too . . . but we had to split up."

"Tavra!" Maudra Laesid exclaimed, raising a brow. "That Silverling's still around?"

"Sort of," Amri muttered under his breath.

Naia's mother clucked her tongue, and Chapyora lowered her head. Astride, she tugged on the eel's mane until she reared, high above all the Gelfling in the pavilion.

"Drenchen, we return to the borderland. Quickly! Can't let these Spriton have all the glory with this fire of theirs, can we?"

The Drenchen roared, raising their spears.

They followed Maudra Laesid out the way they'd come, feet clamoring like drums alongside Chapyora's giant, slithering body. When they reached the edge of the thicket, they found more Drenchen waiting. Some of the warriors gasped and waved when they saw Naia, and she waved back from where she walked beside her mother. She recognized their faces, though every one of them had grown and changed since she'd last seen them. Older, tougher. Wearier. How long had she been gone?

"Mother, we heard from Maudra Mera that skekSa the Mariner has been looking for us. She came by Sami Thicket, and I can only guess she'll head for Sog next. Have you heard anything? Has anyone seen her?"

Naia's mother snorted, blowing away the worries that had been settling across Naia's brow. "No. Not a glimpse. Do not worry, Naia. Have you forgotten what the swamp is like? No Skeksis will make it a day's journey inside, let alone all the way to Great Smerth."

Naia wanted to believe it, so for the moment she did. Maudra

Laesid clucked her tongue for Chapyora to slither ahead to join the warriors at the front. Naia settled into a brisk walk. Amri wandered closer after Maudra Laesid left, keeping pace at Naia's shoulder.

"How far is it to Great Smerth from here?" he asked.

"About a day and a half, two days tops," Naia said. "At least, that's what it was last time I walked it. Sound about right, Gurjin?"

Gurjin walked ahead, halfway between them and the next group of Drenchen, as the party headed south. He grunted and nodded.

"I guess."

In the distance, the sky brightened. They'd been up all night. Naia yawned.

"I hope Tavra and Onica made it to Domrak," Amri said.

"Me too. But if Rian and the Grottan lit their fire, then at least we know all is well there," Kylan said. "Only two fires left. After the Drenchen, only one. And Rian's found a sword."

"And that is what worries me," Naia added. "What are we supposed to use a sword for if we don't bring it against the Skeksis? Especially if Rian's the one wielding it. He's the only one I can think of who wants to kill Skeksis more than me . . . or wanted to, anyway."

"Maybe it's not what we think," Amri suggested. "There's so much in the Tomb of Relics, it's hard to say what anything really is, no matter what it looks like. There are swords and tapestries, paintings and carvings and amulets . . . and rubbish. Lots and lots of rubbish. The only thing we can know for sure about it is that it was covered in dust and cave creature droppings."

Naia couldn't help but laugh a little. "Can you imagine serious Rian, sent by Aughra to the Tomb of Relics looking for a sacred weapon and having to go through all that?"

"Yeah, poor guy. I don't wish that much hollerbat poop on anyone. Except maybe a Skeksis."

Naia's laugh grew. It felt good, as if she had almost forgotten how. Even Kylan was grinning. Amri scooped a clod of soft soil from the ground at his feet, throwing it out into the field. "Take that, Chamberlain!"

"Will you keep it down?"

The brief elation died in an instant, as if Gurjin had thrown a spear and struck it down from the air. Naia bit her tongue.

"We're just joking around."

"It's the middle of the night. Your voices are echoing all across the plains."

"It's *dawn*," Naia said. "I can hear birds."

Sure enough, the suns were peeking over the horizon, and the birds and other critters were coming to life, singing from the tall grasses and clusters of trees. Gurjin pinched his lips together and turned away with a grumble.

Naia glanced at Amri and Kylan, who shrugged. She picked up her pace, trotting to flank Gurjin. He didn't look at her as she walked beside him. "What's going on? We lit two fires, and your best buddy Rian found a magic sword. I would have thought you'd be happier about all this."

Gurjin sucked in a big, slow breath and let it out. He shook his locs out with his hand and rolled his shoulders.

"Sorry. It's nothing."

"Is something wrong? Is it about Mother, or . . . ?"

He finally met her eyes, the same blue as hers, his forehead wrinkled with concern. He licked his lips, hesitated, then said, "When we get to Sog, Naia . . . just don't be surprised if it's not how you remember it."

"What? What's that supposed to mean?"

Her feet felt stuck in the grass, and in that moment he picked up his pace to catch up with the other warriors and their mother up in the front of the line. Naia's feet moved again when Amri and Kylan met her. The three of them walked together, though now all the joy felt as if it had been sucked out of the fledgling day despite the blue and violets that crept across the sky.

"What does that mean?" Amri asked.

"I don't really know," Naia said. Up ahead she could see the distant, foggy line of green and gray where the fields sank into the jungle. The Swamp of Sog hovered ahead, the marshy borderlands within their day's journey. Whatever Gurjin had meant, it was only a matter of time before she would find out.

CHAPTER 18

The journey south was a strange one, accompanied by dozens of Drenchen warriors and Maudra Laesid's personal entourage. Naia recognized all of the Gelfling who marched with them. They all smiled and greeted her, though if they had questions to ask her about her travels, they didn't ask. Maudra Laesid was always urging them onward, discouraging idleness and small talk.

What struck Naia the most about it all was how their number changed the journey itself. When Naia had first emerged from the swamp on her own, the vast plains of the Spriton lands had seemed endless and infinitely daunting. Now, with so many Drenchen walking beside her, and having seen so much more of the world than she'd ever expected, the plains seemed small. Gentle and forgiving, especially compared to the brutal cold of the north or the arid, draining heat of the sandstorm-ridden desert.

How many of these Drenchen had left Sog for the first time to march north with her mother? Even now they treaded across the dry soil and grass without sandals. Naia's feet ached in her shoes, remembering how uncomfortable and often painful the walk had been, full of sticks and brambles and sharp rocks.

"It's finally happening, eh?" Amri asked.

Gurjin had gone up ahead to walk alongside Chapyora, as if putting as much distance as he could between the four of them without running all the way back to Great Smerth on his own. Naia wasn't sure what had gotten into him, but after their confrontation she let him have his space. Still, Amri's comment was a welcome relief from the quiet.

"Yep," Naia replied. "By this evening we'll be in Sog. Ready? You'll have to take off your cloak, you know. It's too warm and humid, and we'll be doing a lot of climbing."

"Sounds like my kind of place," he said. "So you walk among the trees? I thought maybe we might take boats or something."

Whatever had come between them before—the strange aloofness he'd shown when they'd been with the Mystics—was slowly wearing off over time. Now when she looked up, she saw *him* again. Looking back at her with those eyes like the night.

"No. The waterways are inconsistent, some deep and some too shallow to swim in, and they're always changing. It's more reliable to travel in the canopy. I hope you're not afraid of heights."

"Not me! What about you, Kylan?"

Kylan shrugged from Naia's other side. He, too, seemed uncharacteristically light-footed. "It's closed-in places I don't like. I've wanted to see Sog for a long time."

It felt as if a long-lost light was streaming out of her heart, and Naia could barely contain it.

"I can't wait to show you," she said.

The earth became wetter as they walked through the day, with marshes and ponds and lakes springing up more frequently until they were wading through reeds, up to their ankles in peat. The air was thick and wet, abuzz with darting bugs, and once when Kylan tripped over a big root, his yelp scared up a flock of a hundred squawking, blue-feathered bog-birds.

When the peat gave way to clear, fresh water, Naia found a raised apeknot root. The smooth-barked trees sprang up around them like gnarled warriors, guarding the swamp and welcoming her home. Naia hopped up onto the root and untied her sandals. Amri and Kylan did the same when they saw what she was doing. Loop by loop, they loosened the cords until the sandals came off, stowed in Kylan's traveling pack. The cool water and spongy peat pressed against the full sole of her foot. It felt like home.

"Oh!" Kylan said, half in surprise and half in dismay. He took another step, sinking into the water, mud, and peat up to his knees. "Oh."

Naia laughed as Amri pulled off his cloak. He hung it on the tree root so it draped like a ghost, dark fabric blowing in the light wind. Below, he had on a simple jerkin and leggings in Sifa colors, probably borrowed from Onica's ship. Without the voluminous black cape and hood, his athletic figure was more apparent, with strong limbs, feet, and hands for climbing as swiftly as any rock lizard.

"We'll carry on through the marsh until we reach the Tall Pass," Naia said. "There, we'll ascend into the canopy for the rest of the journey to Great Smerth."

"The Tall Pass," Kylan murmured. "That's where you and Tavra and your father encountered the Nebrie, isn't it?"

Naia nodded. She'd shared the memory so many times, with so many Gelfling, but it still surprised her when Kylan recalled it. She wondered if the big Nebrie's body was still there, or whether it had been completely foraged by scavengers and decomposed, returned to rest in the swamp and Thra.

"The same," she agreed.

The small apeknots in the marshland perimeter grew in height and girth, but still something bothered Naia as they followed the Drenchen deeper into the swamp. She'd heard birds before, but now there were none singing. It was silent. The apeknot leaves, long and flat and dangling, languished where the trees' branches met. Tired and weak, luster faded. Here and there the smooth bark peeled in big strips, baring the tender heartwood beneath, not from grazing creatures but from lack of nutrition.

Kylan and Amri didn't notice as Naia did; they had never seen the swamp before, especially not in all its lush glory. They didn't notice how much darker the trees felt, how quiet everything was. How the scent in the air smelled *dim*, if that were possible. As if the life and light were flickering.

Perhaps she was imagining it. It had been unum since she'd left, but the seasons didn't stop turning just because she'd been away. Although the colder seasons didn't affect the swamp as much as they did the northern regions, the trees and creatures still felt the effects. When she'd lived in Sog and seen the swamp transition into winter, it had always been gradual. Flowers folding up, opening for shorter periods each day. Animals hunting less and sleeping more. Perhaps the stillness and quiet seemed so jarring because the seasons had changed while she'd been away.

"Wow," Amri said, looking up.

Overhead, blue and green flowers grew in ivies up the sturdy trunks of the apeknots. The sun shone through their petals, casting dappled lights the color of Sifa sea glass across the pools of water that ringed the swamp floor. They had reached the border of the swamp.

Naia closed her eyes and breathed. The sounds of dripping, flowing water were all around, like a constant rain. Birds *were* singing. The Drenchen had dispersed, no longer walking in a single group, scattering through the apeknots and other trees, disappearing and reappearing as they passed in and out of the sun and shadows.

"All the songs of Sog are wrong," Kylan murmured. He walked through the water and mud without hesitation now, having rolled up the cuffs of his leggings to keep them from getting dirty. *At least for now*, Naia thought to herself with a smile.

"What songs?"

"Any songs. They always sing of the swamp being putrid and stinking of gas, but I don't smell any of that."

Naia laughed. "We're not deep enough. I promise, you'll know it when you smell it."

"I read in the Tomb that the swamp drains out to a southern sea," Amri said. "But the maps never go that far, and no one's ever come back with records."

"It gets very wet if you go much further south than Great Smerth," Naia replied. "Come to think of it, even the Drenchen don't go that far. All our hunting grounds rotate north of Great Smerth, where the game is. Further south and it becomes a lake-land, but the water is brackish and stings after a while. It would make sense if the lakes become the sea there, but I've never gone."

"It's all so fascinating," Amri mused. "Long ago, the Gelfling were explorers. Travelers. Bards, like Gyr, or adventurers like Jarra-Jen. But now we stay where we're put. In our little regions, separated from one another. And it's been that way for so long, it's almost as if we've forgotten as a people how to go outside our own caves. Or swamps, as it were."

"Or fields," Kylan said. "We've become cut off from one another. Even those clans that meet to trade, or that share borders. The Skeksis had a part in it, but the seven clans went along with it on their own. It's easier to remain where you know the land, where things aren't unknown or scary . . . but it's caused us to be in this predicament, too. Where the clans don't trust one another, or even seem to know how to travel beyond the land they know."

"It's changing, now," Amri said. "Finally. A Spriton from the plains has crawled through the caverns of Grot. A Grottan from Domrak has sailed from Ha'rar across the Silver Sea. A Drenchen has touched the waters of the Dousan Wellspring, in the middle of the dry-as-bones desert!"

Now here they were, a group of Gelfling working together, not because they were of the same clan but because they all had the same goal. Because they agreed what was important and worth protecting. And now they had all grown so close, Naia couldn't imagine a day without them by her side.

She looked up when she realized Amri and Kylan had stopped, both staring straight ahead.

"Whoa," Amri said.

Two huge trees seemed to materialize out of the swamp mist, branches reaching out to one another. They looked almost like Gelfling clasping hands, except the apeknots were two of the oldest known in the swamp, wide and tall, their tops growing straight through the canopy.

Naia showed them the step-way carved into the bark of one of the trees, made trine upon trine ago by her Drenchen ancestors. She and Amri and Kylan followed the long line of Drenchen as the party climbed up, emerging at the top on a network of walkways and paths made of tree limbs bound by vines and thick rope nets. It had been so long since Naia had been up in the arms of the apeknots that when she reached the landing, she paused to look down across the swamp. Amri and Kylan looked with her, taking in the undulating emerald and turquoise.

A whisper brushed Naia's ears, like the echo of a long-ago moan. It reminded her of Vassa, skekSa's ship. It wasn't a sound in the ear, though, she realized as her eyes landed on a dark spot in the swamp near a toppled tree. It was a sound in her memory. The phantom moaning of the darkened Nebrie, whose tusks had snapped the ancient apeknots as if they were saplings. The dark spot near the tree was just a pool of water, but when Naia peered closer through the mist, she could see white bones breaking the surface.

"The Nebrie?" Amri whispered.

Naia shivered and nodded. The Nebrie's skeleton had been pecked clean by animals of the swamp, most of its body sunk into the mud and silt below the water's surface. Animals died in the swamp all the time; it was the natural cycle of life. No different were the Gelfling, who were born of the earth, lived of the earth, and when they died, returned to the earth. But the darkened Nebrie that had broken Tavra's wing and nearly killed Naia's father had been forced out of that cycle. Enraged by the darkening in the crystal veins that spanned in interconnected lace beneath every pool and bank of peat.

And not just the swamp. Everything in Thra thrived when it was connected, died when it was broken apart. Radiating with life when whole, but fractured by even the tiniest of cracks.

Naia looked away. Ahead she could see Gurjin and her mother, crossing the foot-paths further into the swamp. She waved to her friends and the three of them followed together. The day went by overhead, and the swamp faded into a cooler evening.

Just as the moss on the trees began to glow, Naia caught sight of warm firelight below. The branch beneath their feet ended, the path continuing on a wooden walkway of planks and rope. The walkway creaked and swung as they walked across it, but Naia didn't need to hold on to the hand-rope like Kylan and Amri.

Her pace quickened and she broke away from them, walking swiftly toward the sound of drums and Drenchen voices. Firebugs danced in the air, and the scent of smoked blindfish wafted up from the hearth fire below.

The apeknot canopy gave way, and Naia's heart burst at the

sight of the enormous tree in the center of a torchlit glade. Tears pricked the corners of her eyes as she took in the tree's whorled, twisting bark and sturdy branches, holding the wooden and carved Drenchen homes like clusters of bird nests made of wood and net.

The day had finally come. Naia had returned to Great Smerth.

CHAPTER 19

The drums stopped a beat when the Drenchen playing them saw who had returned, a moment later striking up into the most energetic and resounding rhythm Naia had ever heard. It was a victory march. A return song for Naia and her mother as they descended from the trees toward the Glenfoot, a wide pavilion at the foot of Great Smerth in the center of the Drenchen village. Built of planks and mud brick, the Glenfoot had served as the meeting place for the Drenchen for generations. Naia felt the weight of her ancestors more than ever as she arrived, on foot beside Maudra Laesid, who sat perched on Chapyora's mighty neck.

"My Drenchen! We return, and with Naia and Gurjin, safe and well. I have beheld the fires of resistance which we have heard of only in song. The Spriton fire, and the Grottan. Only two fires remain, and it will be the Drenchen whose torches join the resistance next."

A volley of cheers and shouts erupted across the Glenfoot. Maudra Laesid beamed and clucked her tongue, taking her spear again as Chapyora lowered her head so she could dismount. Without looking back, Maudra Laesid headed for the carved gate that led inside Great Smerth.

Under her breath, in a voice less proud, she said, "Come, my children. We will find your errant father."

Just as Naia made to follow her, Gurjin caught her arm. A tickling in her mind, like a bug crawling across the back of her neck, felt as if it was about to bite.

"Wait, Naia. Before you go in. There's . . . something I haven't told you," he said, words stilted between rigid teeth.

As much as Naia wanted to know what had been on Gurjin's mind, his sudden confession still didn't end with whatever it was that he was keeping to himself. Naia waited for it to come, but it didn't. Despite their fight and their silent agreement to move past it, there was still space between them. She still didn't know exactly who Gurjin was.

"Yeah," she said. "I know. I guess I'm going to find out."

The great hall filled the belly of Smerth, lit by luminescent moss and a dozen small torches. The heartwood that had housed the big chamber was ribbed and carved with the faces of creatures of the swamp: the tusked Nebrie, the flying muski eels, the swoothu. Maudra Laesid approached the round table that spanned the length of the room. Seated at the far end, in his own chair beside the *maudra's* empty one, was Bellanji. Naia's father, whom she'd last seen bleeding of a terrible wound in his side.

When he saw Naia, he leaped up, footsteps like thunder as he swept past Laesid, snatching Naia up into a hug so big, she felt like a childling for a moment. She hugged him back, trying not to let the emotion of seeing him again overcome her. It wouldn't do to cry in front of all the Drenchen, not even for happiness.

He set her down again, and she saw he hadn't shown so much

restraint, his cheeks glistening. "My little Naia. Not so little anymore. Welcome home," he said.

Their reunion was brief, interrupted by Maudra Laesid seating herself.

"Bellanji. We need to talk."

"I assumed so, since you've returned. Are you ready to apologize?"

Naia arched a brow. She had seen her parents argue before; in a Drenchen household, hard-talk was the way of it, and although Laesid and Bellanji often agreed in the end, the path there was not always a smooth one. Still, the pained look on her father's usually jolly face seemed different, as did her mother's pensive, hard eyes. This was more than a common debate or disagreement. Was this what Gurjin had been trying to tell her?

"Maybe," Laesid replied. "Sit down. Gurjin, Naia. Kylan the Spriton and Amri the Shadowling. Sit at my table so we can discuss what will become of the Drenchen. Kipper, call in Eliona and Pemma as well."

One of the Drenchen guards nodded and scampered off. Naia went to her chair, beside her mother's, while Gurjin took his spot beside Bellanji. It was the chair Eliona had often occupied, after Gurjin had left to become a guard at the castle. Naia wondered if Eliona would ask for her seat back when she arrived, or whether she'd taken the next one down.

"Your sisters?" Kylan asked from where he sat beside Naia. She nodded. Before she could say any more, Kipper came back with them. Eliona, Laesid's middling child, had shot up like a sapling since Naia had left, now nearly as tall as their mother. Pemma, the youngest, stood beside her, and Naia sighed with a tiny regret. Pemma's wings had blossomed, the color of fresh lake grass dappled by morning shadows. While Naia had been away, she had missed her youngest sister growing up.

"Naia!" Pemma exclaimed. "You're back!"

"We can catch up later," Naia said before her two sisters further delayed their meeting, though she ached to shower them with hugs and kisses. "We've important news to bring everyone and important business to complete."

"Indeed," Laesid said. "As I said to the others on the Glenfoot, Bellanji: We witnessed the Spriton turning against the Skeksis. Maudra Mera rallied her clan, and a great fire ignited in the Spriton hearth. Moments later, the fire shone again, and we got news that a similar fire had been lit in the Grottan caves by Rian, Gurjin's friend from the castle."

"We've been traveling to the clans lighting the fires, since Mother Aughra told us it was the way to resist the Skeksis," Naia explained. She didn't know how far and fast news had spread of their travels, so she quickly told her parents and sisters of their journey to Cera-Na, the Dousan Wellspring, and Ha'rar. All listened keenly to her telling, which, although not nearly as eloquent as one of Kylan's songs, still got the job done. At the end, Laesid rubbed her chin between her thumb and forefinger.

"It would seem the fires are a sign from Thra, of our connection to the eternal flame which binds all life of the world," she said. "They ignite, and our connection to our sister clans grows stronger."

"When we lit fires before, we could see glimpses through to the other fires. But we weren't able to speak through them. Not until this time, with Rian," Naia said.

"The more fires light, the stronger the link becomes," Kylan murmured. "Could this be the reason we're supposed to light the fires? Aside from merely bringing the word to all the clans and compelling them to unite with one another—is the purpose of the fires so we can communicate between the clans across the distance?"

"If that's the case, it could be that once all the fires are lit, the seven clans will be able to make a proper plan," Amri said. "Without the Skeksis knowing. If we were to convene in one place physically to have such a meeting, surely they would find out. But if we can speak through the fires of Thra, we might be able to make a plan without them finding out."

"Yes," Naia said. "The clans have been separated and in rivalry for as long as I can remember. Never full war, but certainly ebbing and flowing tides of animosity. Now we know this is not the natural order, but the Skeksis' will. These fires of resistance are the antidote to the Skeksis' segregational meddling. The fires bring us together, as one, as we are perhaps meant to be."

For the first time, it felt real. It felt like the truth. Like something that was right, that made sense, and most importantly, was maybe even possible. As Naia spoke the words inside the great hall of her Drenchen home, she felt, for the first time, like a real leader.

"Which brings me to our next challenge," Laesid said. She

looked across her shoulder to Bellanji. "How fare you who stayed with Great Smerth while the rest of us took up arms to protect our clan? Is your plan working, or have you admitted failure and come around to my way of thinking yet?"

"No," Bellanji replied. "In fact, we are far from failure. Eliona and the other healers have found success where you promised we'd find none."

Laesid's eyes widened in surprise. Naia looked back and forth between her mother and sisters, then to her father, whose thick brows were drawn tight and resilient against her mother's blunt sarcasm. What had happened since she'd been gone?

"Success?" Laesid asked. "How so?"

"We've been trying different approaches, Mother," Eliona said. She, like Bellanji, had a stubbornness to her claim, though now that Naia looked closer she could see weariness across her younger sister's brow. "At first, as you guessed, it didn't work. But we didn't give up. And now, with hard work and perseverance, a few of us have managed to slow down the darkened vein that runs below Great Smerth."

Naia's heart banged once, like a Drenchen drum. All her confidence fell away like leaves from a tree in winter.

"What are you talking about?" she asked numbly.

Suddenly all eyes were on her. All eyes except for Gurjin's, which intently studied the whorled lines in the wood of the council table.

"You didn't tell her?" Laesid asked her only son.

"I was going to," Gurjin replied, crossing his arms and twisting his ears back. He flinched when Laesid struck the table with her fist.

"Then tell her now!" she cried.

Gurjin gulped, brows knotting and unknotting. Naia held her own hands in fists. It was the only way to keep from shaking, to keep herself contained while she waited for her brother to speak. Wait for the dreadful words she could almost hear, though they hadn't yet been spoken.

"When Mother and I left for Ha'rar," he began, "in response to the message from the windsifter that the All-Maudra was dead. My plan was always to part ways with her when we got to Ha'rar and go looking for you. I know we agreed that we should split up, because the Skeksis wanted us together and alive, but something had happened in Sog that was more important."

Light flashed in Naia's mind, but it was tinged with darkness. The crystal cluster in the Mystic Valley, bruised and bleeding. The vein under the swamp bed where she'd encountered the darkened Nebrie. In the Crystal Sea desert, poisoning flocks of Skimmers.

"The darkening," Naia whispered. She couldn't let the word go unsaid any longer. "It reached Great Smerth. It reached . . . home."

She had traveled nearly the entire Skarith region and never crossed a place that hadn't been affected by the blight. She had been naive to think it would not come here. She needed confirmation, but the only acknowledgment was that no one replied. Her mother looked more grim than ever, her father's beard-locs quivering with a turbulent mix of emotions.

"We tried to heal it," Gurjin continued. "But not even

Mother's *vliyaya* was able to cleanse it. The veins that run below Great Smerth have been blighted."

Naia looked up, into the big cavern carved into Great Smerth. The enormous tree she'd been born in, grew up in. Lived in every day of her life, surrounded by the warm gold heartwood, until she'd left.

"We knew it was only a matter of time," Laesid said, stern and quiet. "When the darkened veins reached the heartwood, we knew it was over. Great Smerth is dying, and there is nothing we can do to stop it except take our fight out of Sog, cross the plains, and attack the Skeksis while we still can."

"Or so your mother thought," Bellanji replied.

"I was not—and am not—about to waste our time trying to heal something which cannot be healed!" Laesid boomed. "This is a blight of the Crystal, Bellanji. I told you before, and I'll tell you again. It cannot be cured at this extremity. It must be stopped at the root. Though it breaks my heart to leave Great Smerth, who has protected the Drenchen for generations, we may have to. If we do not join the other Gelfling and find a way to heal the darkened Crystal, *all* of the great trees will die. And the lesser trees as well. And everything on Thra!"

"But Eliona slowed down a part of the darkening with Kipper," Pemma said. "I saw it!"

Naia wanted to hush her sister, to keep her from entering the water that was heating between their parents. But she was still reeling from the news. How long did Great Smerth have? How long would it be before the branches withered and died, its heartwood rotting? Its bark falling in long, blackened strips like the apeknots at the edge of the swamp? She recognized it now, should have recognized it before—the silence and the groves of ailing trees. The darkened veins below the mud were ripe and toxic, sapping the essence out of the swamp that had given her life. Though Naia's mind spun like a ship on the waves of a whirlpool, every time she looked up, all she saw was Gurjin, sitting across from her, arms folded.

"We went to the vein in the blindfish cellars," Eliona said. "Kipper and I tried healing it with a blue stone cudgel. We cracked the vein and tried healing it at the place where it splintered."

"And?" Laesid asked.

"The purple blight in the splinters faded," Bellanji said. "I saw it myself."

But Maudra Laesid did not buy it, and neither did Naia.

"But you say it's only slowing it down," Naia said. "That's not healing it. That's not final. You're describing the amputation of an infected finger, not a healing of the infection itself."

"Not only that, but this vein feeds Great Smerth," Laesid added. "Or it did, before it was darkened. Breaking off the crystal veins is the same as breaking Great Smerth away from the Heart of Thra."

"The Heart of Thra which has become darkened!" Bellanji cried. Naia knew his anger wasn't toward her or her mother, but it bit nonetheless. "Would you rather Great Smerth die quickly and in agony?"

"Of course not!" Naia cried. "But Mother's right. Thra is sick. We can't cut Great Smerth off from the Crystal, and we can't heal the Crystal by healing Great Smerth."

"So what are you saying?" Gurjin demanded.

"You know what I'm saying, Gurjin!"

"We have to abandon Great Smerth," Maudra Laesid interrupted. Nearly commanded. "As I said, and as I have ordered the Drenchen already. I do not relish it, but it is the only course of action."

"Then I'll say as I've said again!" Bellanji bellowed. "I will not leave Great Smerth, not to fight the Skeksis and not even to join you, whom I love with all my heart! I will stay here with the healers and do what you will not. To save the tree that gave us life."

Maudra Laesid stood abruptly, shoving her chair back and snatching her spear.

"I have traveled a long way without rest, only to have this argument again. And yet I leave this night at the same impasse as on the night I left with the warriors. I must rest. But we will meet again tomorrow, and the next day, and the next, until I can convince you of this tragic thing we must do to save the Drenchen and join the Gelfling resistance."

Bellanji stood, too. Usually he might offer his arm to Naia's mother and they would walk together to their bedchamber to retire for the evening. But not this night.

"Then I will see you again in the morning, Laesid, and convince the mother in you not to abandon the mother tree that surrounds us even now," he said.

Then the two parted ways, Maudra Laesid heading up the spiraling staircase with Chapyora while Bellanji stomped out the front gate. Naia got to her feet before Gurjin could beat her to it. She could barely wait until her parents were out of sight before the terrible feeling in her chest came out.

"I can't believe you didn't tell me the darkening had reached Great Smerth!" she cried.

"I'm sorry," he said, but he didn't sound sorry. "You would have just blown up, the way you're blowing up now. I was waiting for the right time!"

"The right time? The right time would have been right away, not as we're walking into the hall!"

Amri and Kylan, Eliona and Pemma remained silent as the big room seemed to shrink. As she looked into Gurjin's eyes, she saw her own face looking back. She and he, reflecting each other like two halves, even after all they'd done apart.

"How could you keep this from me for so long?" Naia whispered. "After everything you said about trust . . ."

"Well, maybe I was wrong."

Gurjin's voice cracked when he answered, and she felt a pinch of remorse. This hurt him, too, and all she was doing was yelling at him. It was his fault that he hadn't told her, but it wasn't his fault this was happening. It wasn't his fault that the Skeksis had done what they had, and that the reach of their destruction on the Crystal had finally reached the one place Naia had believed to be safe.

"I need to see it," she said. It was like her heart was talking without waiting for her mind to catch up. Then her feet were moving, walking at a quickening pace. Out of the great hall, away from her friends and brother and sisters. Anywhere but there.

CHAPTER 20

Only a few perimeter torches were still lit by the time Naia exited the great hall, ignoring Kylan and Amri calling after her. The rest of the swamp had vanished into the night fog, with one or two golden flickers hanging in the trees where Drenchen had fires lit in their hanging huts. Two guards stood at either side of the great hall's gate, nodding briefly to Naia when she burst out onto the Glenfoot. She skirted past the guards and followed one of the big old roots that curved down from the Glenfoot, sloping like a slide toward the deep water that pooled around Great Smerth's base.

The fishery was below, a network of reed pens to keep fish where they could spawn and live happily until it was time to catch and eat them. The root path twisted in an easy spiral and along the water, trained and shaped over hundreds of trine. Naia had always taken it for granted, as a child even believing it had grown that way naturally. But now as she followed it closer to the water, she wondered if the technique of training the root had been given to the Drenchen by Aughra—and if Aughra, in turn, had learned it from the urSkeks when they had arrived on this world. The more she knew, and the more she opened her eyes, the more it felt as if there was nothing that was untouched by them.

The fish were nearly invisible in the dark water under the tree, floating lazily, since all the evening insects had either flown away or been eaten. Naia climbed down a rope ladder, dropping away from it and diving into the water. It wasn't too deep. During the day it was easy to see the bottom, when the water was clear. Now it was dark, but she had played in the fish cellars many times as a child. Finding her way by touch and using her wings as fins, she swam down to where the mud had been cleared and large, flat stones were stacked into cellars for blindfish to hide in.

Light glimmered between the stones of one of the cellars before she reached it. It was dim, its color difficult to make out in the nighttime water. Naia's presence woke some of the blindfish, spooking them out of their silt beds so plumes of soft mud clouded the water. By the time it cleared, Naia reached the underwater cellar and looked inside.

A crystal vein was exposed in the mud, about the width of Naia's finger. It was just a ridge, peeking above the silt—not a cluster like what she and Amri had seen in the valley of the stones. She waved the last clouds of mud away and let out a big bubble of relief. The vein was clear, its light the color of the suns. It went straight under Great Smerth, buried in its roots somewhere far below in the mud and water of the swamp.

Naia brushed away the silt on one end of the vein, revealing a jagged portion of rock where the vein suddenly ended. There were cracks in the stone where it had been struck by Eliona and Kipper's cudgel, and where the fracture broke the rock, it broke the crystal vein, too. On the side that was closer to Great Smerth, the crystal was very dim but clear; on the other side, no light showed in the vein, dark or light. It was proof of Eliona's words: They had severed the tree from the darkening.

Naia gazed at the broken vein. It was bittersweet to behold. Though the darkening was stopped from spreading into Great Smerth, it also meant this vein was broken off from the Crystal. How many more veins spread under the earth and water? Here, and everywhere else in Thra? The Crystal was what bled life into the land. It wasn't possible to cut it away. Not like this. What Laesid had said was true. This was not a lasting solution.

But Bellanji wasn't wrong, either. If they could slow the sickness, then didn't they owe it to Great Smerth to do whatever they could to protect its life as long as possible? Naia didn't know what to do. Though she had wanted to see the vein for herself, even knowing Eliona had been telling the truth didn't give her any more answers. If only Naia could be in two places at once, doing two things at the same time. Healing Great Smerth *and* the Crystal. One hand healing the fingertips of Thra, the other pressed against its heart.

Naia let out a big sigh of water and bubbles. Even if she could be in two places at once, she was no longer a healer. Not enough for something like this. The blue light hadn't come to her no matter how many times she'd tried, not since she'd failed at healing Amri in the cave.

The water shifted from her sigh, blowing back mud and spooking a little blindfish that hadn't woken when she'd first entered the cellar. It wriggled sluggishly, then shook itself free from the mud, long whiskers perking around its eyeless face, six white fins illuminated by the crystal vein's light.

Naia watched it, tilting her head. Blindfish were skittish and difficult to catch because of it. That was why the Drenchen kept the cellars, to make fishing easier. But this blindfish didn't try to swim away like the others. It drifted listlessly in the water in front of her, as if dazed, or maybe still asleep.

Then it darted forward and bit her.

Naia yelped as its tiny teeth pricked her arm. She swatted at it, hard, and it finally flicked its fins and disappeared into the dark water. Blindfish barely had any teeth and its bite hadn't even drawn blood, but the edges of Naia's ears still buzzed with alarm. Blindfish never bit, and especially never bit Gelfling.

A terrible feeling melted across Naia's shoulders like a current of cold water. She reached out and pressed her fingers into the soft mud where the blindfish had been buried, clearing it to the bedrock. As she did, a familiar violet haze filled the cellar.

No, no, no . . .

She stood on the lake floor and spread her wings. With a few powerful thrusts, a wave of water burst through the cellar, blowing the mud out the holes between the stones until the bedrock was bare for her to see.

The vein had surely been broken by Eliona and Kipper's blue stone cudgel. But the complete result of their operation had been hidden by all the mud. Where the darkened vein ended, hairline splinters raced out in wide arcs, fresh and bright and violet. They stretched through the bedrock, reconnecting on the other side of the crystal ribbon, bleeding their darkened blight into it just as badly—if not worse—than before.

Naia knelt above the veins, paralyzed by fear and horror. They were the same veins that crossed the swamp and the plains, traveled through the Dark Wood. Spread from that place where the Crystal was kept, where it shone down into the chute of fire and lit the world with its light and the light of the three suns. The veins were connected, as all in Thra was connected—the veins were part of the Crystal, as all the creatures of Thra were part of one another. Though she was far from the Crystal itself, its song reached her even here. It was a melody without harmony, a song broken into discord. The Crystal, reverberating with its powerful voice, incomplete in ruins without its missing shard.

Where was that shard that had gone flying from the wound in the Crystal? Lost forever? Without it, could the Crystal even be healed, or was it doomed to remain incomplete forever, all thanks to the Skeksis?

And the Mystics, Naia reminded herself. They were the same. Creatures from beyond Thra in a world that was not theirs. And now they were destroying it, bit by bit. The proof was just below her fingertips.

How dare they. How dare they hurt what I love.

Blue light glowed through the muddy haze. In her grief, her *vliyaya* had sparked to life. She gazed upon it, weakly pooling in her hands, lighting the water that swirled slowly through the cellar. Its dim light shone off the crystal veins like moonlight. The ability to heal. The will to mend.

Why had it come back now? This special fire that had been given to her by Thra?

Perhaps it was time to give it back.

The crystal sparked the same way it had in the Mystic Valley, but this time Naia was ready. She gritted her teeth against the initial jolt of energy and pain, pushing her hands through it until they were flat against the darkened crystal. The lake vanished, racing away from her as she fell into the crystal vein, her mind overwhelmed by the droning, crackling, *humming*—then she was flying through the earth, along the rivers of crystal veins, fast as light and pulled by an irresistible, powerful force.

She saw it. The Crystal of Truth, spinning in the chamber at the center of the Castle of the Crystal. Dark amethyst and red, the last ounces of purity all but gone from its rugged, faceted body. The color was the sign of its pain. The sign of its torture and madness, the blazing color of its corruption.

Naia felt the light in her hand streaming out, taking with it her own life force. Pulled in like a fish on a line, bleeding her of it. The Crystal, that once gave life, now wrathful. Dying. Empty.

But if that was what it would take . . .

NAIA!

The watery fish cellar crashed back around her, and Naia felt hands on her arms, yanking her back. She heard a terrible noise and thought maybe Great Smerth's roots were collapsing above, plunging into the fishery on top of her.

The thundering that pounded against her ears and against every bone in her body focused until Naia realized that the sound

came from inside her. Her heart, pounding desperately, trying to keep her alive when she had nearly opened the gate and let the Crystal take everything she had.

Currents flowed against her cheek. Before she knew what was going on, she broke the surface of the water. She heard coughing and retching and finally saw who had dragged her from the Crystal.

"Amri," she began. "Why—you could have drowned!"

He coughed up a last mouthful of water. She flinched back when he glared at her, tears glistening on his cheeks between the droplets of lake water.

"What were you doing?" he shouted. He knelt beside her and grabbed her shoulders, shaking her. "What were you *thinking?*"

"Isn't it obvious?" she mumbled. Under normal circumstances she might have argued. But now, drenched in water, having nearly given her life's essence to the darkened veins—and seeing the pained look in Amri's eyes—she didn't know how to feel. She just felt tired. Fearful and helpless, if those were even separate feelings and not just two halves of the same thing. The tears from before tried to come again, but it was hard to let them when Amri was there.

He didn't let go of her shoulders, gripping her like she might float away at any moment.

"Naia. I know you want to heal the Crystal. We all do. And save Great Smerth . . . but . . . you can't. Not this way. Not at the cost of yourself."

"I just thought if I could do it, then maybe . . ." She shook her head. She looked up, away from Amri and into the graceful, twisting forms of Great Smerth's roots overhead. The tears did come, then, if only one at a time. "I thought Great Smerth would always be here. I thought the swamp was safe from the Skeksis. I never thought . . ."

Everything about Amri softened. His eyes and his voice, his grip on her shoulders.

"I know," he said quietly. "I thought the same about Domrak."

Domrak. Naia shuddered. Beautiful blue-walled Domrak, glowing with moss and lake creatures, filled with the haunting song of the Grottan musicians by the hearth. Maudra Argot's chamber had been lined with clear crystal. Were those crystal veins dark now, too?

"I'm sorry. I didn't mean to . . ."

"No, no," Amri said, stopping her. "Rian lit the fire there. The Grottan will endure. I know they will."

"But you still lost your home. I knew it, I just never . . ." Naia struggled to find the words. She sighed. "I knew it was difficult for you. But I never thought about it happening to me, or my clan. As much as I've seen hardships fall on the Gelfling's shoulders, I never put myself in their place . . . in your place. And now that I am in that place, I don't know what to do."

The confession came out jumbled. Not like hard-talk at all, tentative and guilty. Naia almost didn't want Amri to hear her this way, see her this way, but she didn't know what else to do. She felt as if she had tried everything else, but it hadn't eased the pressure building inside her. Nothing had, until now. Not trying to heal the Crystal, but stammering simple, blubbering words to a Shadowling as the lake waters lapped at their ankles.

"I don't know what to do," she said again, and the pressure eased some more. She leaned into Amri until her forehead was against his shoulder. Though his clothes were still damp with the lake, beneath the scent of the water he still smelled like candlewax and stone. She took a big, shaking breath and shouted: "*I don't know what to do!*"

It didn't echo in the narrow place between them, enclosed by Amri's arms around her shoulders and the silvery curtain of his hair. She felt as if the emotions were draining from her, freeing room in her chest so she could finally breathe again. Breathe, and speak easier, even if the words were unflattering and embarrassing. In the safety of the night and Amri's quiet regard, they spilled out one after the other.

"Then what?" Amri asked softly.

She leaned back. She knew how her gut wanted to answer the question, so she said the first thing that landed on her tongue: "Then what's the point? Aren't I a failure if I can't lead? If I can't heal? If I can't defeat the Skeksis? We can't fight them, but I feel like it's the only thing I know how to do! But if I can't kill them, and I can't heal Thra—then who am I?"

"You're . . . Naia."

The answer was blunt and simple. Amri flicked an ear. She couldn't see his face too well in the dark, but she could hear his breath quicken a touch, his fingers twitching on her shoulders.

"And . . . I think you're amazing. When you're brave, it makes me feel brave. When you're strong, it makes me feel strong. That's what being a leader is—leading by example. You're committed to doing the right thing. Doing good . . . even when you fail. And even when you fail, you keep trying. You bring flowers out of ash."

It felt as if the warmth from his hands was spreading into her shoulders and chest, soft and gentle like the light from a candle. That was what Amri was, she realized. A little fire that never went out, that was always by her side. Not so bright that it drowned out other light, but more than enough to illuminate a path in the night. Gentle and discerning, steadfast and loyal.

"We're going to find a way," Amri said.

"We don't know how to give up, do we?" she asked, letting the warmth reach her lips where it came out as a smile. He chuckled.

"I think that's mostly you . . . But it's probably the thing I love most of all."

It got quiet between them.

"You mean as a friend, of course," she said hesitantly. She was unsure, particularly about one specific word he'd used. "Because . . . we're friends."

She waited for him to say *Yes, of course.* As he might as well have, when they'd stood at the top of the ridge in the Mystic Valley, looking out across the entire world.

Amri shifted nervously. "Oh. You mean that thing I said back in the valley—"

"I just want to know," Naia blurted. "I don't understand. I thought up until then that we . . . But then I woke up and you were all different. And then you started to warm up again, but you never . . . And now you almost drowned trying to save me, and . . ."

"That's not what I—" he choked out. "Naia, there's—"

"I thought maybe you just didn't think there was a difference between like and—"

"Of course I think there's a difference!"

She shut her mouth, realizing they were yelling right into each other's faces like she and other Drenchen used to do as childlings. Amri was no Drenchen, but there under Great Smerth, soaked in lake water, he'd found his voice.

"Of course I know the difference," he repeated, softer. "Naia. I really like you. You know, as more than a friend. But after you got hurt . . ."

He was still hiding something, but at least he wasn't lying.

"Tell me. Please?"

He let out a big, guilty sigh. Before he spoke, she realized what had happened. His hesitation to reveal the truth gave it away. She remembered the voices she'd heard in her dream of the river. Remembered someone who hadn't wanted Amri to come south with them.

"What did Gurjin say to you?" she asked, plainly enough that it left little room for Amri to try to make up another excuse. He sighed. All the pretenses rolled away from him, like when he'd taken off his cloak as they'd entered the wetlands. Finally, the truth came out, and he was her Amri again.

"He just told me that now wasn't a good time," he said. "He said you had other things you needed to do, and that I shouldn't be jeopardizing our mission by distracting you." He shrugged.

"It's not like he threatened me or anything. It made sense. And it was my fault you were so badly hurt. So I went along with it . . ."

Amri trailed off when a trembling rumble rolled through the swamp beyond the curtain of darkness. Naia twisted her ears, straining to hear it. It sounded like a boom and a crash, like a tree toppling. Silence followed, and she thought maybe it was nothing— but then it came again. And again. Amri cleared his throat.

"Are those normal swamp noises?" he asked.

As much as she wanted not to be bothered at a time like this, Naia couldn't deny the bad feeling in her gut.

"No. We should go back."

Naia wiped her cheeks. They stood, and Amri followed her back up to the Glenfoot. The Drenchen sentries had drawn their spears, lighting new torches.

"What's going on?" Naia asked as she and Amri reached the gate.

"We don't know," answered one of the guards. He turned to his fellow and ordered, "Ring the alarm. Call the *maudra* and Bellanji."

As the other sentry scampered up the rope ladder to one of the lookouts on a branch above, the entire Glenfoot shuddered with a high-pitched whine. Naia turned toward the sound, chills racing up her back as she tried to see through the shadows.

Naia's parents joined them within moments of the alarm bell clanging, Bellanji with his long spear and Laesid on Chapyora's back. Lights flickered throughout the glade as the Drenchen awoke.

"What comes?" Laesid demanded. "Who trespasses in my swamp?"

Amri grabbed Naia's arm, clutching her tightly as his Grottan eyes pierced the night. Naia already knew, deep in her belly, who it was, but it wasn't until he said her name that every muscle in her body tightened.

"A Skeksis Lord," Amri said, gulping. "skekSa, the Mariner."

CHAPTER 21

The Drenchen came out onto the Glenfoot as the rumbling grew. The smooth wood of the platform shivered under Naia's bare feet, as if Great Smerth were drawing itself up for battle. Kylan and Gurjin came running from within Great Smerth. Naia exchanged glances with her brother; whatever troubles were still between them, they would have to wait.

"The Mariner!" Bellanji cried. "What is she doing here? And how?"

"She's after me and Gurjin," Naia said.

"She's riding something," Amri said, peering into the blackness beyond the torchlight. "I think it's a creature. Long legs . . . It looks like it's running on the water!"

"Arathim?" Kylan asked.

Bellanji let out a tense huff of air from his nose. "There are big crawlers in the deep south of the swamp that skate atop the lakes and gobble bogs," he said. "If that's so, we'll have to kill that skating swamp-mucker, too."

Maudra Laesid drew her spear. "Drenchen, ready yourselves. Anyone without a spear, unfurl your nets. Prepare to take this underwater if we can, where we have the advantage. Tonight we kill a Skeksis."

Lightning bolted down Naia's back, urSan's face flashing in her mind's eye. She grabbed her mother's sleeve. "Wait, Mother—"

"Here she comes—"

Saplings at the perimeter of the glade toppled as a large nine-legged creature burst into the torchlight. It was as big as an armalig carriage, with a spiny shell and nine segmented legs ending in wide bubbles of skin, keeping it afloat on the water despite its weight and the burden of the Skeksis that was crouched over its knobby thorax.

skekSa the Mariner stood atop the giant skater when it slowed, floating across the rippling water that pooled around the Glenfoot. In one of her three claws she clutched a rein of leather and chain, fastened to a muzzle of iron that held the skater's barbed mandibles like a cage. She yanked on the reins, and the skater let out a strained hiss like steam from a kettle.

The scales on her face glittered green in the torchlight, feathers streaming from the crest on the back of her head. She had lost her hat somewhere during her journey from the north all the way to the south, her black cape littered with swamp mud and foliage instead of sea salt, but she was no less intimidating as her gaze settled on Naia and Gurjin.

"Found you at last," she growled.

Many of the Drenchen had never seen a Skeksis before, and the silhouettes of their spears quivered as they beheld her monstrous form, her hooked beak, and her ancient eyes. They were brave, though unsure, despite their advantage of numbers and terrain. Even Naia's parents were uncertain. Unlike Naia and her friends, they had never faced a Skeksis in battle.

Nevertheless, Maudra Laesid was fearless. She called on Chapyora to rear up, leveling her spear. skekSa's skater fidgeted under Chapyora's shadow, held barely under control by the chains in the Skeksis's claws.

"Begone from my swamp, skekSa," Maudra Laesid said. "Or we'll make fish food of you."

"Mother, we can't," Naia said. "We can't kill her. If we do, a friend of ours will die. Someone who's helped us—"

"Then the Lord Mariner should surely give up her mission to kidnap my eldest children, shouldn't she?" Maudra Laesid boomed. "So that she doesn't force me to end her life tonight!"

skekSa's smile split her beak.

"Oh, I love a good threat," she said. "You are not kindhearted at all, little Gelfling! Not at all, when it comes down to it."

"Mother, please," Naia hissed, but Maudra Laesid's spear did not lower.

"I'm sorry about your friend, Naia. But she will kill many more friends of yours tonight if we do not kill her."

"But this isn't right!"

skekSa drew the blade at her hip. It was a different sword from the one she'd used in Ha'rar, probably taken from her stash of treasure. Where were the rest of those jewels and metals and artifacts now? At the bottom of the sea, or had Vassa finally rid itself of the Skeksis that had been living in its belly?

"Now!" Bellanji cried.

A net came down from the canopy, fast from the rocks tied

to its ends. skekSa roared when she sensed it, leaping from the back of the skater in time to avoid being caught in the web of rope and rock. The skater screeched, free from the Skeksis's hold on its reins but immediately entangled in the net. The rocks hit the water and sank, dragging the struggling creature in a spray of thrashing legs and swamp water. Naia watched it go under, spirit straining along with the poor thing that had never wanted to be there in the first place.

So much senseless violence . . .

"Look out!" Amri shouted as skekSa reached into her cloak.

Too late. skekSa hurled a volley of round black eggs up over the Glenfoot. They struck and exploded in balls of green fire, blasting huge portions of Great Smerth's outer bark into splinters. The fire that curled out of the places where the thunder eggs struck was hotter than torch fire, catching on even Great Smerth's ancient, water-filled body.

"Put out the fire!" roared Bellanji. "Put it out before the tree comes down!"

Maudra Laesid called upon them from the other side: "Spears! *Bola!* NOW!"

skekSa was a blur of feathers and claws, leaping with extraordinary speed through the heavy smoke that pooled across the Glenfoot. Despite their renewed courage, the Drenchen scattered away from her when she landed.

The Drenchen split, some rushing to draw water in a vain attempt to quench the green and yellow flames. Others picked up their weapons and came to Laesid's side, surrounding the drenched

Skeksis as she caught her breath, claws spread and fangs bared. Naia strained to find Gurjin and Kylan and Amri in the commotion.

"*Naia.*"

skekSa straightened to her full height, knocking back her cloak. Naia reached to her belt as the Skeksis approached, but there was nothing there. No *bola*. No dagger.

But she wasn't alone. Amri had found a sword from one of the Drenchen, brandishing it like Tavra had taught him, with his body angled with the blade raised as he stepped up beside Naia. The Mariner glared at him.

"Get out of my way, little apothecary. You are smarter than to get between me and my prey."

"Nope," he said, eyes bright with fearlessness. "I don't want to hurt you, but I'm not going to let you hurt Naia, either!"

Naia breathed again when Kylan stepped beside her. And then, on her other side, Gurjin. He pushed his dagger into her hand, bracing himself with a long spear when she took the familiar blade from him.

skekSa brought her sword down at Amri. He swung his own, catching her blade from the side and twisting. His entire body shuddered from the impact. There was no way his thin sword could withstand the blow, and he knew it. As his blade broke, he sprang deftly away, slashing out with what remained of his shattered sword. Looking back, he saw a deep gash across the back of skekSa's hand.

skekSa grunted and swore, swinging a claw at Amri and knocking him off his feet and into the water. Ignoring Kylan as he leaped off the Glenfoot to help Amri, the Mariner pushed past the Drenchen armed with pointed spears until she towered over Naia and Gurjin. She barely flinched when Gurjin thrust his spear at her, catching it in her free claw and breaking it at the shaft with a terrible *SNAP*.

"No! Stay back!" Naia commanded as the other Drenchen stepped forward, finally finding their courage. She held out a hand to her mother and Chapyora, begging them not to attack. The billowing firelight rippled off every quill and feather of skekSa's furious visage, as if her entire body were boiling with rage.

"I'd wear your twin skins on my coat tonight," skekSa growled, raising her sword. "I'd roast the two of you on the hot coals of this ugly old tree. But lucky you. I fear the Emperor's wrath more than I desire revenge—"

A shadow darted from the canopy, diving at skekSa's face with a stream of angry, chattering squeaks. skekSa squawked in surprise, thrashing with her claws as the flying eel bit and scratched. Feathers flew from skekSa's brilliant plumage until she finally stumbled away. The eel took one last chomp before zipping away, flying to Naia with a puff of victorious fur.

"Neech!"

Naia hugged the eel and bit back a tear. But they had no time for a lengthy reunion. Maudra Laesid ordered sharply, "Now! Pin her traitor bones to the bottom of the lake!"

Naia's protest was drowned by the battle cries of the roaring Drenchen.

For every spear tip that touched skekSa's armor, six broke in her claws. Naia's hand sweated against her dagger as she waited for an opening. One would have to come eventually—after all, it was her that skekSa wanted. Not the other Drenchen warriors, led by her father, who threw themselves upon her with a renewed vigor. Not her mother, who swung a poison-spiked *bola* at her shoulder as Chapyora circled to attack.

Gurjin tugged on Naia's arm. Kylan and Amri, soaked with swamp water, were struggling back onto the Glenfoot. Naia and Gurjin hauled them up, protecting them while they coughed water and weeds.

"You all right?" she asked.

Amri looked at her. "Could be better—"

A dozen Drenchen leaped from the trees, each with the loop of a net in hand. The net swallowed skekSa, dragging her flat against the Glenfoot dais. But not for long. With an ear-numbing roar, skekSa shredded the net with her claws and sword. She hurled the remains of the net, and its weighted stones crashed across the Drenchen and knocked them in a tangle into the lake. skekSa whirled, finding Naia again, shoulders heaving with snarling breaths. Her bellow shook every plank of the Glenfoot.

"I don't have time for this!"

Naia braced herself as skekSa rushed at her. Drenchen drove their spears at her as she passed, but only two touched and neither stuck. Maudra Laesid's poison-thorn *bola* smashed down, striking skekSa in the shoulder and cracking off a piece of her armor in a spray of metal and black blood, but it didn't stop the Skeksis monster charging toward Naia.

"Naia, get out of there!" her mother cried.

Naia didn't budge. She pushed her foot into the solid wood beneath her heel, bracing every muscle. She didn't know how to stop skekSa. She didn't know how to muffle the roaring flames that consumed Great Smerth overhead. She didn't know how to stop the cycle of fear and hate and violence. All she knew was that she had to protect her friends. Kylan. Amri. Gurjin. Great Smerth and all the Drenchen.

A tiny blue light glowed in her hand, hidden by the hilt of the dagger.

"What . . ."

Water erupted from below the Glenfoot. A gray-and-silver form arched out like a leaping fish, slamming into skekSa and sending them both rolling in a grappling tangle of weeds and cold droplets, hands and claws, feathers and mane and tails.

"What is that?" exclaimed Laesid. "What's going on?"

"urSan!"

Amri called her name right as the two big creatures split apart, blood streaming from both of their shoulders, urSan's wound mirroring skekSa's where she'd been struck by Laesid's devastating thorny *bola*. Though skekSa's dark skin hid the effects of the poison, urSan's pale skin showed that it was already taking hold: green tendrils shining with fluid as the poison set in.

The injury didn't stop her from standing between skekSa and the Drenchen, though none of her three hands held weapons.

"There is no going around me," urSan said calmly, though her breathing came heavier and heavier. "You will have to go through."

skekSa tightened her grip on her sword. "I searched for you all this time. How convenient that you appear now. My bonded other. Oh, it's all too rich, that you should be the one to try and stop me when it is our shared destiny I am trying to improve."

"I will not allow you to take Naia and Gurjin. They have a task yet to accomplish. I will not allow them to become ingredients for skekTek's wicked experiments, nor droplets in skekSo's decanter. If you continue your aggression here, I will put an end to us both."

"And if I do not continue, we will both find our end anyhow," skekSa replied coldly. "skekZok betrayed me. He told the Emperor that it was my fault we lost the twins. That I'm a traitor! Now I have no choice but to bring them back to the castle, or skekSo will call for my head. Mine, and also yours, as we all now know."

skekSa glared over urSan's festering shoulder at Naia, eyes burning like fires. How long ago was it they'd met on the beach of Cera-Na? That Naia had questioned whether all the Skeksis were as evil as skekMal the Hunter or skekLi the Satirist? They had all been so cruel, so single-minded, until skekSa.

But now . . .

"Why do you not leave this land behind?" Naia asked. "Travel the seas that you love. The world goes on into the horizon, far away from skekSo and the other Skeksis."

skekSa raised herself up, holding her rotting shoulder while her sword drooped. She laughed and spat with such disgust, Naia was surprised her saliva didn't scald the wood it landed on. She coughed and vomited, shuddering from her oozing wound. Drenchen surrounded her on every side, and she fell back upon a knee.

"I wanted to! All I wanted was to be rid of this wretched landlocked place, travel the sea, and find my fortune—but you betrayed me! Just like everyone has betrayed me. urSan, the Sifa, the Gelfling—skekZok. Now I'm truly alone. Ah, urSan. At least if I die here, I'll have the pleasure of seeing you die, too."

The planks of the Glenfoot cracked when skekSa tossed her sword to the ground. She looked upon the glinting spearheads with a challenging smirk, a jade gaze that finally rested on Naia with the weight of nine hundred suns.

"Get that sword away from her," Maudra Laesid ordered.

Naia let out the breath caught in her throat. Gurjin handed his spear to another Drenchen warrior and approached the Skeksis's blade, ears angled and alert as he stooped to pick it up. It was so big, he could barely lift it, even in two hands. Once he had it, he stood before skekSa, close enough to look her straight in the eyes.

"It's over," he said. "The Drenchen—"

"*Gurjin!*"

skekSa's claw shot out, snatching Gurjin around the waist and yanking him back to her so quickly, he dropped the sword. Before urSan could react, skekSa leaped backward, stealing Gurjin into the lake below with an enormous *SPLASH*.

CHAPTER 22

Naia raced to the edge of the Glenfoot, nearly dropping her dagger.

skekSa surfaced on the other side of the lake, on a raised root of a large apeknot. She had Gurjin wrapped in her arm, her wrist around his neck, one of her smaller claws holding a short dirk to his belly.

"Don't move or I'll open him up right here," she crowed, though her voice and entire body was wrecked by the poison of the wound in her shoulder. The glade came to a standstill, except for the roaring of the flames and the shouts of the Drenchen who were trying desperately to extinguish them. Their shadows danced along the gentle ripples of the lake, the heat of the fire washing overhead, carrying huge flakes of black ash and soot.

"Let him go," Laesid said. "Let him go, or your death will be more painful than you can imagine."

"Then I'll make sure his is the same!"

skekSa pricked her dagger into Gurjin's side enough to draw blood. He grunted in pain, though he couldn't staunch the bleeding with his arms pinned by skekSa's grip. His blood soaked into his wet tunic, creeping like a spreading illness.

Naia looked to urSan. "Can you stop her? urLii and urVa were able to halt skekLi with their song—"

urSan shook her head grimly. "I cannot. If it happened as you describe it, it was because two urRu's song overpowered the single Skeksis . . . in this place, we are equal." She spread her arms, though the demonstration of balance was flawed by her missing hand.

"Is it true?" Bellanji asked. "They're connected?"

"Your friend who would die if we killed skekSa," Laesid murmured, sizing up urSan. She leveled her spear, and a dozen more followed in the hands of the Drenchen warriors that surrounded Naia and the Mystic. "If hurting this beast could hurt that one—"

"How quickly they turn on us, urSan!" skekSa sang, flourishing with her dagger. "Oh, how quickly the little Gelfling betray us! As soon as they know how we are connected. As soon as the Sifa saw the shape of Emperor skekSo in my face, they turned on me. It is only fitting that the Drenchen see my shape in *you*."

urSan didn't retreat, regarding the Drenchen and their spears with a stoic, wise face. She did not raise her fists against them, rather opened her hands and looked to Naia.

"We have no more time," she said.

Naia felt short of breath, as if skekSa's claw were wrapped around her throat as well as Gurjin's. "What are you saying?" she stammered. "You can't possibly be telling me to—"

"Now what will you do, Naia?" cried skekSa. "Oh, she's opened her hands to you. Will you take her life to save your brother's? Sacrifice your goodness by killing—or perhaps it's not a sacrifice at all! Perhaps it's merely the brave thing to do. Destroy these *beasts* come from another world and another time. Ruining this place and your sacred Crystal. Perhaps you see in her the evil you see in me. Perhaps you think that it would be better to do away with us all—the Skeksis and the Mystics both. Kill, then. Kill us both. Wreak your violence and your war. Show me the darkness within you. Unleash it. Oh, it would be my honor if you would."

"Does she want to die?" Bellanji gasped in disbelief.

"She wants Naia to doubt," Kylan replied sternly. "Naia knows better than to listen."

Naia did know better, but she couldn't look away from the dark spot on Gurjin's side. It was growing, dripping across skekSa's clawed feet and onto the surface of the root she stood upon.

"urSan . . ."

The Mystic returned Naia's gaze with one of calm acceptance. Whatever Naia chose, she would allow. Even if Naia chose to bury the dagger in her heart.

Don't.

The strained voice was Gurjin's, but it had come not through her ears, but in her mind. As if they were dreamfasted, as they had before, briefly, but unmistakably. Naia tried not to react, for fear that skekSa might notice. It was no trick of her imagination. She could hear Gurjin from across the lake.

If I don't, she'll kill you! She's so full of hatred that she'll do anything to take revenge—

And you're not like her, he said.

"You are taking too long."

It was the only warning before skekSa plunged her dagger into Gurjin's side. His cry of pain was blunted by the knife in his side, his dreamfasted voice falling away like he'd slipped from the branch of an apeknot. Now he clung to Naia's mind with only a finger's touch. She held on to him with the only thing she had—her heart. She could barely hear him when he said, *I'm sorry I took your powers on the ship. I was just trying to save you. I love you, Naia. I hope you can have them back when I return to Thra.*

Thra. Thra had made Naia a mender, granted her the ability to dreamfast. Not just her own kind, but with all creatures. With the flying eels and the finger-vines. With Olyeka-Staba the Cradle Tree. Thra had given Kylan the gift of song and dream stitching, Amri the gift of rock singing. And to Gurjin, although it had come late, the gift of healing, as it had given Naia and their sister Eliona.

Thra had given its gifts to them all. Not just to Naia—*that* was their bond. The gifts of Thra were to be shared, with Thra and with one another. To unite what was fractured. To heal what was ailing. To save what was corrupt. To mend what had been broken apart. To protect what was most important. That was the key to awakening those gifts. It was all part of the same cycle. The same web that connected the Gelfling to Thra and to one another.

Dreamfast, Naia said to Gurjin suddenly. She reached out to urSan and said the same words aloud to the Mystic: "Dreamfast with me."

"The Mystics and the Skeksis do not . . . ," urSan began, but trailed off and instead offered her hand. Naia took it and shouted across the lake to Gurjin what she had said in dreamfast before:

"Dreamfast with her, Gurjin! We'll do it together!"

Trusting him to find the strength to do it, she faced urSan. She took the Mystic's big hand in both of hers, closed her eyes, and threw open the door between their minds.

At first she was alone, standing at a brink as she had when she'd touched minds with Vassa, skekSa's ship. But the stars that swirled in the galaxy lake rippled *over* her, thousands of inverted waves in the liquid of space. As if the air were on the bottom and the abyssal ocean of the other mind were hanging over her.

Is this . . .

Gurjin stood beside her. In the dream, he was not wounded, though his figure was translucent, as if he might disappear at any moment. *When he loses consciousness*, Naia reminded herself. They had to hurry. They had to get up there, into skekSa and urSan's mind—

THIS WAY.

A hand broke the surface, large and strong. urSan's hand, beckoning to them from above. Together, Naia and Gurjin reached up, clasping the Mystic's square fingers and letting her draw them up, enveloped by the thick space filled with all the stars of the heavens. When they broke through the other side, Naia expected thickness, like water. But it was not an ocean they were entering; it was a space like the cosmos itself.

Stars exploded all around them, the atmosphere alive and alight with the burning colors of the universe. Gold and pink and blue sizzling against the pitch-black of endless space. A vibrant humming crackled through the place, all around them like lightning in a storm. With every burst of light, every snap of energy, images ignited in Naia's mind: fleeting glimpses of urSan and skekSa's arrival in Thra through the light of the Crystal and the Great Conjunction.

She saw an urSkek. Ancient and powerful, with the potential for balance that had not been fully realized. For deep inside this urSkek was lust for individuality. Lust to be recognized as herself, to be loved uniquely. To be separate from the collective of the urSkek race. To be *I* instead of *we; me* instead of *us.*

Naia saw the day the urSkek returned to the castle, as the second Great Conjunction neared. Waiting for the suns to join overhead. Waiting to return home.

Then, chaos. Confusion. And more than anything else, betrayal. Betrayal by the stars and the suns themselves, which should have opened the gateway to send them home once again.

It had been foretold, by the spheres, urSan said. She was beside them, over them, all around them. Not in form but in mind, a shape and a voice that was everywhere at once. *But the spheres had lied.*

GET OUT OF MY MIND.

If the dream was a storm, then skekSa was the thunder. A black-clouded cyclone, roiling bigger and bigger at the center of the space, blocking the light from the stars and suns that spun around them like the figures in Aughra's orrery. It grew until she blotted out the light and the images and memories, trying to push them away. Push them out, eject them from the place they had entered without invitation.

For a moment, Naia lost her place in the dream, opened her eyes. She saw skekSa across the lake, holding her head with one of her smaller hands, though she hadn't yet released Gurjin. They hadn't done it, not yet.

Something moved in the shadows over and behind skekSa. A long, serpentine creature bearing a Gelfling on its shoulders. So distressed by Naia and Gurjin's intrusion, the Skeksis Mariner didn't notice.

Naia closed her eyes, tightening her grip on urSan's hand. Plunging herself back into the dream.

Just a little longer . . .

Back within the dream-space, skekSa's storm had nearly surrounded them, twisting and snarling and slashing. Naia held on to Gurjin as they stood in the center of it.

GET OUT, skekSa thundered. *GET OUT!*

urSan materialized beside them, protecting them with her arms as skekSa's storm closed in. Naia huddled against the Mystic as the storm smothered out the last remaining memories and lights. Soon there would be only blackness, only skekSa's rage, and they would wake—

Remember who you were, Naia begged. *Remember what you loved . . .*

A final memory flashed across the dreamscape, blue and green and glittering. The ocean they had loved when they had been one. The Silver Sea filled with infinite mysteries. The Gelfling rising from the land, eventually attaching and venturing onto the sea. Teaching them how to read the stars, to chart a course with no land in sight. How to read the clouds in the sky and the rough patches of water that rippled across great calms.

When they went to the castle during the second Conjunction, it was those moments that they remembered. Waiting for the suns to join overhead, ready for the shaft of light to open the gateway back to their world. They felt a seed of hesitation nestled deep in their breast. The tiny, four-fingered print of the Gelfling on their heart. They had recognized them for who they were.

Were they really ready to leave all that behind?

I LOVE NOTHING.

skekSa's face burst from the cloud, as big as the sky in the dreamscape itself. Gnashing beak and shining scales like knives, eyes cold and burning all at once. The memory dissipated, broken away until the only thing holding them in the dream was urSan's arms. Naia held on to Gurjin, but even he began to fade.

It's time to go, urSan said. Naia saw blood on her shoulder.

The dream fell away to the sound of skekSa screaming.

CHAPTER 23

Chapyora's sharp teeth were buried in the Mariner's shoulder, Maudra Laesid's spear penetrating a narrow gap in her shoulder armor. Naia's mother gave a sharp whistle and Chapyora snatched Gurjin from skekSa's writhing arms, spreading her gliding fins and bursting away into the lake.

Laesid remained, standing on skekSa's back with her single leg, driving her spear deeper into the Skeksis's back. skekSa's scream went from surprise to pain to rage as she tried to reach the Drenchen *maudra*, grasping and grappling and failing.

"*Get off me! Get off me, you swamp-sucking mud-brained blindfish!*"

Laesid did not let go of her spear. Didn't look away from the Skeksis until Chapyora breached the surface of the lake, gently lowering Gurjin into a puddle of lake water and blood as Naia and Eliona rushed to heal his wound. Blue light flowed forth like a summer storm, rushing from her fingertips and lighting her entire body. Gurjin's eyes flew open at the incredible speed with which his wound closed.

"Your power . . ."

"You never took it from me," Naia assured him. "You awakened your own. To protect me. And all this time I've been so preoccupied blaming you for it. But now I remember what I'm here for. Why I have this power—why *we* have this—"

"*GET OFF ME! I'LL KILL YOU!*"

skekSa threw herself backward, trying to smash Laesid against the trunk of the big apeknot she stood beside. Laesid was too nimble, holding the spear jutting from the Skeksis's back and swinging to the side so the only thing that crashed into the tree was skekSa's shoulder.

Naia rose to her feet, leaving Gurjin with Eliona.

"Finish healing him—I've got to stop Mother!"

skekSa let out a piercing, ragged scream of frustration. The Skeksis were powerful, strong, and huge—but they were not used to being challenged. Even now, Naia's mother used it to her advantage. It looked almost as if she were dancing across skekSa's shoulders, deftly avoiding her claws and slashing knife.

"Mother, stop!"

skekSa cried out in pain when Laesid drove the spear in even deeper. Beside Naia, urSan dropped to her knee, blood pooling around her shoulder and rippling down her arm. Naia knelt by her, though she knew there was nothing she could do. Nothing she could do except stop her mother from killing skekSa.

But if skekSa survived, then what? It was the same terrible dilemma it had always been. This time it brought tears to Naia's eyes.

"Mother—" she cried. "Mother, don't—"

"I'm sorry, Naia," Laesid called back. "I understand what urSan means to you. I understand what the Mystics mean to you.

But we have to put our clan first. We have to survive as Gelfling. Look at Great Smerth. Look what she's done to your brother. Look what she's done to our home!"

Naia looked back. Gurjin's chest rose and fell under Eliona's healing hands, becoming steadier, lit by the blazing fire of Great Smerth burning all around them. Even if they stopped the fire now, so much damage had already been done.

"But it's not right," she said, but she couldn't find the strength to shout loudly enough for her mother to hear. She could only remember what Gurjin had said in their dreamfast.

You're not like her, he'd told her. Not like skekSa. And what Amri had told her, when he'd pulled her from the lake. Her eyes landed on the Shadowling, whose pale skin and silver hair were smudged with mud and crimson. He held the sword he'd used to protect her, though its tip nearly touched the scorched planks of the Glenfoot.

The one he'd used to protect. Not attack.

Doing good . . . Bringing flowers out of ash.

"Eliona," Naia said. "Can Gurjin sit up?"

"Yes, but he's weak."

"Then he'll have to be strong for just a little longer," Naia said. "You two. Quickly, this way. Any Drenchen with the gift of healing. Join me. Help me save our *maudra* and Great Smerth."

Naia pressed her hands down on the wood of the Glenfoot. It was a part of Great Smerth, as every root and apeknot in the swamp was. As Laesid plunged her spear into skekSa, killing both her and urSan slowly, Naia raised her voice. Called out in a song that came from deep in her heart, whose words she had heard on the tongue of Onica the Far-Dreamer and Mother Aughra the Helix-Horned. The voice that sang the song of Thra.

"Great Smerth. Smerth-Staba. Tree that has protected me and my clan. Like a mother in our beloved swamp. Even now as your body is overtaken by flames . . . Deatea. Deratea. Kidakida. Arugaru."

She felt someone kneeling beside her. Amri and Kylan, pressing their hands against the bark of the Glenfoot, though neither of them were healers. Saying the words.

Naia looked up as Gurjin joined them. Battered and bloody but determined. He fell beside her on his hands and knees, bowing his head as his healing light joined hers.

"Deatea. Deratea. Kidakida. Arugaru . . ."

Eliona came next. Then Kipper. Even Naia's father. All the Drenchen, though they did not all know how to heal, heard the words and repeated them. Did as Naia did, although they had no idea why. They saw her and they saw Gurjin, and they did as she called on them to do.

Great Smerth groaned. A sound like the singing of the earth, the creaking of its massive limbs. Naia felt tears on her cheeks at the sound of its voice, old and tired and in pain. Sick, though it wanted nothing more than to be healthy, to spread its boughs across the Drenchen glade. To provide shade and food and shelter. That was what the world wanted to be; that was Thra's only desire. Great Smerth had been a gift to that end. Thra, trying to care for the Gelfling, as they had cared for it.

Naia had nearly forgotten skekSa's screams until they suddenly stopped. Maudra Laesid had ceased her attack, frozen on the Skeksis's back and staring at the Drenchen gathering at the Glenfoot as blue light spread from the roots and trunk of Great Smerth into the water. Racing through the lake toward the root where skekSa stood. Where the light touched, the water cleared, the fire waned. Green life sprang forth, vines and saplings and branches.

skekSa yelped as one of the vines grew so fast it tangled around her foot. She bashed the growth away with a claw, but it was soon replaced with another. Rapid as spring came after winter, the apeknot where she stood burst into life, tangling around her with vines and roots and leafing, blossoming apeknot shoots.

"No!" skekSa snapped, suddenly coming alive with panic and confusion. "No! What is this? *No!*"

But it was not enough. Even the combined efforts of the Drenchen healers could not grow the tree fast enough to bind the Skeksis. She tore through the feeble foliage, tangled but not stopped. It was only a matter of time before she ripped herself free.

Laesid's attacks eased when she saw what was happening. As the growing plant life overtook skekSa, binding her arms and legs in its quickly strengthening forms, she slipped off the Mariner's shoulder.

"What's she doing?" Gurjin grunted, brow streaked with sweat.

"Do not stop, my Drenchen," Laesid called. She stood before

skekSa, leaning on her spear, body filling with light. Her calm composure did not break when skekSa's claws burst out of the growing tendrils, plunging around Laesid's neck and torso.

"Continue this and she dies!" skekSa bellowed, shaking every tree in the glade.

Do not stop.

Her mother's voice was in Naia's mind. In the air. In the trees and the water and the earth below the lake. Despite skekSa's claws piercing her breast and back, Maudra Laesid held up a hand bursting with silver-blue light. Naia felt tears on her cheeks as she understood.

"Mother . . ."

Laesid pressed her hand against skekSa's gnashing beak. The tree that fought to come alive around the Skeksis exploded with life, hundreds of stems and boughs rising and flowering at incredible speed. They tethered skekSa's legs and bound her beak, twisted around her arms even as the blood from Laesid's wounds dripped upon the leaves that sprang open by the dozens.

Within moments, a new tree stood where there had been none. skekSa the Mariner was no more.

"Mother!"

Naia leaped into the water, swimming faster than she ever had before to reach her mother on the opposite side of the lake. Despite his injuries, Gurjin jumped in after her, reaching them moments later.

The infant apeknot had not consumed Maudra Laesid. Its tender branches cradled her, lowering her gently to the soggy peat when Naia and Gurjin got there. She pulled her mother's head into her lap, tears mixing with the lake water as both streamed down her face. Warm blood soaked through her mother's beautiful gowns and into the thick moss that sprawled across the toughening roots of the new apeknot.

"Mother, be calm," she said, though Laesid was already much more calm than either she or Gurjin were. "We'll heal you. You'll be all right."

"You can heal these wounds, but I will not survive," she said, nearly silently. There was no fear in her voice. "I gave my life willingly. What happens with it now is up to Thra."

Naia felt as if she would be overwhelmed by the emotions inside her, hope and fear, worry and pride—and worst of all, the dreaded sensation of loss that was already taking over though her mother was not yet gone.

"But . . . you can't . . . ," Gurjin began, but stopped. She could, and had.

"My children. My gentle, kind, fierce children . . ." Laesid put a hand on each her children's cheeks. Naia leaned into it, though the heat was fading already from her fingertips. "The two of you will light the world with your fire. The new fire of the new generation of these changing times. It is the proudest legacy I could have wished for. The old trees may not survive the darkening. But the forest is everlasting."

As the last words escaped her lips, her eyes closed and her hands dropped. The tree above them trembled with a last surge of energy, straining toward the sky and coloring as white and blue flowers opened along its branches. Maudra Laesid was gone.

Naia closed her eyes as she breathed in the scent of the blossoms, the still and quietness of the entire glade. She could not even hear skekSa within the thick wood of the tree.

"Naia . . ."

Gurjin sounded far away, though he was right beside her, cheeks wet and eyes red. She, too, felt as if she were underwater. Everything was blurry, even as the sky lightened. Somewhere, a bird sang. Cautiously and nervously, a single note calling through the swamp as if to say *I am here. Am I the only one?*

Across the lake, back on the Glenfoot, Bellanji stood with Kylan and Amri and the rest of the Drenchen. Many of the warriors had fallen to their knees, laying down their spears as they saw what had happened. Chapyora reared, spreading her fins, but Bellanji caught her mane before she could dive into the lake again to join them. And as for Naia's father himself, there was no hiding the naked pain on his face, falling like the cold light of the oncoming morning.

"You've got to say something."

Gurjin was right. They were all watching. Waiting. *Needing.* Behind them all, Great Smerth's body was blackened from root to vine, bare of leaves on many limbs, creaking in the early wind like a charcoal skeleton.

Naia gently lowered her mother to the soft moss that covered the apeknot root where she'd died. Gurjin held her there, bowing his head as Naia rose. She gazed across the lake to the Drenchen. Stood below the youngest tree in the swamp. One strong enough to bind a Skeksis, though it would be trine upon trine before it rivaled Great Smerth in size.

But even if the tree grew. Even if the shard could be found and the Crystal could be healed. Even if the darkening were stopped, and Thra could recover, one thing could never be brought back. Naia's mother was gone.

She opened her mouth, but no words came out. In the deafening silence that followed, she heard her own heart breaking in her chest. Tears rushed forward before she could stop them, plain for everyone to see. She tried to speak again. When she failed the second time to drag up the reluctant words from her belly, she couldn't face them any longer. Those waiting faces, all wrecked by grief, looking to her for comfort.

Lost in her own pain, Naia had no solace to give. She turned away and ran.

CHAPTER 24

Naia fled into the apeknot canopy, every step feeling heavier with guilt, but she didn't stop. Her feet found a familiar bough and she leaped, fluffing her wings enough to soften her landing on the rear sill outside her mother's chamber.

Her mother's chamber. The chamber where the Drenchen *maudra* kept her medicines and the sacred scrolls, and met with her private council. It was where Naia had always found Laesid before, since she had been a childling. Where she'd run to when she'd gotten hurt exploring the swamp, or when Neech had broken a fin. Where she'd come when she'd first seen Tavra coming through the Swamp of Sog, so many unum ago.

Now it was cold and empty, part of the wall blackened from fire. The wood medallions that bore the ancient symbols carved and dream-etched by elder Drenchen were scorched, some beyond repair. It pained Naia to see, but all of that could be mended, with time. What brought her to her knees in grief was knowing that she would never find her mother waiting for her in the chamber again, no matter how much time passed.

Naia wept. More than she ever had before, as if the tears were unending. As if she might never be free of the sobs that gripped and shook her entire body. Alone in the chamber smelling of wood and smoke, while the triple suns' light brightened the wide balcony outside. To the suns, it must seem like just another day. The spheres of the sky cared little for the lives of the Gelfling. After all, it was the suns whose conjunction had brought the urSkeks, and whose light had given birth to the Skeksis. If the Three Brothers cared at all, they would have taken the awful creatures away, or maybe never allowed them to arrive in the first place.

She heard steps and tried to press the tears from her face the way she might try to wring a cloth of water, but quickly gave up. There was no hiding it. The collar of her tunic and the wood below her hands were soaked with the salt water. Gurjin stood in the doorway of their mother's chamber, one hand on the frame and the other wrapped tightly around his waist where the worst of his injury been healed by Eliona and bandaged.

Mother's chamber. The thought came to Naia again, dry and brittle like a last leaf clinging to a branch in autumn. She sighed and the leaf blew away. *My chamber, now.*

Gurjin didn't say anything. There wasn't anything to say. Once he knew she'd seen him, he entered and sat beside her, his own eyes red with mourning.

"How's Father?" Naia asked. "And Eliona? Pemma?"

"The same as us," her brother replied. "Same as everyone. Marley had to take Chapyora under lead and away. She kept attacking the tree where skekSa is . . ."

Naia swallowed. At least there was that.

"And it's holding?" she asked. "And urSan?"

"The tree is holding. urSan says she can sense skekSa inside, but she won't be escaping anytime soon. Great Smerth and Mother saved us, even despite all that's happened to it."

Naia shook her head. Great Smerth had endured so much, and with the darkening, still had much left to survive. And if the darkening ever overtook the new tree, its hold on skekSa would weaken. If they didn't heal the Crystal, it was only a matter of time.

But now she knew there was hope. She grabbed Gurjin's hand and held it tightly in hers.

"I'm sorry I pulled away from you," she said. "I felt like we were growing apart, and I was afraid of that."

He squeezed her and said, "Me too. And I'm sorry for keeping things from you. I was trying to protect you. Or I thought I was. But in a way it wasn't much different from what you were doing."

Naia chewed on her lip. "You mean not telling me about Great Smerth? And . . . Amri?"

"Yeah." Gurjin groaned, rubbing his face with his hands. It was the same thing Naia did when she was distressed. "I couldn't stop thinking about Rian and Mira. He was so attached to her, and she was attached to him. And after she died, it just . . . destroyed him. You love so strongly. You love our home and you love your friends. I couldn't bear to see you break if they were to be taken away. Not when you're so strong. But now I know that's *why* you're strong. And now I know that's what you need most to be *maudra*, both to the Drenchen and the rest of the Gelfling."

Maudra.

The word was so familiar, yet felt so strange. It was her mother, not her.

"Gurjin, I don't know if I can do it. Go down and face them. They're going to want me to tell them everything is going to be all right, but how can I tell them what they want to hear when I don't know it for certain? How can I be strong for them when I feel like I'm breaking on the inside? I'm not Tavra or Ethri. What if I'm not ready?"

He held her by the shoulders and looked straight in her eyes. She could see the same uncertainty deep inside him, could feel the slight tremble in his hands.

"You are," he said, shaking her gently. "You've as much training to be *maudra* as either of those two." When Naia didn't answer, he lowered his voice and added, "Mother made sure of it."

Gurjin dropped his arms when Kylan and Amri appeared quietly near the entrance to the chamber. Naia recognized the iridescent black garment folded carefully in Amri's arms. Her mother's cloak, sewn in the shape of beautiful Drenchen wings, laced with shining ribbons and glittering beads.

"Your father has taken her to be prepared for burial," Kylan said softly. "The rest of the Drenchen wait on the Glenfoot."

Naia couldn't take her eyes off the cloak, feeling as if she might be overcome with grief all over again. She had longed to wear the beautiful thing ever since she had been a childling. She had never thought what it would mean on the day she put it on.

Amri stepped forward, holding the cloak with plain and clear reverence, eyes on Naia.

"Go on," Gurjin said.

Kylan and Amri took hold of either clasp of the cloak, and

Naia turned her back toward them. Gently, the two placed the *maudra's* cape across her shoulders, holding it so her wings could peek through the slits sewn for them. It was light, made of woven fabric that would not weigh her down while gliding or hold water long after swimming—barely a whisper on her shoulders, yet it felt heavy as the world. With a practiced certainty and confidence, she stepped out onto the balcony that overlooked the Glenfoot.

The Drenchen had gathered below, some standing, though many were sitting, holding their faces in mourning. As the day grew and filled the glade with light, the ruined state of the place became more evident. Blackened boughs and roots still smoked, filling the air with the musty, damp, burned smell of Great Smerth's injuries. Fallen debris, branches and the like, floated listlessly in the lake. Where the ancient tree had broken open, darkened veins were exposed, making Great Smerth's other, greater illness more obvious.

Faces turned up when she stepped to the edge of the balcony where her mother had stood so many times, Naia lingering back in the chamber. Wondering when her time would come to be the one to stand before their clan. Now was that day, and she tried not to regret that it had come about like this.

"Drenchen," she said, her voice sounding weak and tired. She clenched her teeth and gripped the carved rail of the balcony, trying again with more force: "Drenchen!"

"Better," Gurjin said, and she smiled. She let go of the rail and let out a breath, addressing the Drenchen clan that waited below.

"A traveler came to our swamp from the furthest reaches of

the north. The next day, I left Great Smerth and Sog to find my missing brother."

It felt like an old song when she told it that way with all the Drenchen listening with quiet faces. Yet there was no other way to tell it. That was what had happened. That was the day that everything had changed for her, though in the lifespan of Thra and against the lifetimes during which the Skeksis had ruled, it was so very late. In the end, though, it was why she had left the Swamp of Sog—and how she had returned.

"Since then I've traveled across the Skarith Land. Through the Spriton Plains to Stone-in-the-Wood. Climbed the Grottan Mountains, all the way to Ha'rar. I've seen the Crystal Sea and the Dousan Wellspring, my toes have tasted the salt waters of Cera-Na on the Sifan Coast. One by one, five of the seven Gelfling clans put down their weapons, their anger, and their fear. One by one, they held one another instead. Each time at the end of a great speech given by an even greater *maudra*. Yet here I am, standing before you, with no great speech to tell and so much sadness in my heart."

Even the birds quieted. Down below, one of the Drenchen elders held his hand to his mouth.

"We miss her, too, Naia," he said, and Naia tried not to lose control of her flighty emotions when he added, "but we also believe in you."

"As Laesid believed in you," added another.

"And as Gurjin and your father believe in you," said yet another.

"You don't need to make a great speech to light this fire."

Naia looked over her shoulder as Bellanji joined her at the balcony, face wan with grief and the ribbons stripped from his locs in mourning. She tried to stay strong as he stood beside her, though seeing her father transformed into such a somber character made her feel like a stone sinking into the deepest part of the lake. If he couldn't smile, then how could she?

"Father . . . I don't know what to say."

Like the clouds parting after a storm, the smallest of comforting smiles bent the edge of his lips. He thumped her on the shoulder and pushed her forward.

"All you need to do is say who you are, and what we shall do next."

Naia stood at the precipice of the balcony, toes curling over the edge. It was almost dizzying, though she knew that if she were to fall, her wings would ease the descent, and the Drenchen below would catch her.

Golden light caught her eye. Across the lake, visible from her high vantage on the balcony, was the new tree. The sapling apeknot, flourishing in the bright sun. New and green, both fragile and resilient.

It was that tree Naia set her sights and heart on. Believed in it, as it had believed in her. She gathered all of her strength up in one breath, then let it out, as big and fierce as she was able.

"I am Naia, new *maudra* of the Drenchen clan. And on this day we lay down our spears and hold one another—"

She took the dagger from her belt and hurled it over the heads of the Drenchen. All eyes were on it as it twirled, sparkling, before disappearing into the deep water of the lake below the Glenfoot. Fingers spread and palms empty, Naia held her hands aloft so all could see.

"We join the resistance. We will protect Thra. We will heal the Crystal."

"Blue Flame Naia!" cried Gurjin, throwing his fist in the air. He grabbed Naia's hand in his other. As their knuckles pierced the sky, glowing blue, the Drenchen roared her name again and again.

"Blue Flame Naia!"

Sparks flew from the smoldering hearth on the Glenfoot below.

The Drenchen gathered around it, holding out their hands, eyes alight with focus and unstoppable intent. Naia held Gurjin and stepped off the balcony, alighting with him on the scorched Glenfoot among their clan before the hearth.

Drenchen found one another, and when the last palms touched, the hearth burst into light. Gasps of shock and awe hissed against the rushing of the hot flames as the story of the Drenchen fire was dream-etched, hot and cosmic, into the Glenfoot and across Great Smerth's ash-coated body. Naia and Gurjin's return to the glade. The darkened veins beneath Great Smerth. Their confrontation with skekSa, and Maudra Laesid's last sacrifice.

"Naia?" asked a familiar voice from within the flames. Maudra Mera, peering out from the brightness from Sami Thicket, surfaced in the roiling fire even as the faces and voices of the other clans awakened within it. "Naia, is that you?"

"Yes," Naia replied. "The sixth fire is lit. Here below Great Smerth."

The fires rippled with color as Gelfling across all of Thra gasped with happiness and relief. Naia saw glimpses of the many places where the fires had been lit, as far as Ha'rar and as near as Sami Thicket. Within the fire, the world suddenly seemed safer. The other clans closer.

"Maudra Ethri?" Naia asked. "Rek'yr and the Dousan? Shadowlings, Silverlings, Menders, all?"

"Yes, we are here," came a cool voice. Maudra Ethri's emerald eye glittered through the fire, a streak of green. "Waiting near Ha'rar on the *Omerya*."

"And we, too, near the Wellspring," said another with a splash of gold and indigo, and Naia thought she glimpsed Periss's and Erimon's tattooed faces as well. "Waiting for the sign. Of the seventh fire, I presume."

The seventh fire. Only one left, and everyone knew where it had to be lit. Maudra Mera's voice broke the murmurs yet again, calling to Naia with an edge of importance.

"Naia. I am glad for the Drenchen fire, but we cannot relax now. My scouts have recovered a number of Stonewood refugees from the border of the Dark Wood. They said they saw—" Her voice was drowned in a wash of heat. The fire was fading. Most of what Maudra Mera had to say was lost, though the final part came through:

"We must finish what we have begun. And quickly. It's beginning!"

"We will!" Naia called to her. The fire faded, and she wasn't sure if her promise had gotten through. But it didn't matter. Maudra Mera would know soon enough. She turned to the Drenchen that circled around them and the hearth that had so recently been blazing with flame.

"We lit the sixth fire here," she announced, "but there is still a seventh yet to light. A final one to unite the rest, and we know exactly where to go. Anyone who can still fight, prepare to depart. I need half our healers to stay here and try to mend Great Smerth if you can . . . The rest, come with us. We leave immediately for Stone-in-the-Wood."

Even though the Drenchen burst into movement, it still felt painstakingly slow. Only a few of the muski were large enough to ride, and Chapyora was still too distressed over losing Laesid. They would be going north on foot.

"Maybe we should go without the rest," Gurjin said lowly as they prepared their things to leave. "We could travel faster."

Naia disagreed. "I don't know what Maudra Mera meant when she said it was beginning. But we can only guess she meant our rebellion against the Skeksis. We need to light that seventh fire, and that means finding and helping the Stonewood survivors. Whether it's Maudra Fara or the refugees or Rian or all three. We're going to need all the help we can get."

As their party gathered on the edge of the Glenfoot to leave, Naia frowned as her father strode forward. He was dressed in his battle armor, made of fish scales and lake-crab shells. Despite his armor and spear, Naia saw a tremble in his hands, and the places where tears had streaked through the soot and smoke on his cheeks.

"Then off we go," he said, but Naia didn't budge. She took in a deep breath and stepped before him.

"No, Father. You're staying here."

Drawing in another last taste of sweet Sog air, Naia unclasped her mother's cloak from her shoulders. With a flourish that caught the afternoon light, she unfurled it until it rested gently across her father's shoulders, as if Maudra Laesid's wings embraced him once again.

"But—"

"You will stay here and protect those who stay to keep Sog safe," Naia said, putting her hands on her father's where he clenched his long spear. One by one, his fingers relaxed. "That is what Mother would have wanted."

He let out a gruff, impatient sigh but, other than that, did not protest further. Naia held her breath when he lowered his long spear, holding it out to her. She took it in both hands, feeling its weight as her father turned away from her, addressing the Drenchen who were staying in the glade.

"Our *maudra* and our healers go to mend the wounds of Thra," he boomed, his voice echoing through the great apeknots and Great Smerth itself. "Send them off with all your might!"

The cheers of the Drenchen were like wind in sails as Naia led the way north toward the Spriton Plains.

After a full day of travel, the peat gave way to solid earth, marsh, and reeds. Naia led the Drenchen out of the apeknot canopies, and they continued along the ground. She tried not to worry about how they could cross the vast fields and meadows in time to find the surviving Stonewood before the Skeksis did. Her body and heart ached, but she knew she could not rest. Not when they were so close to completing their task.

Kylan tilted his head, perking an ear as they stepped out from the constant shade of the apeknots. "Do you hear something?"

"Sounds like hooves," Amri said, stopping beside them. He knelt and put his pale hand against the wet earth, the back of it just covered in clear marsh water. The ground rumbled below Naia's feet.

"Brace yourselves!" she called back. "Something comes!"

The drumming sound cascaded from a distant tapping to a rolling thunder. Naia stood fast as they waited, though for what, she didn't know. Skeksis carriages, drawn by troops of armaligs? An army of armored Arathim, crawling across the plains with venom dripping from their sharpened spikes? Or something worse, something darkened, some new invention of the Skeksis that the Gelfling could never dream of?

Galloping figures broke over the rounded hills, and Naia nearly dropped her spear as her muscles relaxed with a wash of relief.

"I guess we'll be making good time after all," Amri said with a wide grin.

Dozens of graceful white Landstriders crested the hill, the sun shining off their gauzy fur and lighting the pinks in their wide, pointed ears. Half were mounted, half with saddles bare, all with long, powerful legs that were the swiftest in the Skarith Land. Naia couldn't help but laugh with relief when she saw Lun and Gereni waving from the shoulders of their Landstriders.

"What are you all waiting for?" Lun called, chest puffed up with pride. "Get on!"

CHAPTER 25

"Maudra Mera sent us to get you. The rest are headed toward Stone-in-the-Wood, to protect the Stonewood hearth until we are able to light the fire."

Naia had never wanted to hug the little Spriton *maudra* more than at that moment, so it was good she had sent a messenger instead of coming herself. Instead, she gave Lun a brisk nod.

"Thank you, Lun," she said. "We're ready."

The last time she had been on a Landstrider, she'd been only half-conscious, with Kylan at the reins. The memory was all a blur, and yet when the rest of the Drenchen were paired off on the backs of the majestic beasts, she found herself in the saddle with the reins in her hands, looking down at Gurjin and Amri. Nearby, Kylan was on the shoulders of his own Landstrider, looking more comfortable than she'd seen him in a long time.

"You look like a natural," he said to Naia, leaning down to pat his mount. She tried the same thing, feeling the big creature's powerful muscles twitch, shrugging its coat beneath her hand and the saddle. So high up, she couldn't hear Gurjin and Amri as they exchanged words below. A moment later, Amri grabbed hold of the saddle ladder hanging below her, making quick work of the climb and sliding lightly into the saddle behind her.

"Hi," he said. "Uh . . . Huh. The saddle is smaller than it looks from down there."

It was. Naia could feel Amri against her back, though there was a small pommel in the middle of the saddle made to accommodate two riders. The Shadowling was warm, the sure hands that had taken him swiftly up the ladder suddenly unsure. She grabbed his hand and pulled it around her waist.

"Hi," she said, smiling back at him. She tried to say it with confidence and nonchalance. Her cheeks warmed as he wrapped his arms carefully around her. "Tighter than that or you'll fall off," she warned him.

"Oh."

She swallowed when he tightened his arms, his embrace firm but not too firm, his hands slender but strong.

"How's this?" he asked quietly, nearly right into her ear.

"Fine," she mumbled.

"What, no *better now that you're here?*"

"I said it's fine!"

"Ready?" Lun called, his Landstrider prancing on the hill ahead.

None of the Drenchen replied with confidence. In earlier times, Drenchen Gelfling would never have found their way on the backs of the Spriton Landstriders, just as a Spriton would never have climbed on the back of a flying eel. But these were not earlier times. Naia clucked her tongue as she might have if she were on Chapyora's back. To her relief, the Landstrider turned, though lazily. Maybe she'd get the hang of it after all. And if she could, they could.

"Don't let a silly thing like this stop you," she called to the Drenchen. "Let's ride!"

The soft, endless-seeming hills of the plains were like waves as the Landstriders raced across them. Though their long legs made them awkward and jarring to ride at slower speeds, once they reached a full gallop, their gait was even and smooth and impossibly fast.

Within what felt like moments, they passed the small forest in which Sami Thicket was enshrouded. The clouds overhead were arcs of white, streaming north as if even the winds in the sky were guiding them toward the Dark Wood where Stone-in-the-Wood and the final Gelfling fire waited. Sog rushed away, veiled again in fog, and Naia hoped there it would remain. Safe, she wished with all her heart. In the care of her father, Great Smerth, and the other Drenchen who had stayed behind.

"Naia?"

Though the others called out in whoops and cheers, Amri's were the only words she could hear against the wind that rushed across their ears and off the Landstrider's mane. Now that the Landstrider had found its stride, Amri's arms remained looped gently around her waist. In case of unsteady ground, or maybe for some other reason.

Either way, Naia didn't mind.

"What?"

"Do you think it'd be a bad idea if I were to have a turn at the reins?"

Naia laughed. "A bad idea? Ha! I don't know what I'm doing at all—the Landstrider is making all the calls. Aren't you, big guy?" The Landstrider grumbled deep in its throat, and Naia grinned. "Come on, Amri. Take your turn."

The Landstrider slowed enough that they could switch spots, holding on to the leather straps of the saddle and harness until Amri was perched up front with the reins in hand, Naia in the rear seat with her arms around him.

"This is amazing!" he exclaimed. "I never thought I'd ever have the chance!"

He bounced the reins, and the Landstrider picked up its speed, suddenly leaping over a tuft of earth so high and fast that Naia's wings instinctively sprang out from beneath her cloak. They caught the wind and filled, lifting Naia up off the saddle. She yelped and grabbed Amri's shoulders, holding him tightly to keep from blowing away.

"Whoops!" he cried. He tugged on the reins to slow the Landstrider.

"No—it's all right!"

"Are you sure?"

With the wind rushing below her wings, arms linked under Amri's, Naia's heart filled with a burst of exhilaration. Amri's ankles were tucked tightly in the saddle stirrups, wiry body firmly attached to the harness. As long as she held on, she wasn't going anywhere. She grinned.

"I'm sure! Keep going!"

Naia had always envied Tavra and Tae's flight-worthy wings. Though her Drenchen wings doubled as fins underwater, she

couldn't fly like they could, only glide. But she had watched Tavra's skill in the air a hundred times, and could watch her a hundred times more, every time overwhelmed with envy and amazement.

Now, hands wrapped in Amri's cloak, buoyed by the Landstrider's tireless pace, she knew how it must feel. As if the top of the world had opened up, beckoning her into a new, boundless realm in the sky. Up among the clouds, where the light blue of the sky turned to purple and black and filled with stars . . .

Naia folded her wings slightly. The stars, from where the urSkeks had come. Space, which held infinite worlds, of which Thra was just a speck. Amri felt her land back into the saddle and looked at her over his shoulder.

"Something wrong? I haven't seen you smile like that in . . . maybe ever."

She alit on the saddle, kneeling behind him and sighing.

"It doesn't seem right," she said. "Having fun at a time like this. Even as we try to stop what might be unstoppable."

Amri put his hand on hers, where she wrapped it around his chest.

"Or maybe," he replied softly, "it's the best time. Because we might not have a chance later. And anyway, what else is resistance if not loving in the face of danger?"

Naia looked over her shoulder. The Spriton and the Drenchen Gelfling shared the saddles of the Landstriders, each helping the other, all facing ahead toward their common destination. Stone-in-the-Wood. The final fire.

"Naia, there's something I wanted to ask you."

She had the feeling she knew what he was going to ask, but that didn't stop her heart from pounding. From the thrill of flying or from the anticipation of the question he was about to ask, she didn't know. She was surprised he couldn't feel it through his shoulder where she leaned against him.

"All right?"

His hand tightened on hers, briefly, then let go.

"If we make it through, and light the seventh fire. And beat the Skeksis. And all that stuff, you know. I was wondering . . ." He hesitated, fidgeting awkwardly, finally coughing out the rest of it: "Wondering if I could go with you."

"Go with me?" It wasn't exactly the question she'd been expecting, but her heart fluttered all the same. "Go with me where?"

He shrugged. As he spoke, he gained confidence, as if realizing there was no turning back now. "Wherever you go afterward. Back to Sog, to somewhere brand-new. I don't care where. I just want to be by your side."

Naia opened her mouth, but all that came out was a strange, unsteady gasp. She forced a laugh to cover the flustered warmth in her chest.

"Oh, Amri. Are you finally saying you have feelings for me?" she asked, ribbing him with a hand, but he didn't laugh or squirm. Instead, he straightened, nodding once with the most serious expression she'd ever seen on his usually laughing face.

"Yep. That is what I'm saying. And don't feel like you have to say anything or return my feelings. That's not why I'm telling you. It's expected, maybe, or boring to do it now and this way. But there it is. I guess I just wanted to tell you in case something happens in Stone-in-the-Wood."

Naia nodded against his back. Ahead, a dark line was growing on the horizon. The Dark Wood was fast approaching, inside the course of the afternoon thanks to the relentless speed of the Landstrider cavalry.

"Amri, I have never met someone as adventurous and funny as you," she began. She felt him tense in her arms, ears angling out to the side. "And you've been a most wonderful friend."

"I see . . . ," he murmured, volume falling.

She wrapped her arms around him, hugging him more tightly and warmly. She had never held someone that way before, knowing he had feelings for her and that it meant something to him. Realizing, as his warmth spread into her own body and lit her nerves with a thousand tiny blue fires, that it meant something to her, too.

The Dark Wood loomed just ahead of them, tangled with thorny brambles and impenetrable sentinel trees.

"*And*," she said, whispering into his ear, "if we come out of this alive, I think we should continue this soft-talk and see where it leads us."

The Dark Wood fell over them like night. The Landstriders were just as unstoppable within the forest as they were on the open plains, breezing between the trees on their long legs that never seemed to trip. Naia didn't know how to prepare for what lay ahead when they reached the Stonewood village. She didn't know what they would find.

"Whoa, whoa!"

Lun and Gereni pulled on their reins, braking at the head of the herd until all the Landstriders slowed. In a small clearing of the wood, gathered around a crop of dark blue boulders, were more Landstriders and Gelfling in tattered clothes and smoldering armor. Naia leaped down from the saddle when she recognized Maudra Fara and Maudra Mera, rising to meet them from among the mottled group of Spriton and Stonewood.

"Naia!" Maudra Mera exclaimed. "Thank Thra. I see Lun and Gereni got to you after all."

"Yes, and just in time. Maudra Fara! I'd heard you were taken captive by the Skeksis."

Maudra Fara, tall and proud though she had seen brighter days, nodded solemnly.

"I was." On that topic, she had nothing else to say, gesturing instead to Maudra Mera. "I have been searching for my Stonewood since then. They have been hiding in the woods since we lost Stone-in-the-Wood. Alone and cold and afraid. And yet here came Maudra Mera, marching back to the place we had to leave behind."

The Stonewood *maudra*'s brow was hard and unimpressed. Whatever Maudra Mera had said to her had not been persuasive, and Naia was not surprised. The Stonewood in the clearing were injured, malnourished, and weak. The battle with the Skeksis had taken a toll on their bodies, and their minds were still reliving the nightmare of losing their ancestral home. If Naia had been in Fara's place, she was not sure she would have listened to Mera, either.

"But Fara is stubborn as ever," Mera said. She tilted her head. "Where's your mother? I would have thought she would certainly join us at the chance to stand against the Skeksis."

"My mother is here in us," Naia said as Gurjin joined her. She held her chin up when Maudra Fara's and Maudra Mera's eyes softened with understanding.

"I see," Maudra Fara said. She placed the flat of her palm on Naia's forehead. A moment later, Maudra Mera did the same. "Then you know the pain that rises in my heart and prevents me from doing as Maudra Mera suggests. We have already lost once to the Skeksis in Stone-in-the-Wood. I could not bear to bring my clan there to lose a second and final time."

The last time Naia had seen Maudra Fara, it was in Stone-in-the-Wood. The stern *maudra* had known she and Kylan were on the run from the Skeksis, and friends of Rian's and Gurjin's. Back when they had only been known as traitors. Maudra Fara had thought it too dangerous for Naia to stay within her village. She had even turned her back on Rian, one of her own, for the sake of the rest of the Stonewood.

Rian. Rian, the Stonewood soldier who had tried with everything he had to warn the Gelfling of the Skeksis' betrayal—and been called a traitor in return. Exiled by his own people, forced to bear the burden of the terrible truth alone. His face had not been in the flames, as it had when he'd lit the Grottan fire. When she looked, Naia couldn't find his sharp, determined eyes looking at her from among the Stonewood refugees. The seventh fire was theirs, and Rian's—so where was he?

The answer was clear in Naia's heart. He had been tasked by Thra, the same as she had. Though she hadn't heard his voice or seen his face, she knew without a doubt exactly where they would find him.

"Rian," Naia began. "Rian is waiting for us. For you, his *maudra*. We have to join him. So he can join us. So we can all awaken the power that Thra has given us. It worked in Sog. It has worked every time the Gelfling fires light. Thra is greater and more powerful than even the Skeksis. This is what Aughra has been trying to tell us all along."

"Aughra!" Maudra Fara exclaimed. "You must already know what I think of that old witch. Haunting the hills near my Stone-in-the-Wood. She may have been brilliant once, but she no longer wants to offer the Gelfling any wisdom."

"Rian said the same thing, and I thought so, too—but now I believe her voice was lost, because *we* turned away from *her*. Away from Thra. When the Skeksis divided the Gelfling, we began to fight among ourselves. We became fractured and weak. But that can change. I know you are tired, but we are here to support you. When we unite, I'm sure we will hear her wisdom again. The voice of Thra. It will heal us all."

Maudra Fara was like one of the stone pillars that stood atop the rise in Stone-in-the-Wood. For an instant Naia wondered if she could not be swayed. Then Maudra Mera grabbed Fara's arm, pinching it with her strong little fingers.

"I never thought I might say this, but I agree," Mera said. She hesitated, then added, "I've seen the fires—two of them. They are of Thra. They may even be the fires of prophecy . . . Maudra Naia is right."

A chill went up Naia's neck. She held Maudra Fara's hands with a last plea.

"Please, Maudra Fara. Heal the rift with Rian. He is waiting for you."

After a long moment, Maudra Fara nodded.

She turned toward the Gelfling who waited in the shade of the stone, weary and worn and afraid. Yet when they saw the three *maudra* standing before them, wings half-splayed and eyes shining with confidence, they rose to their feet. Emboldened.

"Riders, warriors," Maudra Fara called, "anyone who can. Get on a Landstrider and ready yourself. To Stone-in-the-Wood we go, to find the one we spurned from the nightmare he has called upon himself."

Sunlight broke through the trees as the Landstriders found a path cleared through the wood. The scent of fresh smoke and the distant clashing of weapons were the first signs that they were close. Then through the green and gold leaves, Naia glimpsed a tall, rigid shadow, like a mountain amidst the trees. The ancient tower of boulders that marked the center of the once proud home of the Stonewood Gelfling. It was fleeting, at least at this distance, but unmistakable.

They had reached Stone-in-the-Wood.

CHAPTER 26

Only ruins remained of the once mighty village, lasting proof of the day Maudra Fara had declared war against the Skeksis. Naia gasped, holding back involuntary tears of emotion as she took in the crumbled houses that lay in shambles among trees blackened and spindly from fire. The only thing that looked untouched was the rise at the back of the clearing, a mound of boulders that had given Stone-in-the-Wood its name. Now it gazed across the remnants like the marker of a hundred graves.

He was where she knew he'd be. In the center of the village, sitting with a single companion in the dirt near a pyre of black stones that made up the Stonewood hearth. His cheeks were scratched and bloodied, his tunic torn. He was with a girl with pale skin and big black Grottan eyes.

Rian stood when the Landstriders, the Spriton, the Stonewood, and the Drenchen entered the clearing. "Naia—Gurjin—Maudra Fara—"

Maudra Fara flew from the back of her Landstrider to meet him, striding over the stones and broken rafters and shingles. Rian looked unsure as she approached him, as if she might even now try to turn him away. He held a long golden-hilted sword, though he didn't raise the weapon as Naia and the others dismounted from the Landstriders.

"You're here," Rian stammered. His eyes darted from Maudra Fara to over her shoulder, where he caught sight of Naia and Gurjin. Naia nodded to him, saw Gurjin do the same. "Maudra Fara . . . Look! I got the sword. The one Aughra sent me to retrieve—she says it can stop the Skeksis. She says it will be our salvation!"

He held up the sword. It was Gelfling-size and asymmetrical, a double-edged blade that reflected the light of the flames like sunlight on polished iron. This was the sacred artifact Aughra had sent Rian to find in the Tomb of Relics. The answer to their questions, the object of their many dreams, though how such an instrument of war could help them heal Thra, Naia didn't know.

Maudra Fara looked upon the blade and sighed.

"Oh, Rian. I am sorry you had to do this alone. I should have been the first one to believe you, but instead I turned you away. And because I did, so did everyone else . . . But all that was a mistake. Now I am here, even if I may be too late."

A tense quiet followed, until the Grottan girl at Rian's side nudged him gently. The trepidation fell away from him like an unamoth shedding a cocoon. He stepped out of it, transformed by the moment, into his *maudra's* arms and embraced her.

"It's never too late," he said.

Smoke rose from the piles of stones that had once been Stonewood houses, from beneath the debris and charred trees. The sky flashed as if there were a storm in it, blue embers and light falling like rain across the stones and the broad leaves of the forest trees. The fires radiated green and pink, blue and gold. They did not consume, as the Skeksis torches had. Where the tongues licked, life sprang like water from a deep well. And as the color washed across the clearing, on the remains of every wall came the etchings. Burning and sizzling and complete, the stories of the seven Gelfling clans: Sifa, Dousan, Vapra. Spriton, Grottan, Drenchen. Stonewood.

The fire burned in its thousand colors, longer than it ever had before, louder with its drowning song. It reminded Naia of the dream-space that Aughra had awakened in them. So many hearts and minds, almost dreamfasted with one another, despite the distance between them. All together for the first time, in a place that had been destroyed by war. The menders, all there, listening.

Naia forced herself to breathe again, though every crackle of brilliant flame took her breath away. The warmth showered her cheeks and dazzled her eyes, the embers landing within her heart and revitalizing her. They had done it. After so long fighting with only hope as their guiding star, they had done it. The fires of the Gelfling had been lit.

"You should say something," the Grottan girl said, startling Rian from his awe.

"What?" Rian asked. "What . . . do I say?"

No one answered at first. Not even Maudra Fara or Maudra Mera. Naia put a hand on Rian's shoulder and told him what she had been told so recently.

"Your truth," she said. "You are the one who saw. You are the one who was cast out. Now, we have come to you. We believe you.

We are with you. Tell every Gelfling of the Seven Clans what you have seen, and what we will do."

Rian drew himself up, facing the fire.

"Gelfling of the Seven Clans," he began, awkwardly at first. "My name is Rian. If you're gazing into these fires now, then you already know what I am about to tell you. But it needs to be said, so I will say it again. And again, until I cannot say it any longer.

"The Skeksis have betrayed us. They killed the All-Maudra. Broke the Crystal and caused the darkening. Have been feeding on our essence. I was sent by Mother Aughra to retrieve this sword, foretold to hold the power to overturn the Skeksis."

Blue flame rolled along the gleaming metal of the golden-hilted sword. As he held it before the flames for all to see, it began to ring. Quietly at first, then rising so loud it was howling, vibrating with the song, its glimmering intensifying until it blazed so white in his palm it cast their shadows long and hard across the crumbling stone walls of the village.

"The Skeksis have kept us divided for a thousand years because they fear what would happen if we were united. Because they know that it is our calling to protect Thra and the Crystal that they have corrupted. And they were right to be afraid. You, the Gelfling of the Seven Clans, have lit your fires of resistance. I stand here in Stone-in-the-Wood, at the hearth of the seventh fire. As proof of our promise that we will resist the Skeksis and heal the Crystal . . . not as many, but as one."

The voices came. The cheers of the seven clans. The fire blazed and the strange sword sang, and Naia felt the heat and the sound resonating in her heart, as if she were but one of a thousand flickering fires burning in a single hearth.

Yet in it, something was strange. Foreign, like someone watching her from behind. As if the fire itself had been tainted by the darkening, some smoldering ember burning black and corrupt amid the other shining coals. Whispers, in crooked, sharp tongues, and terrible black eyes.

"*Interesting.*"

The single word rolled out of the fire like black smoke. Malice and contempt, corruption and wrath. This was no Gelfling voice. Naia had heard it before, in the castle, at his banquet table. His word—his law—pervaded all of their world, it seemed. Now he intruded into their most intimate place, the Gelfling fires of resistance.

The roaring of the hundreds of Gelfling voices hushed.

"Emperor skekSo," Rian growled. "How—"

"How?" skekSo scoffed, the word dripping from his tongue like poison. "These fires were given to you by the Crystal of Thra, which has given itself to us. To *me*."

"It didn't give itself to you," Naia spat into the fire. "You took it. Just as you take from it even now!"

He ignored her as if she hadn't spoken.

"Rian. Rebels. Gelfling traitors," the Skeksis bellowed. "Give up this farcical resistance. If you do not, we will crush you. All the Gelfling songs—if any Gelfling are remaining to tell them—will tell how you were responsible for destroying your own race. Do you understand?"

"I understand you are afraid of what I have, Emperor skekSo.

"This is the weapon Thra has given us to stop you," Rian continued, voice full of fire. He brandished the sword, thrusting its gleaming edge in the fire. "And I will not back down. We will not give up. We will rise against you until you have returned the Crystal to Thra!"

The violet and black flames surged so tall and hot that even Naia had to step back. What she saw next put a shudder down the full length of her back.

Emperor skekSo, bedecked in his obsidian robes, gazed back at them through the fire. To his left and right were the hulking black figures of the other Skeksis, backs and shoulders heaping with armor. The Emperor's eyes glowed fuchsia, purple, and red—reflecting the light of the glowing thing into which he was staring. The thing that had allowed the Skeksis to take dominion over all that which was not theirs: The blighted Crystal of Truth. The Dark Crystal.

"We will see you soon, Rian," Emperor skekSo said.

Then the sparks and tongues of flame subsided, and the channel through which they had been connected to the other Gelfling clans was gone.

Naia stared into the hearth where the fire had been, no one sure what to say or how to say it. She struggled to recapture the flying feeling of victory she'd had in the moments before the Emperor had spoken. She jumped when Amri grabbed her hand and squeezed.

"We still lit the fire," he reminded her quietly. "We still united the Gelfling. No matter what he said, skekSo can't take that away from us. Not now, not ever."

"He's right," Maudra Fara said. She took a survey of the Gelfling there, a scattered collection of Stonewood, Spriton, Drenchen, and exactly two Grottan. "What's done is done. The Gelfling are united and the Skeksis know. These things cannot be changed. So now, we will do as Rian has said we will. Resist until we can resist no more. Here in Stone-in-the-Wood, we will make our stand."

"We've lit the fires as we've been asked," Maudra Mera agreed. "If Thra truly has answers for us, it must sing to us now."

"How long do you think it will be before they get here?" Naia asked.

"If they left immediately by armalig carriage, less than a day," Rian said. "But without Gelfling guards at the castle to help them prepare, it will be longer."

"Then we have some time," Naia agreed. "Maudra Fara, please trust me to heal your weary. Rian, you and Gurjin should brief whoever can fight on what to expect when the Skeksis arrive."

"That we can do," Gurjin said.

The ruins were quiet as the Gelfling prepared. Maudra Fara and Maudra Mera lit a fire in the old hearth, a fervent red one that brought a much-needed warmth and dryness to the clearing. Naia assigned Drenchen healers among the Stonewood refugees, sending others to the lake adjacent to the village remains for fresh water. At her back, she heard Rian and Gurjin explaining the Skeksis' heavy metal armor and strategizing how the Gelfling might use the tree cover and rocky pathways of the wood to their advantage.

Naia took a quick count. They had several dozen, between the three clans, and not including those too wounded to fight. That many, with the help of Great Smerth, had been enough to stop skekSa in Sog. But when skekSo came, he would not be alone. It was not impossible that he would bring every other Skeksis with him, from the sharp-eyed Chamberlain to the huge, hammer-fisted General.

Could the Gelfling truly endure them? Or was this the end? The future was terribly uncertain. There was no promise that they would prevail. Only that the confrontation would happen.

"Naia?" Amri's voice brought her mind back to the present. He had removed his dark cloak and rolled up his sleeves, was covered from waist to shoulder in smudges and streaks of black soot. He waved, so she rose and followed him through the skeletons of two crumbled houses to a trench caused by a felled tree. In the pit of dirt below the drying, frayed roots, the Grottan girl was working tirelessly with a pile of black, twine-wound balls.

"I don't think you've been properly introduced," Amri said. "This is Deet. Deet, this is Naia! Drenchen *maudra*."

"Hello!" Deet called up. Her cheeks were covered with dirt and soot from the black dust she was working with, but her dark eyes glittered with a hopeful smile. "Rian's told me about you. It's so nice to meet you!"

Amri hopped down into the pit and Naia did, too, when he gestured. The acrid, sulfuric scent in the pit from the dust reminded Naia of something she'd smelled before. She tried to place it, splashing through the waters of her memory until she saw skekSa, hurling her explosive eggs into Great Smerth.

"Smoke bombs," Amri said, a proud smile crossing his face.

"I used to make them, back in Domrak. We used them in smaller sizes to clear hollerbats when they'd roost in the chimneys," Deet explained.

"Like what skekSa used?" Naia asked.

"Yes," Amri agreed. "Deet and I compared notes. I think these will work quite nicely to give the Emperor and the other Skeksis a big surprise."

Naia felt lighter. "This is good. I'll tell Rian and Maudra Fara. We'll figure out the best way to use these. Thank you, Deet. Amri."

The two Grottan nodded, eyes twinkling. Naia took hold of a root that dangled into the pit and climbed out.

She found Rian taking a short break, sipping water from a skin carried by one of the Drenchen. The golden-hilted sword leaned against a tree near his hip, shining like a sliver of sunlight.

"How's it going?" she asked.

"As well as it can, considering our circumstances," he replied. "I'm sorry to hear about your mother. My condolences."

Naia nodded her thanks. She wasn't truly prepared to talk about that yet.

"Amri and Deet showed me what they're working on. I think if we can ambush the Skeksis as they approach, we might have a fighting chance. But I wanted to talk to you about something else.

Something we've got to agree on, before skekSo and the others get here."

Rian's brow rose below his dash of blue hair. "Which is?"

"We can't kill them. Not a single one."

He started to protest, eyes wide, but he closed his mouth slowly in understanding.

"I see. Because of the Mystics, you mean."

"Yes, but not just that. The Skeksis have divided the Gelfling and pitted us against one another for a thousand trine. Just like you said. They did it to keep us weak. But the weakness came not just from being broken apart, but from the rivalry it caused. The corruption of the Crystal is because of its wound and the missing shard, and that wound has been deepened by the hatred and greed and fear of the Skeksis. They want us fighting—against them or against each other, it doesn't matter. But we can't give in to that."

Rian curled his lip in, eyes going far away. "So they'll come here and we'll be martyred."

"No," Naia said. "But that's our challenge. To stand before them and to prove we are stronger. That we can persevere. To do all that without succumbing to the darkness in our hearts, and without losing our lives."

"I hear what you're saying, Naia, but it's just . . ." He shook his head, eyes locking on to the sword. "Aughra sent me to find that, you know? A sword. A weapon. What else is there to do with a weapon but harm?"

If only Aughra were here to explain, Naia thought. So many answers had come, from the fires and the Gelfling themselves.

She had fought so hard to find those answers, to earn the wisdom and the explanation. And yet it still came to this, a strange and dangerous riddle.

Rian let out a weary sigh.

"Why would she send me to retrieve a blade foretold to stop the Skeksis if she didn't want me to raise it against them?" he asked.

"I don't know," Naia said. "We'll have to find out."

That night, she sat before the Stonewood hearth with the others as they rested, and Kylan sang the ballad of the Gelfling Gathering that he'd first told in Sami Thicket. Naia listened to him tell the song, hearing the lyrics that had been only a dream so recently. Now each part had come to pass, like a prophecy unveiling itself, one flame at a time.

As the embers dimmed and the Gelfling prepared to return to their work, Naia took a sip of water and stretched. It would be a long night, one which would turn into morning before she knew it. She handed her waterskin to Amri when he came over. His cheek was smudged, his fingers and knuckles raw from working with the black dust all day.

"You should try to get some sleep," he said.

She snorted. "I can't. We have so much to do. Even if we all work through the night, we'll never be as ready as I wish we could be."

"I know. But you have to let the others help prepare. Your duty will be to lead, and you have to be rested to do that."

He said it so firmly, she wondered if he might be right. She looked away. "I'm not sure I can sleep even if I try."

"Even if you can't, at least give your body a rest. Just for a little bit. Come on."

He held out his hand, and Naia realized she couldn't say no.

They found a bed of moss below a tree on the border of the village ground. The stars were out and were it not for the ghostly silhouettes of the collapsed buildings all around, it might have seemed like any other night in the Dark Wood. They sat together, and Amri fluffed his cloak on his knee.

"I'll keep an eye out in this dark for you, and I promise to wake you if anything stirs."

Naia had never laid her head in a boy's lap before, but it was surprisingly comfortable. His cloak smelled like fresh earth, familiar and soft. She closed her eyes when she felt his hand rest upon her shoulder. Thra's endless turning seemed to slow, the rest of the world and all her worries vanishing. There were no Skeksis here. No darkening between them. For once, it was just the two of them, and in the safety of that moment, she fell asleep.

CHAPTER 27

They all awoke long before the first scouts reported back. Naia looked up from the ditch she was digging, alongside Gurjin, Kylan, and others equipped with spades and makeshift tools scavenged from the village.

A Spriton girl appeared, out of breath from her sprint through the Dark Wood canopy.

"We counted twelve, in six armalig carriages," she said. "As Rian guessed, they're coming along this path. They'll be in for a surprise indeed."

Naia thanked the scout and sent her on her way to warn the others back in the village. She wiped the sweat and dirt from her brow. The ditch was not complete, but the Gelfling who'd worked through the night on it had done well.

"It's good enough," Gurjin said, catching her glance. "No way the carriages will be able to cross."

"We can only hope," Naia agreed.

"Part of me wishes we could stay and watch it work. I'd love to see the look on the Emperor's face when he realizes he'll have to walk."

"I'm sure we'll see his face sooner than we like," Kylan said. He glanced at Naia and then suddenly hugged her. She returned it, though briefly, holding him at arm's length afterward and fixing him with a stern glare.

"You stay safe now, you hear me? Keep the others safe. Don't come after us. No matter what. Promise?"

Kylan sighed and nodded. He pressed his hand against his *firca*.

"Just . . . don't die. All right?"

"We'll do our best," Gurjin chuckled. "But no promises."

They and the other Gelfling climbed out and up into the trees, scampering across the boughs, hidden by the gnarled branches and thick leaves. Naia glanced back, but Kylan was already gone, to protect the children and those who were still too wounded to fight. At least she could feel relief about that. If anyone survived their confrontation with the Skeksis, Naia hoped it was her song teller.

Rian was waiting in the center of Stone-in-the-Wood. The hearth had been relit and glowed orange and red at his back, casting light down the golden-hilted sword in his hand. The rubble was cleared, only a few Gelfling in sight. The last of them were armed with leafy branches, which they used to brush out the footprints that they had made overnight.

Naia scanned the tree line as she approached Rian. She couldn't see through the leaves even though she was looking. That was good.

"Are you ready?" she asked.

"As I'll ever be," Rian said, voice tight.

"We'll be right there. Ready."

They clasped hands. Naia wished for a moment she had more time to know the ex-soldier. Maybe if they survived the day, they'd have that time.

"I know it," he said firmly. "Thank you, Naia. And best of luck."

"To all of us," she agreed, and went to join the others in the trees.

Waiting was agony. Watching Rian pace, alone in the middle of the clearing, was almost worse. Naia's hands sweated against each other, and it took every ounce of willpower to keep still. Their plan relied on surprise—one of their few advantages, and if any of them gave themselves away, they would have to flee. Abandon Stone-in-the-Wood a second time, take untold casualties as they were hunted by the Skeksis.

No, they had to win. They had to turn the Skeksis away and reclaim this place as one they would protect, where the Skeksis were not welcome and would never be. Prove to all the Gelfling that hope was not lost. That there was a way to endure without falling into darkness. That the song of Thra was more powerful than even the darkness the Skeksis had brought upon it.

Naia closed her eyes and pressed her hand against the bark of the tree.

Mother Aughra, she prayed. *Mother Thra. We fight for you today. We will show the Skeksis that we will not submit any longer. We will stand until we can stand no more. Let our footprints be left in stone as proof we did not give up.*

She opened her eyes and twisted her ears when something stirred in the brush. Shadows, tall and hulking, moved within the wood. Amri, crouched beside her, reached out and gave her arm one final, comforting squeeze.

The Skeksis had arrived.

Tall and armored, moving slowly and steadily like the arced shadow of an eclipse across a moon. Naia recognized Lord skekZok and Lord skekVar. skekSil, the Chamberlain, in his ruby and amethyst dress, close to the right hand of the Skeksis who stood in the center front. Whose voice had broken the Gelfling from their awe, whose metal helmet gleamed as if it were devouring the light of the now-dying Gelfling fires.

Rian faced them as they approached, seemingly alone. The color had drained from his face, but he did not give ground. Not even as Emperor skekSo, bedecked in a frothing cloak of black pinions on top of shining iron armor, stepped to the front of the Skeksis line. He held a scepter in one claw, his cruel beak plated with a mask of dark metal. His shadow engulfed Rian as he drew up to his full height, and yet the Stonewood did not step back.

"skekSo," Rian said. He tightened his grip on his sword, though he did not raise it. Not yet. "So you came after all."

"It's just you?" skekSo exclaimed. He raised his head, casting over the ruins and through the trees. Naia held her breath. There was no way he could see the dozens of Gelfling waiting, was there? She gripped the smoke bomb in her hand, ready to give the signal the instant she saw any spark in the Emperor's eye. But his gaze landed back on Rian, the spiked hackles around his neck only partially roused.

"What a waste of our time," he growled. "*WHAT A WASTE.*"

skekSil the Chamberlain's high-pitched voice was like a bug in the Emperor's ear as he wrung his claws together. "My lord. Do you wish us to take him captive? Hmmmm, back to the castle for skekTek to drain?"

"We have plenty of captives remaining at the castle," Lord skekUng grumbled in reply. "*I* say we make an example out of him. Like you should have done properly the first time." The last he spat to skekZok the Ritual Master, who turned away with a snarl.

Emperor skekSo nodded slowly, running his claws over the head of his scepter. His breath came noisily through the armor plate across his snout, furious at the thought he'd brought all of his lords to this place to deal with a single Gelfling. But the fury was turning hungry. Lusting for any revenge he might be able to take, now that he had Rian in his reach.

With the second of his four hands, he waved dismissively.

"We will do both. Take him alive. We will kill him back at the castle. And be quick about it. This has already been too much a waste of our time."

It was his mistake. Naia raised the smoke bomb and screamed, "*NOW!*"

The earth itself seemed to erupt with black smoke as smoke bombs rained upon the Skeksis. Naia lost sight of the figures below as the clouds of thick smog rose, smelling of sulfur and burning moss. The Skeksis cried out, thrashing in the stinking darkness, suddenly broken from their intimidating formation in surprise and confusion.

That was where Naia wanted them. She pushed her fingers in her mouth and whistled.

Winged Spriton led by Maudra Mera and Maudra Fara bearing Drenchen nets leaped from the trees, flinging the nets upon the Skeksis. The Gelfling darted above the boiling chaos below as other Gelfling on the ground emerged, snagging handfuls of the rope nets and pinning them into the earth with spears and staves. The ropes would not hold forever—even now, they snapped and sliced between Skeksis claws and blades.

But the effect would last. As the Skeksis broke themselves free, one at a time, they spun away from one another, scattering in disarray and anger. They were no longer collected, smug, proud. Now they were enraged, primal. Naia beheld the scene from above, as Gelfling with spears jabbed between the scales of the Skeksis armor. One at a time and without fail, the Skeksis reacted, lashing out at the nearest Gelfling, pursuing them with snarling fangs and talons. Even massive Lord skekUng fell to their design, charging after a group of Spriton and Drenchen with a thunderous bellow.

By the time the smoke faded, the Skeksis had fully broken from formation. Only Emperor skekSo remained, with the Chamberlain at his back. The Emperor's armored carapace heaved with breath, steam jetting out from his mask as if an inferno raged inside him.

"Emperor," the Chamberlain began, but the Emperor held out a claw. Opened his dagger-toothed maw and screamed.

"KILL THEM ALL!"

Rian let out a piercing battle cry and charged. Startled by

the ferociousness and speed, skekSo was barely able to raise his scepter in time to block Rian's shining blade. The force of it on his unprepared parry knocked him back half a step, more than Naia might have predicted. When Rian brought his sword against the Emperor a second time, sparks flew and even the Chamberlain backed away.

skekSo snarled and shoved at Rian's blade with his scepter with enormous strength, sending the Stonewood flying backward. Naia finally left her perch, spreading her wings enough to glide until she landed with a *whump* beside Rian, helping him back to his feet. A moment later Amri and Gurjin joined them.

"Vermin!" the Chamberlain cried from behind the Emperor's back. "Fools!"

He shut up when the Emperor lashed out with his scepter, even at his own ally. The Chamberlain whimpered and shrank back, though he still lingered when the Emperor thundered toward Naia and Rian. Though his footsteps shook the earth, up through her heels and into her legs and back, she clenched the soil with her toes. She had made a promise.

"You should have stayed hidden," Emperor skekSo roared, volume rising with every step. "You should have stayed scared. *But now, you will all die!*"

Naia opened her mouth to reply, but the wind was knocked out of her as a black blur crashed out of the wood. The huge black shape whirled through the village, a storm the size of a Skeksis, in a pitch-black cloak broken by twisted, skeletal spikes. It finally stopped, crouching in a steaming mound of darkness between

Rian and the Emperor. It twisted its head, and Naia saw a glint of white. A shard of bone, fastened to the monster's face with twisted metal spikes. The remains of a mask he had worn until she had cracked it so many days and nights ago.

The Emperor's mouth split in a toothy, glistening smile as he looked upon the monster.

"skekMal," he growled. "Take care of this."

"*Gelfling,*" the Hunter hissed, a plume of hot steam rushing from his ragged lips. He twisted until he faced Rian and then reared up to his full, tremendous height. "What's this it has in its hands? A pretty sword. A pretty trinket."

"This is no *trinket,*" Rian said. He faced skekMal, pointing the shining beacon of a blade at the Skeksis Hunter's heart, its double edge reflecting the light of the triple suns above.

The Emperor's voice tore through the silence as if it were flesh.

"Yes, skekMal. *Now.* Take that traitor fool. Make an example of him where everyone can see."

"With pleasure, Emperor."

"*Rian!*"

skekMal hurled himself forward with unsated hunger, jaws open as if he might devour Rian whole. Naia leaped, trying to intercept, but she was too slow. Her fingers brushed Rian's sleeve before the Hunter tore him away, mounting the Stonewood tower like a hulking black Arathim.

CHAPTER 28

"Now what will you do, Drenchen?"

Naia's neck ached to look away from skekMal as he climbed the rise with his captive. Emperor skekSo folded his hands across his scepter, tilting his head so his helmet shone like dark ice. Though the Chamberlain stood at his back, gripping his dagger, neither Skeksis moved toward her and Amri.

"Fight us? Then where is your weapon? Or is Rian's little toy the only weapon you stupid Gelfling have?"

All around them, in pockets of battle throughout Stone-in-the-Wood, Gelfling and Skeksis voices screamed almost in unison. Trees near the border of the clearing had been lit up, choking the air with whorls of ember and stinking black smoke. Naia flinched as the Ritual Master smashed his scepter into a band of Gelfling rebels, killing one instantly and wounding the other two. Across the clearing, the Chamberlain knocked a Spriton off his Landstrider—Lun—and plunged his twisted dagger into his belly. Where his blood fell, the earth darkened.

And above them, skekMal had reached the summit. Naia could only watch from where she stood below as he tossed Rian to the ground. Rian had managed to keep hold of his sword somehow, and climbed to his feet. From the tilt of his shoulders, though, Naia could see he'd been hurt during skekMal's violent ascent. Still he faced the Hunter, and though every Gelfling in the wood could see him, he faced the Hunter alone.

"When the Hunter kills him, this battle will be over," skekSo said. "This battle and this resistance. This rebellion. Over, in one move. Tiny flames die so quickly."

"Rian won't lose," Gurjin said. Naia clenched her fist. She could hear skekMal's snarls and screams, the clanging of metal as he clashed weapons with Rian.

"The Gelfling and the sword have called upon Rian as their champion, and he will win," she said. But even as she did, fragments of doubt came swirling back. Could Rian defeat skekMal? And what if he did? What would happen if that magic blade sliced the Skeksis Hunter's throat? He would fall then and there, in front of everyone. In front of his lords, and they would see Rian standing over him.

All while somewhere in the Mystic Valley, urVa's blood would quench the golden dust. And deep inside the Castle of the Crystal, the Heart of Thra would remain the same, as broken and incomplete as before.

Emperor skekSo snorted a jet of steam. He tossed back his cloak, drawing a sword in one hand, balanced by the scepter he held in the other. His two remaining claws were free, twitching talons eager to snatch and tear.

"Too bad you won't live to see how wrong you are," he said.

He attacked. Straight at them, swinging his scepter. He had speed, and strength, but as Naia leaped up and Gurjin and Amri fell to the side, she could already tell the Emperor was not as practiced in battle as skekSa. His strikes were uncontrolled and reckless, making up in anger what he lacked in calculation. Naia held only a stone, using it to block his blade when she couldn't avoid it.

"DIE!"

The single word echoed through the clearing.

Even the Emperor turned away from Naia to see who had issued the dreadful command. At the top of the rise, in sight of all who watched, skekMal the Hunter brought his sword down on Rian.

Metal flew in splinters, reflecting the afternoon sky. The azure light flickered as it struck the shards of the now-shattered sword blade that exploded out from between Rian and skekMal. Rian stepped away as metal pieces crashed to the ground.

Then all went still. The reverberation of Rian's sword breaking echoed like a funeral song, a dirge that made Naia's bones want to weep. Everyone heard it and everyone stopped. The Skeksis, weapons raised for slaying Gelfling. The Gelfling of the seven clans, scattered between them, many climbing the rise of stones that towered at the center of it all.

skekMal let out a booming laugh, holding up his weapon. Its scarred blade remained intact, whole and proof of what it had just destroyed.

And in Rian's hand was a hilt with a jagged twist of broken of metal.

Every face that could turned upward. Every eye saw Rian,

staring numbly at what remained of the golden-hilted sword, falling to his knees in disbelief.

"Naia!" Amri called out.

A shudder went down her spine as she felt ugly breath on her neck. Before she could get out of his reach, the Chamberlain grabbed at her from where he'd been lurking. She twisted against him and beat him with her stone, but he had three other claws with which to grab. He latched on and held her up, away from Gurjin and Amri.

"Here, my lord!" the Chamberlain cried. "Here!"

Naia gritted her teeth as he shook her violently, then threw her. The world swung and swamped like a boat on the sea. The only way she could tell which way was down was the dirt in her mouth as she collided with the ground. She heard Gurjin and Amri call her name, saw them thwarted by the Chamberlain as they tried to get to her. Saw in her memory the terrible flash of light as Rian's sword broke against the Hunter's blade.

She pushed herself up as the Emperor's shadow hovered nearer. Clutched her stone and dug her fingers into the earth and met his eyes, even as he raised his sword to kill her.

"I won't give up," she said. She felt a tear that had finally slipped past her lashes, one of grief and anguish, that had seen what she had seen. The tiny drop of water slipped off her cheek onto the ground and disappeared. "You can kill me. But you can't change me. The forest is forever."

Orange and red wings flashed in front of the sun. The Emperor's cries were garbled as a Gelfling shot through the air.

With a mighty cry, Maudra Fara struck him in the face with both feet, hard and fast as a *bola* stone.

"Naia!" she shouted. "Go to Rian!"

She groaned as the Emperor's talons pierced her body. At first Naia thought she was gone, but before she went, she drove her spear beneath the Emperor's metal mask and jerked, snapping it off his beak with a grisly spray of gore.

"Go to Rian," she said again over the Emperor's screams. "Go—"

Her final command ended abruptly on the Emperor's sword. Naia pulled herself to her feet. She wanted to go to the Stonewood *maudra*, even if she could do nothing for her. But Fara had wanted her to go to Rian, and . . .

"What's that sound?" the Chamberlain squawked suddenly.

Amri and Gurjin finally broke past him as a strange lull interrupted the din of the battle. It was a rumbling in the earth, a vibration in the air. A wind gusted and the treetops churned as dozens of shadows raced across the sky. Even the Emperor was at a loss, clutching his bleeding face where Maudra Fara had ripped his mask from his head. Naia and skekSo both looked up in a daze, at first not sure what they were seeing. But when a volley of egg-shaped satchels dropped behind the Chamberlain, exploding in flame and red-hot fire dust, she knew.

"The others," she gasped. "They came—"

Wings of every color filled the sky: Sifa and Dousan, Grottan and Vapra. Fire and swords rained upon the Skeksis, spears and arrows flying from the Gelfling who rushed from the woods on foot and on the backs of Landstriders dressed in the indigos and silvers of Ha'rar. Rainbow light filled the smoking ruins, flashing off iridescent wings and the banners of seven Gelfling clans.

The Skeksis cried out in shock and rage as fire dust crashed upon them, burning their eyes and inflaming their senses, each fending for themselves against the burst of Gelfling forces strengthened from the air and with the speed of their fearless Landstrider mounts.

"No—"

Naia backed away from Emperor skekSo. He sighted her, but this time he didn't even have the chance to raise his sword. A helmeted Sifa soldier on a Landstrider struck him so heavily, he was knocked to his knees, his sword flying from his claws. As he reached for it, another Landstrider tackled him from the other side as it galloped across the clearing. He went flying in a rolling cloud of dirt and pinions.

The first rider wheeled her Landstrider about with perfected ease. Naia had never seen a Sifa on one of the tall beasts before, let alone such an expert rider. When the soldier raised her visor, though, she understood. The sunny, freckled face was a welcome one.

"Go!" Tae called down. She turned her head so Naia could see the crystal spider clinging to her hair, whispering in her ear. "Tavra and I will take care of these Skeksis fools!"

"Naia, wait, please—" Amri grabbed her arm when she turned to go. He knew what it might mean. He knew what she was willing to do.

"I have to go," she said. "I have to protect Rian. I don't know how, but I have to."

"Let her go," Gurjin said, holding Amri's shoulder. His cheek was bruised and caked with dirt and blood, but his spirit had not been broken. Not even after what had happened at the top of the rise.

"*Hmmmmm*," sneered the Emperor, pulling himself to his feet with an awful cough. He spat blood, weaponless, surrounded by the chaos as the battle shifted to the Gelfling's favor. "*Let her* go. *Let her* die up there, too, for all the Gelfling to see."

"Trust me," she whispered. First to Gurjin, then to Amri. "*Trust me.*"

Amri's fingers tightened, then released. Naia gave her brother and her friend a last look, trying to pour every feeling into it, then turned away and ran for the rise.

CHAPTER 29

Naia leaped up the first boulder, and then the second, grappling the hard stone edges and ancient moss. The top of the rise seemed impossibly far, as if it were ascending into the sky even as she raced to reach it. She couldn't see the top as she climbed. Had no idea if Rian had survived the Skeksis Hunter or fallen under his unforgiving claws. Her heart ached at the thought, which seemed as though it might be inevitable—but she swallowed the feeling and climbed instead.

The sound of a horn hammered in Naia's ears. She pulled herself over the top of the rock in time to see a monster's broad, gaping face fly overhead. The shadow of a fledgling Crystal Skimmer covered her before it flapped its wide fins, propelling itself up in a spiral around the rise. On its back, a crimson-cloaked Dousan with tattoos across his shaved head cupped a hand around his mouth, his feet hooked into the harness on the Skimmer's shoulders.

"Need a lift?" Periss called. "Get on! We're coming around again!"

The Skimmer whistled with effort, circling the rise. Naia curled her toes around the boulder, spreading her wings and leaping when the Skimmer banked. She landed with a heavy

THUMP behind Periss and grabbed hold of him as he yanked on the reins.

"Up, up, Massimassi! *Up!*"

The Skimmer blurted an earnest howl, banking once more and pounding the rise with air. skekMal had just reached the summit of the rise as Periss brought his Skimmer toward the peak. He took a short dirk from his pocket and gave it to Naia.

"You sure about this?" he asked.

She pushed the dirk back to him. "I'm sure."

"Then good luck," he said. "Blue Flame *maudra!*"

Naia jumped.

She landed on the flat peak of the Stonewood rise, where more than a dozen ancient obelisks jutted like the spires of a crown. skekMal tossed Rian to the ground before him, letting the Gelfling roll across the dirt and moss and rocks. Rian's knuckles bled, but he still held his sword in his hand. He pulled himself to his knees, an equal distance from both the Hunter and Naia. The three suns blazed from above. One sun for each of them, casting both light and shadow.

"Naia, what are you doing?" Rian groaned. "It's over. Aughra lied. The sword broke. You don't need to die up here, too."

"Get up, Rian," Naia urged him. She didn't take her eyes off skekMal, who watched them with his burning, cold eyes. As if trying to choose which of them to kill first. "Rian, get up. Don't let him defeat you. Prove to him that you'll rise against him. Prove to Thra that we'll resist—even if we die."

Rian swore in protest but pulled himself to his feet. A gust of wind buffeted them all, unfurling Naia's wings and ruffling the blue streaks in Rian's hair. Her empty palms sweated, painfully aware she had no weapon, as skekMal raised his sword like a battle ax.

"First we finish what we started," he said, and charged at Rian.

Naia lunged. Without thinking, diving between skekMal and Rian, throwing open her arms and thrusting her empty hands forth. Closing her eyes as the blue light shined outward, uncalled and uncontained, blazing against the fangs in skekMal's ravenous, open maw.

It was all she could do. To protect Rian. To protect anyone.

The pain never came, and Naia opened her eyes.

skekMal's sword dangled above like it was caught by an invisible hand. He struggled within his skin, twitching and quivering, but he could barely move. Not just his sword, but his entire body.

"What?" he croaked, barely able to even move his mouth. "What is this? *WHAT IS THIS?*"

"skekMal!" the Emperor cried from down below. "What are you doing? Finish them!"

skekMal lurched again, and for a moment Naia thought he might break free of whatever mysterious power had hold of him. Steam poured from his nostrils, as if boiling water were slowly filling his entire being, as he struggled against his own body. Like an unamoth caught in a web, believing that if it struggled long and hard enough, the strands would surely break.

"*Naia.*"

The voice that came out of skekMal's throat was not the hissing, cold one that had screamed at her in the Dark Wood. It was grave, determined, familiar. Naia slowly lowered her hands, unable to look away from the Hunter's eyes as she saw a spark within them. The recognition of another, who had gazed upon her once before with respect and admiration.

"urVa?" she whispered.

"Do not fear," came the Archer's voice through skekMal's lips again. "And do not despair—" Then skekMal came again: *"DESPAIR UNTIL THE END OF YOUR—"*

CRRRR-CRACK.

skekMal screamed as the sound of splintering bones erupted from his chest. Black blood dribbled out of the seams of his armor, in both the front and the back, as though he had been pierced by an invisible arrow.

Tears welled in Naia's eyes. The arrow was not invisible; it was real enough. But it was elsewhere. Where urVa was, far away in the valley, in the place where he had plunged it through his own heart.

skekMal the Hunter could not even pull the shaft of the weapon from his breast. He clawed at his chest, snapping his armor off in twisted plates of spiked metal, but there was nothing he could do. He coughed and screamed, blood spraying from between his pointed teeth.

"Don't despair—*DESPAIR*—raise your voice in *SCREAMS*—song. Sing—*of your annihilation*—and believe . . ."

Then he burst into flame.

When he was gone, the entire wood was silent. Even the Emperor, who stared in shock as his champion was reduced to a pile of smoking bones and singed armor, did not know what to say or do. Gurjin and Amri had reached the dais at the top of the rise, running despite their exhaustion when they saw both she and Rian were still standing. Gurjin was the first to make it, throwing his arms around Naia and Rian all at once and hugging them so tightly Naia was surprised they didn't break.

"I told you to believe me," Naia mumbled into Gurjin's shoulder. She could almost make out Rian's weary smile on her other side, and caught Amri wiping a stealthy tear away just before he winked at her.

Something rang. They stepped back from one another when light sprang forth, vibrating in time with the eerie tone that filled the air. It was coming from Rian's sword.

"Why is it ringing now?" Rian whispered, holding up the broken blade. "After it's been broken?"

Rian stood, raising the hilt. The ringing grew into a drowning song, calling to her, to them all, in a voice Naia had known since she had been a childling. It held every body immobile in its power. Even the Skeksis, whose beady eyes widened and shook as they beheld it—as it beheld *them*.

"What *is* that?" Gurjin whispered.

"I think it's—"

She could hear the song. Vividly now, as clear as it had been when she had stood before the Crystal in the castle. As clearly as when Aughra's message had reached them in the dream-space. As strongly and as unmistakably as it had sung to them in Onica's Far-Dream, when Amri had asked how they would stop the Skeksis.

Now it answered in its ever-present song. The voice that sang the earth to life, that called upon the rivers to flow and the tides to change. Naia knew its name and shivered.

Somehow, the Crystal was here.

Rian lowered the sword and gazed into what remained of the blade, into the glowing pommel and hilt. As he did, the ringing subsided, as if it had been a single note that had reached its end. Rian's ears twisted back and he looked to Naia, as if to ask her how to make it begin again. How to call it to life, to unleash its power once more, again and again, endlessly.

A single, clear note cut through the air clouded with Skeksis breath and the scent of ash and blood. It was strong, like the wind, ringing through the hollow bone of the bell-bird *firca*.

Kylan the Song Teller stepped onto the dais at the top of the rise. The wind blew through his braid, as if sharing breath with him. As if encouraging the song to be a thousand times louder. His fingers played without thought, drifting through the notes as if they came from beyond him. Within him, and through him.

As the *firca* rang with the song that had once moved mountains, the sword Rian held cried out in return, with more volume and energy than before. The Skeksis let out gasps of pain, holding their heads and horns, trying not to shrink away from the light and the sound that filled Naia's heart with a fragile hope. Though she did not want Kylan in this deadly place, she had never wanted to see him or hear his *firca* more.

"No," breathed Emperor skekSo. He stared, transfixed, paling with light and fear, at the thing that burned in Rian's hand. He ripped the dagger from the Chamberlain's claws and charged up the rise himself. "Kill them. Kill them *NOW!*"

Naia advanced at Rian's shoulder, Gurjin and Amri close behind.

"Don't stop playing," she called to Kylan. She took Gurjin's hand in one of hers, Rian's in the other. "Throw down your weapons. Hold one another. The song of Thra. Sing it! Everyone, together, *now!*"

Without waiting for the others, she raised her voice and sang.

She had never been a strong singer, gifted neither with an instrument nor with the talent of story like Kylan, but that didn't matter now. She sang the words that she had heard before. In Mother Aughra's dream-space, and in all the worlds within their world. The song of Thra.

Deatea. Deratea. Kidakida. Arugaru.

Gelfling voice after voice called out after hers. She heard Gurjin's and Amri's beside her. The Stonewood and the Spriton, the Grottan and the Drenchen. All their voices lifted in a symphony. Then the Sifa. Tae, hand in hand with Onica beside Maudra Ethri. And the Dousan—Periss and Erimon had come, with Sandmaster Rek'yr and Maudra Seethi. Scattered across the boulders of the rise, white-winged Vapra alit like a flock of unamoths. Among them, Naia recognized Tavra's sisters, Brea and Seladon. The All-Maudra's other two daughters, united with the third and the rest of the seven clans.

Light burst from Rian's sword, the metal of the hilt melting away as if it were paper smoldering in a candle. What remained, clasped in his fingers, glowed with all the light of the inner sun of Thra. The Crystal of Truth.

It was a crystal shard.

The Skeksis Emperor stumbled backward. His cry of dismay struck out against the chorus of Gelfling voices and the singing of the Crystal. Rian held the shard as it if were the deadliest weapon imaginable. The other Skeksis recoiled as the light radiated in the reflections of their fearful eyes, the shard's deafening song overpowering their cowering hearts.

"Dreamfast," Naia called. She squeezed Rian's hand, and as if by pure instinct, he squeezed back. Following her lead, the Gelfling held one another, some closing their eyes and bowing their heads. "Open your hearts. Hold one another!"

Rian's heart was pounding so hard Naia could feel it through the pulse where their palms were pressed together. Naia let the vibrating song of the Crystal, pulsing through the shard, overwhelm her.

"Do it!" he cried.

For an instant, she saw space.

Infinite stars scattered across an abyss of radiant darkness. Planets—her world, and others—blinking in and out of existence. Each with a heart that beat, giving life, glowing at each world's core. Each with its own song, the lifeblood of all that lived upon it.

This one is ours.

She didn't know whose voice it was that said such a simple

thing. Dreamfasting with so many Gelfling, it was impossible to know. Perhaps it was not one person, but all of them. It didn't matter. It was the truth.

And we have only one, Kylan added.

Amri's voice echoed hers: *And we will protect it.*

Fight for it. That was Rian.

Naia took in a deep breath and let it out, and added:

Heal it.

The earth shook. The clouds knit together in a silver gauze, shedding a shimmering curtain of rain. The droplets sizzled as they touched the stones that littered the ruins where proud Stone-in-the-Wood had once stood.

Steam and smoke issued forth from the broken walls and shattered boulders. The etchings that had appeared when the Stonewood fire had lit—the pictographs showing the tales of all seven clan fires—began to glow. As they had when they had first been carved, though now with a more radiant light than ever before.

New etchings burst from the stones. Images and writing, stars and suns and moons. Light blazed and the Skeksis screamed as it burned them. Pure, bright, white—like the shard that flashed like a star as Rian held it aloft for all to see.

The sound of the earth singing—the infinite voice of Thra—was all that could be heard. Naia felt it along the surface of her skin, straight into the marrow of her bones. She could feel the song as strongly as she could hear it—as plainly as she could see the light radiating from Rian's hand.

It was life. It was power. It was theirs.

The Skeksis heard it. They saw it, and they knew.

And then they ran.

Stumbling and grappling over one another, they clawed their way past the rubble and stones and Gelfling, taking cuts and stabs from the Vapra swords and Sifa blades as they passed. In a flurry of black and indigo and crimson, they fled into the wood in the direction of the castle.

The Gelfling had won.

CHAPTER 30

After the Skeksis were gone, Naia and the other Gelfling gazed upon the etchings.

They covered every stone surface in the ruins, interlaced with the etchings that had already been cast by the lighting of the seventh Gelfling fire. In every nook and every toppled Stonewood structure, pictures of stars and suns and moons were emblazoned like brands. Naia traced her fingers over the shapes—many images, but many words as well—wandering silently from wall to wall. Every etching was different, bleeding into the next, in a chain of hundreds, if not thousands, of passages and illustrations.

Naia had never fully learned to read, no matter how many times Kylan and Amri had tried to teach her. But she didn't need to read to know what she was looking at. She and her friends and all the Gelfling had asked so many questions. Finally, Thra had answered. She knew without a doubt that the answer to every question was here. Somewhere, scattered among the remains, burned by the fires of prophecy.

"Naia! Come look at this!"

Kylan and Rian waved her to a long stone wall that had once been the rear of Maudra Fara's meeting chamber. The other walls around it had been knocked down and destroyed, but the rear wall behind her stone *maudra*'s chair still stood. Five Gelfling figures were etched into the portion of the wall there, and arching overhead, words curved like a domed roof.

Kylan stepped forward, letting his *firca* rest on his chest as he traced his fingers over the still-smoking etchings. As he did, they drew the attention of the Gelfling that wandered the ruins looking for survivors and taking in the wonder of the etchings.

"The legacy of the Gelfling race," Kylan read aloud for all to hear. "What was sundered and undone shall be made whole. The two made one." He glanced at Naia, then at Rian, before he finished: "By Gelfling hand, or else by none."

"Look at those below," Amri said, joining them. Along the bottom of the Gelfling tableau were more familiar shapes, these more ominous: Skeksis. urRu. urSkeks, and the Castle of the Crystal. One thing in particular caught Naia's eye.

"That looks like the shard," Gurjin said.

Rian looked at the thing in his hand, a miniature version of the Crystal of Truth that was trapped deep in the heart of the Castle of the Crystal.

"The shard heals the Crystal," Naia said. "It's the missing piece. The real way for us to mend the Crystal. Stop the darkening and heal Thra again. It's telling us what to do."

A red-haired Sifa stepped beside her, touching Naia's shoulder. Onica the Far-Dreamer gestured, guiding their gaze across the wall with a wise, graceful hand.

"It's more than that, Naia," Onica said. "Thra is older and wiser than we. These etchings are not just the answers to our many questions. How to, and when to. The what, and where. They are more than that. They are the signs of the future foretold. Burned by the fires of prophecy."

Naia shook her head. "I don't think I understand . . ."

"This wall reveals the future which will come to pass. The Gelfling *will* heal the Crystal. The Skeksis *will* be rejoined with the urRu. The urSkeks *will* return to the world from which they came . . . and Thra *will* heal. It is not a suggestion or an instruction." Onica's sea-green eyes passed over the wall once more, a bold smile crossing her lips. Naia shivered at the determination in the Far-Dreamer's brow as a breeze ruffled her crimson hair.

"It is our future," she said. "And our legacy."

"And now the Skeksis have seen it."

The crowd of Gelfling parted around a familiar, waddling figure. She trudged out of the trees that surrounded the ruins, gray and black hair in tangled knots around her whorled horns. Her earthen-tone robes were disheveled, leaves and soil clinging to every part of her. She had been silent when the Gelfling had gone astray. And now that they had turned back, opened their ears to her song, she had returned. Mother Aughra, the Helix-Horned. The voice of Thra.

"They know what it means, the Skeksis. And they fear it. They fear *you*." She stood before the wall, casting her heavy gaze upon it, moving her entire body to turn her head on her short neck. "That's why they ran. That's why they will lick their wounds in the castle!"

"You don't think they'll come back?" Rian asked.

"Not today. Not tomorrow, either. Aughra can sense them. Through the Crystal. They'll barricade themselves inside. You did well today, Gelfling."

She spoke over her shoulder, barely bothering to acknowledge the Gelfling except for the last, almost casual remark. Even so, Naia felt a weight slip from her shoulders. The Skeksis would not return that night. They had time, at least for now.

"Then tonight we recover," Rian said, facing the Gelfling that circled around the wall. "Tonight we tend to the wounded and pay respects to the dead. Build fires in this place and warm our tired bones. For when the Skeksis come after us again, it will be relentless. They have no reason to pretend to love us any longer. They'll come after us with everything they've got."

Naia took Rian's hand once more, holding it out so the shard gleamed in the light.

"But the Skeksis saw the prophecy as we did. They know they can no longer divide us. These signs are proof of our unity, the shard a promise. The Gelfling will prevail."

As the suns climbed and then began to set, all three in the sky at once, Naia busied herself with healing the wounds of the injured. Around her, the Spriton and others rounded up the Landstriders and prepared them for the journey south.

She exchanged greeting glances with Periss and Erimon as they helped the Spriton and Vapra repair Landstrider gear with remnants from Crystal Skimmer harnesses. She even caught sight of Mythra, Rian's sister, as she and other Gelfling helped the Grottan and Dousan prepare the bodies of the dead for their final rite.

When night approached, the edge of the clearing lit with small fires and circles of Gelfling. They shared words and provisions, finding one another. Somewhere, Naia even heard someone playing on a pipe.

They had lost so much. Domrak and Stone-in-the-Wood. Great Smerth. And so many had fallen today, and in the days so recently past. Naia's heart ached when she saw Maudra Ethri, Maudra Mera, Maudra Argot, and Maudra Seethi seated around their own fire, a hollow space between them where Maudra Fara and Maudra Mayrin would have sat.

"Naia!" called Maudra Ethri. Chimes and bells rang like rain against the ocean as she waved Naia over. "You've worked all evening. Sit with us. I've even got a flask of nectarwine."

Naia tried not to show her hesitation as she took a spot with the other *maudra*. The one her mother would never occupy again. Of the seven *maudra* of the once seven clans, only four remained. She took the flask Ethri offered her, tasting the sweet, pungent wine that smelled of fermented sogflowers. She pushed down a cough and handed it next to Maudra Mera, who was not so successful.

"How fare you, young *maudra*?" Argot asked. She held her thin hands out to the fire, legs crossed, her cane leaning against her hip.

"I don't know," Naia admitted. "I'm glad for this chance to rest. The Gelfling need it. But I can't stop thinking about everything we've lost."

"It is important to remember what has been lost," Seethi

said. Naia had never met the Dousan *maudra*, but the time for first greetings had long past. They had seen battle together, and survived together. Now it felt as though Naia had known the blue-and-gold tattoos across the older *maudra*'s face forever. "But it is also important not to dwell on it. To dwell is to become attached. And it would not do to become attached to what is in the past."

Maudra Mera cleared her throat, waving away the last coughs from the nectarwine. "Precisely, Naia. My soggy dear. In these times, it is more important to value what we have. It is what Mayrin and Fara, and your mother, would have wanted."

Naia looked across the faces of the Gelfling around the fires, under the awakening stars in the ruins they had reclaimed. Still touching the dream-etchings from the fires, and the new one brought forth by their collective Far-Dream. Their cheeks were scratched and marred with bruises and blood, many with the weary sadness of battle imprinted on their brows. Yet in every face she saw, there was a flickering. A tiny blue flame within every one of them. As they looked on the prophecy wall they'd created together, and as they stared in awe and wonder at Aughra as she read the inscriptions, her gnarled fingers cupping her whiskered chin.

They had come together. They had protected this place that they had lost. And now, they had brought forth the fires of the prophecy. And Aughra, the voice of Thra, herself. Though the towering figures of the past might fall, the Gelfling would endure. They were the protectors of this land. And they would resist.

"May . . . may I join you?"

The timid request came from a Vapra girl, who stood at the perimeter of the fire just outside the golden light as if she feared what might happen if she stepped within. She looked like Tavra, with long silver hair and pale skin. Naia recognized her from a Far-Dream she'd had long ago. This was Seladon. Tavra's older sister, and the one who had taken All-Maudra Mayrin's place after she had been murdered by the Skeksis.

A strange stillness came over the ring of *maudra*. Seladon had sided with the Skeksis after they had killed Mayrin. But in the end, she had heeded Rian's call. She bowed deeply, folding her hands across her knees.

"I understand if you do not wish me to sit among you," she said, voice muffled but no less sincere. "The crown of the All-Maudra was invented by the Skeksis to drive the clans apart. I accepted it when they killed my mother for fear of what they might do to the Vapra. But I know better now. I hope I can earn your trust, even after all that has happened."

Naia took in her tattered robe and bruises, the weary look across her wide, bare brow. No crown rested there. Just the sign of loss and loneliness. She waited for judgment from the others at the fire, and Naia reflected that the last time she had asked for their blessing, it had been Laesid and Fara who had withheld. Two *maudra* who were no longer with them.

"*Maudra* meant something long before the Skeksis invented the *All-Maudra*," Naia said. "So long as you wish to be true to that, then you are always welcome here."

The smile that crossed Seladon's face was brilliant as sunlight on snow. Maudra Argot even moved her cane, making room, and then they were six around the fire. Ethri nudged Naia with an elbow.

"You see? Waves recede, but only for a moment. The tide is ever changing, and yet it beats upon the shore as it has since the beginning of time. We are all part of the world, as it is part of us. We bear in our breast the sparks of the flame that lives in the heart of the world. Things change, but life goes on. We are that life. We are that song."

Naia's mother's words came out of Naia's mouth, as if Maudra Laesid had been there to say them herself:

"The forest is everlasting."

As if she had summoned them, Gurjin and Amri emerged from the dusky shadows, Rian a step behind. Naia moved to the side to make room for her brother and her friends. Though Gurjin could have easily taken the seat next to her, he went round the fire, wordlessly leaving it for Amri. The Shadowling slid down next to Naia, a pleasant warmth, familiar and comforting.

"So what do we do next?" Rian asked.

Naia realized with a start he was asking her. But for once, the answer came easily.

"Recover," she said. "Fortify. Realize the prophecy by returning the shard to the Crystal. Fend off the Skeksis until the next Great Conjunction and wait until the light of the triple sun unites them into urSkeks and sends them away."

"I have been discussing with Seethi," Ethri said. "We found

in fact we have much in common, the Gelfling of both the Crystal and Silver Seas."

Seethi nodded, quiet as death compared to her Sifa counterpart. "If we must endure the Skeksis for many trine to come, there could be no safer place than aboard the ships on the ocean or in the Wellspring shielded within the desert. We can take the Vapra who are accustomed to the north, along with anyone else who seeks refuge."

"We've brought Landstriders from Ha'rar," Seladon added. "Along with what supplies we could. We are in your debt and at your disposal."

"I would like to offer Sami Thicket to anyone who wishes to come south," Mera began, wringing her hands. "But our village is small, and the Skeksis have traveled easily to us for many trine. It would not be safe . . . I fear not even for us Spriton, any longer."

Argot sighed, tapping her fingers against the head of her cane. "It is the same in Domrak. The caves are in shambles after what the Arathim did. It is not safe. Not anymore."

"Then come further south," Naia said. "Only one Skeksis has ever stepped foot in the glade under Great Smerth, and she was defeated. Though the darkening has touched the swamp, as it has touched everywhere, the forest is eternal. Anyone who wishes to come with us is welcome . . . so long as they can withstand the scent of my beloved swamp."

Naia winked at Maudra Mera. To her surprise, the wiry Spriton sighed and nodded.

"Thank you, Naia," she said solemnly.

That left Rian and the tiny piece of crystal. It seemed impossible, that the little sliver of shining mineral could truly be the missing piece. The evidence of the wound that had weakened the entire world, small enough to fit in a Gelfling's hand, its smooth facets rippling with firelight.

"And I will find a way to return this shard to the Crystal," Rian said.

"You won't be alone," Gurjin replied. "Because I'm going with you."

Rian's ears flattened, though a cautious hope sparked in his eyes. "You are? I thought after all this you'd want to go home . . ."

It made sense, flashing like flint on steel. Naia smacked her palm with her fist.

"He is," she said. "The two of you know every corner of the castle. The Dark Wood can't hide an entire clan, but it can hide two. You'll be safe, and you can make a plan." Naia faced Gurjin across the fire and felt a resonance she'd missed for a long time. Face-to-face with their mirrored eyes, reflecting a moment that had separated them once before in their childhood.

"I will return to Sog and protect the Gelfling who go with us there. And you will go with Rian. Take the shard. Heal the Crystal . . . It's what Mira would have wanted."

"I won't let you down," Rian said. He glanced at Gurjin. "We won't."

"In the morning, then," she said. "The Gelfling can decide as they like. To go north with Ethri and Seethi and Seladon, or south with me and Mera and Argot."

The Gelfling worked steadily through the night. Naia rose with the others when the deep tone of a Dousan horn rang through the clearing. Erimon was calling. It was time for the final rite, to pay respects to the dead. Under the light of the moons, the Gelfling gathered a final time at the Stonewood hearth. The coals had smoldered, and it blossomed with blue smoke when Onica and Maudra Ethri anointed it with Sifa coral dust. Naia linked hands with the others, their voices in a tri-part lament led by Maudra Seethi.

"We return you to Thra," Maudra Seethi sang. To the Gelfling who had passed that day and in the days before. "May you sing the song of eternity in the light of the fire in the heart of the world."

After the rites were finished, an air of relief came across the clearing. As if a breeze had finally blown the last scent of darkness from the ruins, as the moonlight lined every rock and boulder in silver. Naia's ears turned toward the sound of a lute, though the fingers that plucked the strings were not nearly as skilled as the ones she was used to. A Sifa bard was perched atop a boulder, playing and singing a ballad that she felt she had heard once before. Amri listened with a group of other Gelfling, ears forward and attentive.

"Amri," she said quietly, touching his elbow. "Have you seen Kylan?"

"No," he said. "Last I saw he was still looking at the wall at the back of Maudra Fara's chamber."

Naia nodded. Of course he was. She made to go after him, but paused.

"You're coming south with us tomorrow, right?" she asked, anxious about his answer, though she didn't know why. As if he might not be there when she came back.

He only chuckled, brushing his silver hair over his shoulder.

"Um, obviously. You promised we'd have a soft-talk. Remember?"

Naia felt a blush creep up her neck. "As if I'd forget!"

Then she shoved him away and snorted, pushing past him and his sideways grin and heading toward the wall where she'd last seen Kylan.

CHAPTER 31

The wall with the five figures was in the center of the ruins, out of sight from the campfires that flickered along the perimeter. The stench of the battle with the Skeksis had cooled, replaced by the indigo scent of the night and starlight. Naia followed the orange glow of a torch, finding Kylan kneeling at the base of the wall, clearing away vines and recording the figures on the wall in his book.

"Kylan. There you are!" She crouched beside him, nodding a second hello to the crystal spider on his shoulder, shining in the light of the clear sky. "And Tavra."

"The etchings go on for what seems like forever," Kylan said. He sighed and looked into the pages of his book. "I'm never going to be able to record them all. Especially not if we're leaving in the morning. We may know the final outcome, but we can't deny that hard times are yet to come. For all of us. The Skeksis may try to destroy the wall. The song of the prophecy must be preserved. But . . ."

Naia followed Kylan's glance, seeing what he meant. The etchings were sprawled across every stone and fallen wall, some in the dirt that was already muddied from dew and the night breeze. The Gelfling couldn't all remain here. Even if Aughra had said the Skeksis would stay away for now, they would not stay away forever. Especially not if many Gelfling remained.

Still, there was something that connected Kylan to the wall. Something strong as a dreamfast, as if his destiny was intertwined with the lore of the prophecy. Kylan, the song teller from Sami Thicket, whose *firca* resonated with the very shard of the Crystal.

From how he touched the wall, how he could not look away from it, she could tell he knew it, too. That though he might want to go with his friends, he knew this was more important. They both did.

"Then you're staying," she said. "Here, with the etchings."

He jumped, eyes widening at her. "But . . ."

"Someone has to interpret the etchings and record them. If it's just you, here in the ruins, it won't attract the Skeksis' attention. You know your way around this place now. In the Dark Wood. And Sami Thicket isn't too far."

The song teller's ears twisted back and forth, not sure whether to be relieved or worried.

"I will stay with you," Tavra said. Her spider voice was audible thanks to the still of the night. "Onica was drawn to the etchings as well. I think she'd be delighted to stay. The two of us will keep you company while you make sure the song of the prophecy is recorded."

Kylan's sigh ended with a smile.

"It's difficult to say no to the two of you," he said. "Naia, are you sure?"

Naia laughed to hide the opposite feeling that was burrowing in her chest. Even deciding Gurjin and Rian would go to the castle hadn't felt like a farewell. Not really, and certainly not like this. Naia wasn't sure the time would ever feel right to say farewell to Kylan of Sami Thicket. Her friend the song teller.

"I'm sure," she said. "And when you're done here, you should go to see Master urSu in the valley. The Mystics may be able to help us understand the wall. If there's any writing you and Onica can't decipher . . . but it's a big responsibility, Kylan. Maybe I'm the one who should be asking you: Are *you* sure?"

Kylan's hand drifted to the bell-bird *firca* at his neck, no longer bone white, but singed a darker shade, like clay or earth.

"If I'm honest, I've never been so sure of anything," he said. "I'll make sure one day all the Gelfling know the song of how we endured the Skeksis. Forged the prophecy and healed the Crystal. And in that song, your name will ring. As will Rian's and Gurjin's. Tavra's and Onica's and Amri's."

"And yours," Naia said, tears pricking her eyes. She tried to capture his face in her memory. The path ahead was unsure and uneven, and even though the Gelfling were united in spirit, there was still distance between them. It was likely it would be a long time before they saw each other again.

Kylan chuckled. "Don't be silly. It's poor taste for a song teller to insert himself as a hero in his own song . . . I'm glad to have met you, Naia."

"Same, Song Teller," she said, and wrapped him in another hug that she hoped could last until the next time they met.

CHAPTER 32

Morning came softly and quietly.

Naia woke to the smell of the fires being put out, the gentle murmuring of the Gelfling saying their goodbyes to one another. It was time to leave.

Naia busied herself with a Landstrider bestowed upon her by Maudra Mera. Amri was already in the saddle overhead, adorning the beast with braided blue and green ribbon that flowed in the early wind like victory banners. Gurjin and Rian approached. They'd shed their armor and dressed in the lightweight tunics and cloaks they might have worn had they never been guards at the castle.

"Well, this is it, I guess," Gurjin said.

"I tried to find Aughra to say goodbye, but she's gone," Rian added.

Naia scanned the ruins, but she didn't see the hunched back of the old witch. She didn't expect to. But in the air and in the earth, in the last ashes of the fires as they were doused with water from the nearby river, something stirred. The voice of Thra, quiet and constant as ever.

Naia smiled.

"She isn't gone," she murmured. "Just busy. We'll see her again . . . You'll be all right, you two? I'm not going to regret sending you off on your own, am I?"

Gurjin snorted. "Not if I have any say. Though knowing this blue-streaked fizzgig, I might not."

"If anyone can handle him, it's you," Naia teased.

Rian rolled his eyes, blew his bangs back with a puff of air. The shard was nowhere in sight, though the satchel at his belt had a familiar shape and weight to it. He'd keep it safe. He held his hand out to Naia.

"Until next time," he said. "We resist. For Thra."

"For Thra," she agreed. Then before any of them could say anything more, Rian strode off into the wood. Gurjin gently punched Naia on the shoulder, refusing to hug her. Refusing to act as if this could be the last time he saw her. Without words or dreamfasting, Naia knew how her brother felt.

"Later," he said, and then turned from her. Not knowing what to say, she reached out and socked him back. They shared a final look as Naia climbed the rope ladder onto the Landstrider where Amri sat waiting.

Naia and Maudra Mera led the way south out of the Dark Wood. Their party paused when the woods cleared and the Spriton Plains opened before them.

"I've been thinking," Amri said suddenly. "Do you remember what skekZok said, back in skekSa's ship? About how our descendants might not know the names of the clans?"

"Yeah?"

"Well, take a look around. Maybe he was right."

Gelfling surrounded them. On foot and some on Landstrider,

the Drenchen and the Spriton and the Stonewood. There were even some Sifa and Dousan with them, and silver-haired Gelfling, though whether they were Grottan or Vapra, Naia couldn't tell from the lofty saddle of her mount.

It didn't matter, anyway. They were one clan, now. No matter what else happened, that was something the Skeksis could never take away from them.

In the distance, the mist of Sog beckoned. Though Naia had stood on so many brinks before, for some reason this one seemed the most decisive of all.

"I feel like I've never been here before," she said. Sharing the little, vulnerable feeling with the Shadowling at her back. "Never seen it, even though we have. Even though we're going back home. To my home, anyway. And now yours. But everything's different. It seems like a brand-new world I've never stepped foot in, all over again."

"It is new," Amri said. "It's new every morning. It's only our memory that ties us to yesterday. Everything else is different, every time the suns come up."

Naia closed her eyes, feeling the warmth of the three suns as they brightened across her face. She took in the moment, the fresh air across her shoulders. Amri nearby, holding her waist. The Gelfling waiting below and all around. Listening for her signal.

To continue. To go on. To survive.

She opened her eyes. Kicked her heels and whistled, letting the moment pass as her Landstrider raced first into the awakening day.

GLOSSARY

Arathim: A race of ancient arthropods, including crystal-singers and silk-spitters. Their color and shape varies widely from family to family, with number of legs ranging from three to twelve.

armalig: This slow-thinking but fast-moving creature is motivated by food and so easily tamed. Often used by the Skeksis for pulling their carriages.

bell-bird: An ancient, extinct bird whose bones and beaks are said to resonate with Thra's song.

bola: A Y-shaped length of knotted rope with stones tied to each of the three ends. Used as a weapon, the *bola* can be swung or thrown, enabling the wielder to ensnare prey.

Crystal Skimmer: These large, flippered creatures are very social and travel in pods. They are native to the Crystal Sea. Easily trained by Gelfling, these majestic beasts are used by the Dousan clan to cross large expanses of the desert.

daeydoim: Six-legged desert-dwelling creatures with large dorsal scales and broad hooves. Frequently domesticated by desert nomads.

firca: A Y-shaped Gelfling wind instrument, played with both hands. It was Gyr the Song Teller's legendary instrument of choice.

fizzgig: A small furry carnivore native to the Dark Wood. Sometimes kept as a pet.

hooyim: One of the many colorful leaping fish species that migrate in large schools along the northern Sifan coasts. Often called the jewels of the sea.

Landstrider: Long-legged hooved beasts common to the Spriton Plains.

maudra: Literally "mother." The matriarch and wise woman of a Gelfling clan.

maudren: Literally "those of the mother." The family of a Gelfling *maudra*.

merkeep: A delicious tuber. It is a traditional food of the Stonewood Gelfling.

muski: Flying quilled eels endemic to the Swamp of Sog. Babies are very small, but adults never stop growing. The oldest known muski was said to be as wide as the Black River.

ninet: One of nine orbital seasons caused by the configuration of the three suns. Arcs in which Thra is farthest from the suns are winter ninets; arcs in which Thra is nearest are summer ninets. Each ninet lasts approximately one hundred trine.

swoothu: Flying beetlefur creatures with strange sleeping patterns. Many act as couriers for the Gelfling clans in exchange for food and shelter.

ta: A hot beverage made by mixing boiling water and spices.

Three Brothers: Thra's three suns: the Great Sun, the Rose Sun, and the Dying Sun.

Three Sisters: Thra's three moons: the Blue Moon, the Pearl Moon, and the Hidden Moon.

trine: The orbital period of Thra moving around the Great Sun, roughly equivalent to an Earth year.

unamoth: A large-winged pearly white insect that sheds its skin once every unum.

unum: The time for Thra's largest moon to circle Thra once, roughly equivalent to an Earth month.

vliya: Literally "blue fire." Gelfling life essence.

vliyaya: Literally "flame of the blue fire." Gelfling mystic arts.

xeric: One of twelve Dousan nomadic groups, each led by a designated sandmaster.

zandir: A flower native to the wetlands near Cera-Na. Its pollen can cause the lowering of inhibitions and talkativeness, so it is often used in truth-telling potions.

APPENDIX A

THE GELFLING CLANS

VAPRA

Sigil animal: Unamoth

Maudra: Seladon, the All-Maudra

The Vapra clan was an industrious race with white hair, fair skin, and gossamer-winged women. Considered the oldest of the Gelfling clans, the Vapra resided in cliffside villages along the northern coasts, making their capital in Ha'rar. Chosen by the Skeksis after the death of Maudra Mayrin, Seladon doubled as All-Maudra, matriarch leader of all the Gelfling clans. Vapra were skilled at camouflage; their *vliyaya* focused on light-changing magic, allowing them to become nearly invisible.

STONEWOOD

Sigil animal: Fizzgig

Maudra: Fara, the Rock Singer

This clan was a proud and ancient people who dwelled on the fertile lands near and within the Dark Wood. They made their main home in Stone-in-the-Wood, the historical home of Jarra-Jen. Many Stonewood Gelfling were valuable guards at the Castle of the Crystal. They were farmers and cobblers and makers of tools. They were inventive, but pastoral; like their sigil animal, they were peaceful but fierce when threatened.

SPRITON

Sigil animal: Landstrider

Maudra: Mera, the Dream Stitcher

Age-old rivals of the Stonewood clan, the Spriton were a warrior race inhabiting the rolling fields south of the Dark Wood. With such bountiful land to raise crops and family, this clan's territory spread to cover the valley in several villages. Counted among the most fierce fighters of the Gelfling race, the Spriton were often called upon to serve as soldiers for the Skeksis Lords and guards at the Castle of the Crystal.

SIFA

Sigil animal: Hooyim

Maudra: Gem-Eyed Ethri

Found in coastal villages along the Silver Sea, the Sifa were skilled fishermen and sailors, but very superstitious. Explorers by nature, the Sifa were competent in battle—but they truly excelled at survival. Sifan *vliyaya* focused Gelfling luck magic into inanimate objects; Sifan charms enchanted with different spells were highly desired by travelers, craftsmen, and warriors of all clans.

DOUSAN

Sigil animal: Daeydoim

Maudra: Seethi, the Skin Painter

This clan made their settlements on sandships—amazing constructs of bone and crystal that navigated the Crystal Sea like ocean vessels. Resilient even within the arid climate of the desert, the Dousan thrived. Their culture was shrouded and unsettlingly quiet, their language made of whispers and gestures, their life stories told in the intricate magic tattoos painting their bodies.

DRENCHEN

Sigil animal: Muski

Maudra: Laesid, the Blue Stone Healer

The Drenchen clan was a race of amphibious Gelfling who lived in the overgrown Swamp of Sog, deep in the southernmost reaches of the Skarith region. Sturdier and taller than the rest of their race, the Drenchen were powerful in combat, but generally preferred to keep to themselves. Though one of the smallest Gelfling clans, the Drenchen had the largest sense of clan pride; they were loyal to one another, but remained as distant from other clans as possible.

GROTTAN

Sigil animal: Hollerbat

Maudra: Argot, the Shadow Bender

A mysterious, secretive breed who dwelled in perpetual darkness in the Caves of Grot. Generations in the shadows left them with an extreme sensitivity to light—and solid black eyes that could see in the dark and large ears to make out even the faintest of echoes. The Grottan clan was said to number less than three dozen Gelfling, and their life span was said to be unheard of, lasting three to four times as long as other Gelfling.

APPENDIX B

LOCATIONS OF THRA

Black River: The main waterway within the Skarith Basin. It flows from high in the Grottan Mountains north to Ha'rar, where it empties into the Silver Sea.

Castle of the Crystal: Also known as the Skeksis' castle, this obsidian tower is where the Skeksis Lords live, and where they protect—and control—the Crystal Heart of Thra.

Cera-Na: A bay on the western coast of the mainland where the Sifa gather.

Crystal Sea: A desert of crystalline sand just southeast of the Claw Mountains. Frequented by electric storms and sandstorms.

Dark Wood: The large forest that fills most of the Skarith Basin. Also called the Endless Wood, it seems to go on forever.

Domrak: The home of the Grottan clan, a network of caves deep in the Grottan Mountains.

Grottan Mountains: A ridge of rocky mountains on the west border of the Skarith Basin.

Grottan Sanctuary: A deep mountain valley overgrown with giant stone mushrooms. An ancient nesting ground for bell-birds, this is where the Grottan Gelfling often go to meditate.

Ha'rar: The northern, snowy home of the Vapra clan. Made the capital by the Skeksis when they ordained the Vapra All-Maudra.

Kira-Staba, the Waystar grove: A grove of glowing trees growing on the bluffs that overlook Ha'rar and the Silver Sea.

Mystic Valley: A mysterious ravine to the south of the Dark Wood, on the northern edge of the Spriton Plains.

Nenadi-Staba, the Low Tree: A low-lying, gnarled-root tree growing in the wood near Sami Thicket.

Olyeka-Staba, the Cradle Tree: A towering tree in the Dark Wood, said to be the tree from which the entire forest originates.

Omerya-Staba, the Coral Tree: A floating coral tree made of thousands of marine colonies, converted into a living, sailable ship by the Sifa clan.

Oszah-Staba, the Wellspring Tree: A tree growing in the Dousan Wellspring. Its enormous leaves prevent storms from damaging the oasis.

Sami Thicket: A village hidden in a forest within the Spriton Plains, and home of the Spriton clan.

Sifan Coast: A long series of rocky shorelines along the north and western sides of the Claw Mountains. Inhabited by the Sifa clan.

Silver Sea: The frosty, fog-enshrouded sea north of the Skarith Land.

Skarith Basin: The land that lies between the Claw Mountains to the west and the Grottan Mountains to the east. The region within includes the Crystal Sea, the Dark Wood, and the Spriton Plains.

Smerth-Staba, Great Smerth the Glenfoot Tree: An ancient tree growing in the heart of the Swamp of Sog.

Spriton Plains: A vast series of rolling plains and meadows south of the Dark Wood. Home to the Spriton clan.

Stone-in-the-Wood: Home of the Stonewood Gelfling, this village nestled deep in the Dark Wood is large and fortified with stones and rocks. Some say it was the first Gelfling village.

Swamp of Sog: A lush, dense jungle in the southernmost part of the Skarith Basin.

Tomb of Relics: A cloistered hall in the Grottan Mountains where ancient artifacts are kept safe by the Grottan Gelfling.

Vliste-Staba, the Sanctuary Tree: A pink-petaled tree growing on the mountains near the Grottan Sanctuary. Its roots are made of glittering stone and penetrate deep into the mountains.

ACKNOWLEDGMENTS

I remember exactly what I was doing five years ago, to the day. I was sitting in an empty room with my laptop balanced precariously on an old bench I'd found in the garage. We'd just closed on a house and I wanted to take advantage of the unfurnished place to focus on writing. It was just me, my laptop, and Trevor Jones playing in my earbuds.

I was working on cleaning up my revised entry to the Dark Crystal Author Quest. I had learned I was a finalist (one of five) in February 2014, and had until May to submit my updated manuscript. I had no idea what my chances were. The only thing I could do was write the best story I could. And now, five years and four novels later, I'm writing different words—these ones of gratitude:

Thank you to Rob and Francesco, and everyone at PRH, for believing in me and my work, for helping me become a better writer, and for making me feel so welcome in publishing. Thank you, Erzsi—for all you do, but especially for always being there to listen to me freak out on the phone (about both amazing and not amazing things). Thank you to Cory for bringing the text to life in ways more lovely than I pictured in my own imagination.

Thank you to all of the Dark Crystal fans. You're the ones whose songs have kept Thra alive. Thank you to my friends and family who have supported me.

Thank you to Jeff, Will, Javi, Viv, and the rest of the AOR writers' room for being such kind and magnificent song tellers—to Louis, Halle, Blanca, Rita, and everyone else in the Jim Henson Company/*Age of Resistance* family for welcoming me so warmly and genuinely.

Thank you to Claire—obviously for being the best partner that ever was, but in this context specifically for willingly learning everything there is to know about the Dark Crystal over the past five years without complaining or calling me a nerd (except that one time).

Thank you to Brian and Wendy for showing me where the magic comes from. Thank you, thank you, thank you to Lisa and Cheryl for trusting me with this magical, important world. You have made me feel as though I belong here.

And finally, my deepest gratitude to Jim Henson. For without him this would not be, and surely, I would not be who I am today.

Until next time.

Joe

April 11, 2019